THE
TRAPPED
ONES

BOOKS BY STACY GREEN

THE TRAPPED ONES

STACY GREEN

bookouture

Published by Bookouture in 2022

An imprint of Storyfire Ltd.
Carmelite House
50 Victoria Embankment
London EC4Y 0DZ

www.bookouture.com

ISBN: 978-1-80314-354-5
eBook ISBN: 978-1-80314-353-8

For Mom, who left us too soon. I still miss you every second of every day.

PROLOGUE

Jessica raced across the dark woods, praying she didn't twist her ankle. Cold wind hit her face, and her heart pounded so fast she could almost feel the panic and adrenaline rushing through her veins. She ducked behind a thick maple tree and tried to catch her breath without drawing attention to her hiding spot.

Great, white puffs of air floated in front of her. Blood trickled from the wound on her head, and she struggled not to gag every time she tasted it on her lips.

She thought of the poster hanging in her dorm room, the mantra that she'd tried to live by for the past year. "Fool me once, go to hell." Why had Jessica fallen for his lies?

A twig snapped behind her. Jessica peered around the tree trunk, heart pounding, afraid of who—or what—she might see, but the clouds had moved in front of the moon, and she couldn't make out anything beyond the treeline.

A light flickered on inside the big house, and she could see someone walking past one of the big windows. If she didn't go now, Jessica knew she would never get another chance. She took a deep breath and then shot out from behind the tree, racing toward the house. Suddenly, she was bathed in light. She'd triggered the motion sensors. Squinting from the intrusion of light, she staggered up the steps, her feet hitting the back deck with a loud thud. Breathing hard, she raced across the deck to the sliding door. "Please, help." Jessica pounded her fist against the glass, screaming as loud as possible.

A woman with a plump face and gray eyebrows stared at her through the pane, cracking the door. "What's wrong with you?"

"Please, I need help. He's right behind me."

"Who?"

"Just, please, I'll tell you after I'm inside. You don't know what he's capable of."

"Who?" the woman demanded, noticing the blood on her face.

Jessica scanned the dark woods, trying to see through the ghostly trees.

The woman hesitated.

Jessica squeezed her fingers around the sliding door, preventing the woman from completely shutting it. She knew the woman would be conflicted, caught between wanting to help her and to keep herself safe.

"Please help me." Tears oozed from her eyes, mixing with the drying blood.

The woman's gaze drifted over Jessica's shoulder, the worry in her eyes replaced by confusion. "What in the world are you doing out here?"

ONE

Nikki adjusted the earbud in her right ear and zipped her fleece jacket all the way up to her chin. Crisp fall air chilled her nose and fingertips, but the sun felt good on her skin. This time of year, most of the trees around Palmer Lake were naked, allowing the warmth of the sun through to the section of the walking path that cut through the woods surrounding the lake.

The trail system was only a few minutes' drive from the FBI building in Brooklyn Park, and Nikki tried to walk a few times a week. She'd never been much for exercise, but after the events of the past several months, Nikki needed an outlet that involved solitude. A group of wood ducks floated in the water, and a male cardinal called for his mate.

Tyler had once told her that seeing a cardinal meant a lost loved one was watching over you. But which lost loved one? She doubted that it was him. He'd been murdered at the hands of a serial killer Nikki had been chasing, and she reckoned he'd hold a grudge against her about that. He wouldn't watch over her when she hadn't watched over him. She still saw flashes of his body lying on the steel autopsy table, and they were always accompanied by a crushing sense of grief.

She hadn't been able to stop thinking about Tyler this week. His parents had decided to sue for custody of their daughter, Lacey, citing Nikki's job as a significant reason for trauma in Lacey's life.

But that part wasn't the thing that made her blood boil. It was the words they'd used in their statement, asserting that her devotion to her job was akin to an "obsession, leading to a loss of parental time" with Lacey. That she relied on "near strangers" to help care for Lacey, and that her decision to go back to the FBI instead of finding a job that would keep her working regular hours for Lacey's sake made her unfit to parent.

The word "unfit" hadn't been used in the paperwork, but Nikki knew that's what the verbiage meant. Tyler's parents had resented her for the divorce, and they'd been in Tyler's ear over his shared custody agreement with Nikki since the day the divorce became final. His parents lived in the area, and historically they'd been de facto babysitters when things became more hectic, but not since his death. Nikki had made sure they remained in contact with Lacey, allowing her to spend as much time with them as she'd wanted. The Hunts were the only grandparents she had, and they loved Lacey dearly. But they also reminded her too much of her father, and Lacey struggled with seeing them at times. Nikki had tried to explain the situation, but Tyler's parents refused to listen, blaming everything on her.

Now they wanted custody rights.

Nikki had immediately called the FBI's contact in family court, and he'd confirmed that the Hunts' chances were slim, but Minnesota did have something called "interested third party custody" that could be cited when the biological parents were unable to care for the minor. Tyler's parents had the burden of proof, he'd reassured her. Nikki might work a lot of hours, but she also found a support system for Lacey, and they were both in therapy. Nikki still owned her house in St. Paul, but they spent most of their time in Stillwater, and Lacey had bonded with Rory's family, especially his mother. Since Nikki's daughter was nearly six years old, the judge would also make sure her little voice was heard as well.

"Chances of you losing are slim to mostly none," her legal contact had said. "I wouldn't worry."

Nikki kept telling herself that she wasn't worried about losing Lacey, that she was just frustrated with Tyler's parents. This was only going to bring more stress for Lacey, and Nikki had bent over backwards to make sure the Hunts continued to be a part of their granddaughter's life. If their true motive was to piss her off, they'd succeeded.

The sound of footsteps coming up behind her brought Nikki back to the present. She always kept the music low and never used both earbuds when she was out walking alone, no matter the time of day. Nikki couldn't allow herself to be that vulnerable.

"On your left." A slim woman jogged past, her own music up so loud Nikki could hear every word. Nikki wanted to tell the woman to be smarter, to use only one headphone so that she could keep her wits about her, but she knew it wouldn't do any good. It was the middle of the day, and the woman had her phone attached to her arm. It was easily accessible if she needed it, but it also brought a false sense of security. She'd just finished working on a tragic case involving a runner: a poor girl from Iowa had been out running with her phone in the rural area she'd grown up in. Her body wasn't found until a month later.

Nikki glanced behind her, instinctively taking a head count of how many people would be coming on the trail, but the trail was clear. She checked her watch to make sure she still had enough time to get around the lake and then quickened her pace. As she rounded the last curve on the trail, she noticed a man crouched at the edge of the cold water, seemingly lost in thought. The cop in her sized him up: jeans, light jacket, white tennis shoes, cropped dark hair, definitely biracial. Nice bone structure too, she thought.

The man turned his head then, and fresh sweat erupted on the back of her arms. She'd seen this man twice over the past few days, milling around near the office. Had he been following her?

She silently cursed her knee-jerk response. The FBI field office in Brooklyn Center was huge, and Nikki didn't know everyone who worked there. The man could have come to the lake to reset, just as she had. Never mind that he wasn't wearing the usual dress pants and tie; he could be a lab tech working in another field.

The wind shifted, turning the moisture on her skin ice-cold. The man stood and looked at her, stone-faced. Should she wave? She didn't have time to turn around, but she also didn't have much on her to ward off an attack. Nikki felt like a hypocrite for even considering it, but the man's demeanor was too precise. It was almost as though he knew she'd be rounding that corner around this time.

The Beatles' "Here Comes the Sun" blared from her phone, startling them both. The man turned around and walked back to the path, his back to her.

She answered her phone without bothering to look at the caller ID. "Agent Hunt."

"It's me, Kent." Kent Miller was the interim Washington County Sheriff, and Nikki had worked with him on several cases since she'd returned to the area. She hadn't talked to him much since August, when Miller had been investigating human remains found on a construction site.

"Hey, what's up?" Nikki kept the man in her eyeline as she walked toward the parking area. He headed toward the entrance, his head down and hands in his pockets.

"I've got a mess unlike anything I've seen," Miller answered, his deep voice shaky. "It's a triple homicide, with a survivor clinging to life. I need your team's help."

She'd worked with him enough to know he only called when a case was exceptionally bad. Nikki hit the remote start on the jeep and jogged towards the vehicle. "Text me the address," she replied. "Liam and I will be there as soon as possible."

"Did he give you any details?" Liam asked, tossing his work bag into the back seat. She'd texted him on the way back to the office, telling him to be ready and outside. Liam was Nikki's partner on the major crime unit and a solid profiler. He also wasn't afraid to go head-to-head with her if he disagreed with something, and while the trait could be infuriating, it was essential for their unit to be successful. She'd worked with Liam for more than six years, which meant they often spent more time with each other than with their significant others. At this point, they could read each other's moods and facial expressions in a heartbeat. Liam had stepped in and taken over while Nikki was out on leave after Tyler's murder, and the unit ran seamlessly. Few people could have stepped into her job on a moment's notice, but Liam had excelled.

"He called it a mess unlike anything he'd seen," she told him. "Three dead, one survivor in bad shape. Put your seat belt on."

Liam snapped the belt into place. "That doesn't sound good."

"Neither did he," Nikki said. "I've never heard him sound like this, even last winter when we worked on the missing girls case."

Liam retrieved his tablet from his work bag and started pulling up maps of the area. "More woods," he grumbled. "Fantastic."

Forty-five minutes later, they were on the southwest side of Stillwater.

"Looks like the house is at the end of the road," Liam said. "Best I can tell from this map, there's a good-sized ravine behind the house, with plenty of tree cover surrounding it."

The home sat on ten acres, adjacent to city-owned land, in the wealthy Northland Park area of Washington County. "Plenty of places to escape and hide." Nikki parked behind a Washington County Sheriff's cruiser and killed the engine. The house had likely been built in the nineties, and Nikki guessed it was at least four thousand square feet. A shuttered-in ground pool was visible just behind the three-car garage, and a new Toyota Camry had been blocked off with crime scene tape.

She spotted Deputy Reynolds, who she'd worked with on previous cases, guarding the scene. He looked paler than she remembered and relieved to see them.

"He looks like he's about to throw up," Liam said quietly. "That doesn't bode very well."

Nikki locked the vehicle and headed towards Reynolds, her heart rate increasing with each step.

Pumpkins lined the front of the house, and fake webbing stretched across the upper level, complete with a large, creepy fake spider. It reminded Nikki of the old science fiction movies where giant rats and other animals attacked humans. She eyed the spider, half expecting it to move. "Deputy, how's it going?"

"Not good," Reynolds answered. He pointed to the box sitting at his feet. "Sheriff Miller is waiting for you. You'll want booties and gloves. The smell's pretty strong too."

"Thanks for the warning," Nikki said. She and Liam slipped on the protective equipment and made their way to the front door as Miller emerged from the house, shaking his head. His dark skin had a pallor that made her stomach turn. He sat down on the top step, taking deep breaths.

Nikki glanced at Liam and knew he was thinking the same thing: what the hell had happened inside that house?

"Kent, you all right?" Nikki asked, sitting down next to him. She zipped her jacket against the wet fall chill. "We got here as soon as we could."

He wiped his face with a blue handkerchief. "I haven't thrown up at a scene since I was a rookie. Until today."

"Christ almighty," Liam said. "How's the survivor?"

"Still in surgery. I don't know if he'll make it." Miller stowed the handkerchief in his pocket. "There's no sign of forced entry. Survivor's a senior at the university. All three were stabbed multiple times. His mother's body is in the kitchen and his father's near the front door. The third victim fell from the upstairs balcony. Her hands were bound, and she landed on the tile floor in the foyer. It's gruesome. Medical examiner's with her now."

Nikki grimaced. "You have an ID on her?" she asked.

He shook his head. "Not officially, but I checked missing persons cases, and she matches the description of Jessica Chandler, a sophomore at the University of Minnesota who disappeared off campus a couple of days ago. I talked to the detective working her case. She's coming out here to make the ID."

"Have you found any evidence that she was held here against her will?" Nikki added.

"Not yet, but Courtney's been working upstairs for a while." Courtney was their lead forensic investigator, and since many of the county sheriffs didn't have enough crime scene technicians or state of the art equipment, she was often called in to help with a major crime scene before Nikki had even been invited to assist with the investigation. Miller stared ahead, as though lost in the memory of what he'd just seen. "We found the survivor, Bryce, lying on his back in the foyer, not far from the female. He's got a head injury, either from fighting or hitting the floor, plus an abdominal wound. It missed vital arteries, but the paramedics said it's showing signs of infection. He's in surgery for the head wound."

"Any idea what kind of knife?" Liam asked. "Were all three stabbed with the same one?"

"We're not sure yet. Hopefully the medical examiner will be able to figure that out," Miller replied. "His uncle said that Bryce was mostly out of it when he arrived, but he said that when first responders were loading him into the ambulance, Bryce came to enough to mumble 'look out' a couple of times. I talked with the paramedic who rode with Bryce to the hospital, and he confirmed that's what Bryce said, but he lapsed back into unconsciousness after that."

Miller picked up the water bottle sitting on the steps between his knees and took a shaky gulp before clearing his throat. "There's an ice skate between Jessica and Bryce, men's size ten. We found rope and a stun gun in the trunk of a Camry registered to Bryce. We've also spotted marks on Jessica's back and left leg that look like taser burn. Medical examiner will have to confirm."

"An ice skate?" Nikki had never mastered ice skating, but she knew the blades could be dangerous. Last year, a high school student had been cut by a skate during a hockey game collision, and he'd died in the hospital. Nikki had checked off yet another sport too dangerous for her daughter. "Is it possible he grabbed the skate to use in self-defense?"

"Probably," Miller said. "There's a blood trail from the master bedroom and down the stairs, but Courtney will have to test to find out whose blood it actually is." Miller sipped more water.

"You said his uncle found him?" Nikki asked.

Miller nodded. "Vic Weber. When Dave didn't show up for work at their law office and didn't answer the phone this morning, his brother decided to come and check on them. They've been putting off getting a new furnace, and he was afraid something had gone wrong with the old one."

"Carbon dioxide poisoning," Nikki murmured. "It's a genuine concern. Happened to a family when I was in second grade. The only one who survived was the oldest son, because he'd been staying at a friend's place." She'd been in the same grade as one of the victims, the empty desk a constant reminder that a family had gone to sleep and not woken up. She'd had nightmares for months.

"Vic knew the garage door code," Miller said. "He banged on the front door and couldn't see anyone inside, so he went in through the garage door. That's when he found Joan in the kitchen. He called it in right away. 911 was on the phone with him when he found the others."

"Weber Legal, right?" Liam said. "I see their commercials all the time. Didn't they just win some kind of big community award?"

"I don't know," Miller said. "But Dave was a well-connected member of the community. He's also a former Olympic breast-stroker. Bryce swims at the university and went to the Olympic trials last year. His uncle said that he'd just missed the cut." Miller looked down at the steps, shaking his head. "That sounds like a terrible pun."

"Does Bryce live here or on campus?" Nikki didn't know a lot about college swimming, but she knew the practices were often early morning, and the Webers lived nearly forty-five minutes from the university on a good traffic day.

"He's vice president of his fraternity and lives at the frat house, but he does come home regularly," Miller answered, looking through the dogeared pocket-sized notebook he always carried. "He's a member of Sigma Alpha Epsilon."

"Weren't they kicked off campus?" Liam asked.

"Suspended," Nikki said, glad she'd kept up with the alumni news for all these years. "For hazing incidents, but they were reinstated a few years ago. I don't know much about them beyond that."

"His uncle insists that they were a happy family, they have no enemies." Miller shook his head. "But this is a complex scene, which is why I called you guys in. If this is a stranger killing, we've got to put the community on alert."

Nikki nodded. Miller didn't have a lot of resources, and with three dead bodies, one hospitalization and a plethora of different wounds and potential weapons, she understood why he needed her help on this one. "Liam and I will head inside. Join us whenever you're ready."

"Might want to leave your coats out here," Miller said. "Someone set the thermostat to eighty-eight degrees."

"Eighty-eight degrees? My grandma doesn't even set the thermostat over seventy-eight, and her house is sweltering." Liam shrugged out of his coat and draped it over the porch railing, and Nikki did the same, wishing she'd gone with short sleeves this morning instead of the long-sleeved blue Henley.

"Blanchard says the heat will make it harder to figure out time of death," Miller said. "I'm guessing the killer did his research."

Nikki knew he was right: the warmer the temperature, the faster the decomposition process. Bodies in warmer climates passed through rigor mortis much faster than those left in mild climates. "Did the uncle mention a break in their routine? Was there any reason they wouldn't have been home last night?"

"Not with Dave's job," Miller answered. "His brother said he worked until six p.m. He usually gets home around seven. Joan worked at the Stillwater Public Library. She went home early due to a migraine. I checked with her supervisor, and she clocked out around three yesterday."

As soon as Nikki entered, the coppery smell of dried blood overwhelmed her. The two-story house boasted a large open foyer, with stairs that curved into a gallery-style hallway upstairs. Nikki could see a bit of the kitchen toward the back of the house, and the open floor plan allowed them to see Joan's feet in the kitchen. Her husband had been killed near the front door, his body sprawled between the foyer tile and the carpeted great room. The girl who'd fallen over the sweeping stairwell and onto the foyer's ceramic tiles had been covered with a sheet, but Nikki could see the blood pooling over the grout between the tiles.

"What the hell?" Liam whispered, pointing to the wall beneath the sweeping stairs.

Nikki read the words scrawled in black spray paint out loud. "The righteous hate what is false, but the wicked make themselves a stench and bring shame on themselves."

"Who said that?" Liam asked. "Is it from a movie?"

"The Bible, Proverbs 13:5." The dark-skinned woman standing near Dave Weber's body didn't look up from the notes she currently scribbled. Sweat dotted her forehead, and the circles lining her eyes made it clear the doctor had been up for hours. As the state's first female African American chief medical examiner, Blanchard was hard-nosed on her best days, and her determination had earned her the respect of her colleagues. Most scenes were handled by a death investigator who brought the body into the office for her and her pathologists to autopsy. Blanchard's presence at a scene was never a good sign. If she'd come out herself, the depravity of the case was worse than usual.

"Doctor Blanchard, how are you?" Nikki said, her skin already clammy. "Man, it really is like a sauna in here."

"That's why they're coming out of rigor already," Blanchard said.

"In normal conditions, that's around twenty-four hours, right?" Nikki asked.

Blanchard nodded, fanning herself with a gloved hand.

"Temperature definitely sped up the process, possibly by several hours."

"We don't know if it happened last night or this morning?" Liam asked.

"Not yet," Blanchard said. "Wife's in lounge clothes, and he's wearing khakis and a dress shirt. Could have been relaxing for the night or getting ready for work early this morning."

Nikki walked around Dave's body. He was on his side, curled into the fetal position, and Nikki could see superficial stab wounds visible on his hands and face alongside the wound that must have killed him. "These look like defensive wounds. He put his hands up to ward off the attack."

Blanchard nodded. "It looks like the same weapon to me. He was stabbed in the stomach and bled out. Hopefully quickly."

"Any idea what size knife?" Liam asked.

"I won't know for certain until the autopsy, but my guess is the blade is at least ten inches. Courtney bagged the knives in the kitchen, but if you look at the width of the wounds—not the depth—they're closer to the size of a hunting knife."

Nikki knelt down next to Jessica's body. She'd hit the tile floor face down, her neck twisted, and one side of her skull caved in from the impact. Bits of skull and brain matter were embedded into her dark hair. Her arms, still bound at the wrists with thick, brown rope, were pinned beneath the girl's chest. "She reflexively put her hands up to block her fall," Nikki surmised.

Blanchard joined Nikki. "Her hands are drawn into fists and pinned beneath her. She's not as far through rigor mortis as the others. I probably won't be able to check her fingernails until we get her on the table."

"Does that mean she was killed later than the Webers?"

"Not necessarily," Blanchard said. "Body composition and

even location make a difference. She's also the farthest away from the heating vents."

The Webers' house had arched ceilings, and the upstairs appeared to be nearly as open as the lower level. "That's what, nine, ten feet up to the railing?" Nikki asked.

"That sounds about right," Liam said, gazing at the balcony. "She fell face first, so she was likely pushed, right?"

"I'm leaning that way since it appears her hands are still bound," Blanchard said.

Nikki sniffed, trying to place the chemical mixed in with the stink of dried blood and decay. "Is that ammonia?" She pointed to the marker on the bottom step. "Did someone try to clean up blood off the hardwood floor?"

"Way ahead of you, boss lady." A familiar voice called from upstairs. Courtney peered over the railing. At barely five feet, Courtney always had to roll up the pant legs on her Tyvek suit, but her personality made up for the height deficit. "I already took pictures before the effects of the Luminol wore off."

"You find any shoe prints in the blood?" Liam asked.

Shoe prints could be a slam dunk in court or a disaster, depending on the skillset of the forensic examiner and how well the crime scene had been blocked off. Courtney was one of the best examiners Nikki had worked with, but she'd also seen more than one good defense attorney get those prints thrown out because of poor crime scene management, usually by the first responders.

"A partial, but don't get excited," Courtney said. "It'll be at least two days before I even get to it, because there's far stronger evidence to process. The lovely note you're standing in front of looks like generic spray paint you can buy anywhere, but we'll test it anyway. There's a large spot of blood up here in the hall-way, near the master bedroom, and we've found a matching skate. There are droplets down the stairs consistent with someone injured and trying to stumble down."

Nikki picked up the evidence bag containing the bloodied ice skate. "Where exactly were the skates?"

"Master bedroom closet," Courtney said. "I'll test the blood against all of the victims."

"I can tell you the skate isn't the murder weapon," Blanchard said. "It's the wrong angle and diameter. According to first responders, the skate was lying near the survivor, and he had cuts on his arms and hands that looked more like defensive wounds. The wounds to his neck and abdomen appear to have been made by the same knife used to kill his parents, and given the amount of blood, an artery was at least nicked."

"You're saying Bryce probably tried to use the skate blade in self-defense?" Nikki clarified the scenario she'd suspected as soon as Miller had briefed them.

Blanchard nodded. "Based on the report from the paramedics, yes."

"Is there a chance some of the blood on the skate could be from the killer?" Liam asked.

"It's possible," she answered. "Your suspect was likely cut by the skate too, though, so that's a job for your lab to determine. I can't say anything definitively until then, other than the skate wasn't the murder weapon."

"Maybe the killer didn't know he was here," Liam said. "Bryce is upstairs and gets the only weapon he can, but it backfires."

Nikki went to the kitchen and over to Joan's small frame. She lay on her side too, her legs spread as though she'd dropped mid-step. Unlike her husband, her body didn't have a lot of blood around it. "How did she die?"

"Stab wound to the left lung, punctured right through it. Would have been quiet and a relatively quick death."

"Check for hesitation marks when you do the autopsy."

She checked Joan's ring finger. "No rings. Are there any other signs of a possible B and E?"

"No." Miller had joined them, wearing fresh booties. "Back door was secure, and so were all of the windows. Basement walkout is locked too. Mrs. Weber has a lot of jewelry in a box upstairs. Her wedding set might be there."

"She doesn't just have a box of jewelry," Courtney said. "She's got some stuff that should be in a safe—which, by the way, we found in the master closet. No sign of anyone tampering with it. I dusted it for prints."

"Sheriff, did Dave's brother mention why Jessica might have been here?" Liam asked.

"He didn't know her, and he didn't know anything about Bryce having a girlfriend. He said it would have been really out of character for him to bring a girl home to meet his parents. He's not interested in serious relationships, too busy with school and swimming." Miller shook his head. "This is just vague enough that it could have been done by someone who knew them or a stranger who'd just marked them for slaughter."

"I was thinking the same," Liam said. "Someone obsessed with punishing people, no matter how small the infraction. It could have been a perceived slight, even. But whoever did this didn't act on a whim."

Nikki studied the family photos hanging in the foyer. Bryce looked like a younger version of his father, down to the red hair and freckles. Both were tall and lean, although Dave had thickened around his middle. They both dwarfed Joan's small frame.

"Unless we hear about other valuables being stolen, I don't think the motive was robbery," Nikki said. "Especially if Joan's got more expensive jewelry upstairs. The killer had intent."

Was the intent personal or had this family been chosen for their secluded location? Most killers who attacked families put them through some form of torture, often raping the wife. In Nikki's experience, they also tended to spend more time at the scene, because they'd done their research and knew how much of a window they had with the family.

So far, this case appeared to be a mixed bag: obvious planning, but without evidence the killer had done anything more than a blitz attack.

"Miller told us the paramedic saw signs of infection in Bryce's wound." Liam looked at Blanchard. "I know it can set in quickly, but there's got to be a time discrepancy between the murders and his attack, right?"

"Possibly," Blanchard said. "There could be a large gap between his wounds being inflicted and his parents' deaths, but it depends on what type of bacteria caused the infection. Some of them spread very quickly. I'd also like to know why Jessica was tasered *after* she died."

"What?" Nikki asked, shocked. "That doesn't make sense."

"I'll double-check during the autopsy with a better scope, but there are zero signs of healing. It's all burned, which can happen when there's no oxygen to the flesh."

"The taser is in the Camry out front," Miller said. "It was unlocked, keys under the seat. We didn't find any cartridges in the car or the house."

Jessica had been missing for a few days. Was it possible that she'd somehow ended up at this house and the family was attacked out of necessity? Tasing her after she was dead sounded like anger, which meant there could be a personal connection between her and the killer.

Liam seemed to read her thoughts. "If there's a personal vendetta against Jessica, that changes everything."

"We don't know that for sure," Nikki reminded him. "She could have been here and done something to piss the killer off, and he tased her body because of that. Last word type of thing." She understood why Miller had called them in. Reynolds was a good deputy, but he hadn't worked a lot of murder cases and probably didn't have the trained eye to really work through the scene and pick out anomalies, not to mention the initial shell shock of seeing the victims. Nikki looked up at Courtney still looking over the bannister, which had been covered in finger-print powder. "I see you printed the railing. What about the thermostat?"

"Done already," Courtney said. "It's in the kitchen."

"Sheriff, you've confirmed no one was visiting the family?"

Miller nodded. "Dave's brother and partner in the law firm said it was just the two of them, and Bryce, whenever he came home from school, which had become less often. He usually only came home to study for a big test."

Nikki had gone back to Jessica's broken body, noting the oversized hoodie and too-long sweatpants. "Was she wearing shoes?"

"No," Blanchard said. "Just socks, and they appear to be new."

Nikki gently pushed the baggy sweatshirt sleeve up Jessica's right arm, looking for signs of bruises. But as she checked the rest of Jessica's body, she dislodged the tag of the sweatshirt, and could see two letters inked on the white polyester tucked behind Jessica's hair.

"B.W.," she said aloud, looking at her colleagues to see if they understood the significance. "Unless someone wrestled her into it, Jessica and Bryce knew one another," Nikki said, a chill running down her spine. "Enough to feel comfortable wearing his clothes."

TWO

"Her fingers are probably broken along with her arms," Blanchard said, studying Jessica's body. "I'll be able to check her nails once I get her on the table and the hand is more pliable."

"Do you need a sample of Bryce's DNA to rule him out?" Liam asked. "We can get it from the hospital."

"I've got it," Courtney said. "Bagged his razor, hair found on his pillow, and a comb from the bathroom. I also took samples of the blood in the hallway. Assuming it's his, we'll be able to compare things fairly quickly."

"Are you taking his car to the lab?"

"Yes," Courtney said. "It's windy out, and I don't want to lose anything working outside. We'll give it a full sweep later today."

"What about security video?" Liam asked. "There's cameras mounted at the front and back doors."

"We're working on it," Miller answered. "They both record to a personal server. We're working on getting into the system on the laptop we found on the kitchen table."

"We can get a tech to the law office if you don't find it,"

Liam said. "He might have access set up there. Are there any other computers in the house?"

"A tablet. Trying to unlock that too. My deputy that's good with Apple products is out canvassing the area. I don't expect him to find much since this house is so secluded, but maybe we'll get lucky."

"Liam, see if you can help get into the laptop and find the security videos." Her partner knew things about computers Nikki barely understood, and he often saved them the time and effort of bringing a computer tech to the scene. She turned to Miller. "How much did you get from the uncle earlier?"

"Not a lot, as you can imagine," Miller said. "I'm going to the hospital in a little while and probably the law firm. We'll do a full background check."

"Come look at the master bedroom first," Courtney said.

Nikki avoided the area near the evidence markers on the staircase, glad that she didn't have to look at the shoe print even if it might help them figure out who'd killed the Webers. She still had nightmares of the bloody shoe prints on the stairs the night she found her parents. Had Bryce found the same thing at his home?

The Webers' bedroom was a true master suite, with a separate bathroom and a big walk-in closet. Despite a king-sized bed and heavy armoire, the room still appeared large. They also had a private deck with a beautiful view of the ravine behind the house. "What a view."

"Especially with the fall colors." Courtney labeled an evidence bag and sat it out of the way. "There's a gun case in the master closet, but it's locked. If Bryce found the ice skate intending to use it in self-defense, he must not have known the code to the gun safe."

Nikki looked around the room in search of something else that could have been used as a weapon. The matching lamps on the individual nightstands appeared to be made of a solid metal.

She tried to lift one. "Okay, so this is too heavy to move with very quickly. Still, running into this room, these lamps are the first things I'd go for as a weapon."

"I'll make sure to print them too."

Nikki spotted the two-tiered jewelry armoire sitting on the dresser. The lower section contained a Chanel bracelet and several other pieces that appeared authentic. She also found a diamond-encrusted watch that had to be worth at least $1000 in a pawnshop. She rifled through the already-open nightstand drawer next to the right side of the bed. "A nail file, hand lotion and rose-scented shea body butter. Safe to say this is her nightstand. Still no wedding set."

"Maybe they're in the safe," Courtney said. "But then why isn't that other stuff in it? You wear a wedding set every day, usually."

"I always took mine off in the bathroom and left them on the sink," Nikki said, trying not to think of Tyler again.

"I checked all the bathrooms and the kitchen," Courtney said. "We'll keep looking. There's also a home office downstairs. We haven't gotten to it yet, but we might find insurance information on the rings."

"That would be great. I'll ask at the hospital if they found them in Bryce's personal effects when he came in, although that seems like a stretch. Which room is his?"

"Down here."

Nikki followed Courtney to the last door on the left. The room was nearly as large as the master, and even though Bryce lived on campus, his bedroom still appeared very much lived in and relatively neat for a twenty-two-year-old guy. A basket of folded laundry sat on the floor, and the bed had been made. Nikki went to the desk and leafed through the open textbook. Dozens of blank sticky notes had been fixed to various pages, with some passages highlighted, but she didn't see any sign that Bryce had been taking notes.

Nikki picked up the framed photo of Bryce and four other tall, fit guys in Speedos. "Is that who I think it is?"

"The most decorated Olympian of all time?" Courtney nodded. "Sure is. That's taken at the 2016 Olympic trials."

"That's right, you swam in high school and college." Nikki did the math in her head. Bryce would have been fifteen in the picture, barely old enough to be eligible.

"A division two college. Nowhere near this level. He had a trial time for the most recent Olympics too. I found the heat sheets in his drawer. He must have kept them as souvenirs." Courtney chuckled. "Bryce swam the 100 fly, too, in the championship heat. Imagine sharing the pool with those guys."

"Where's his computer?" Nikki asked in confusion. "Most college kids use laptops to take notes." A set of AirPods had been left on the desk, but she didn't see any sign of a phone or computer.

Courtney held up a bagged, wireless mouse. "This is an Apple Magic Mouse. There's also a wireless keyboard in the desk drawer. But no MacBook. I did find a new iPhone in the downstairs toilet. We're trying to dry it out, but Apple says thirty minutes is the max time the new phones can be submerged and still work."

"I wonder if there's stuff on the phone he didn't want anyone to see," Liam said from the doorway.

"Find out their cell carrier and get a warrant for the records. Once we get a confirmed ID on the female in the foyer, we'll get one for hers so that we can cross reference phone numbers. And we'll need to talk to Bryce's fraternity brothers, along with the swim team. They spent the most time with him, so if he showed any sign of doing this, they're the ones who would have noticed." Nikki looked around the room one last time. "I don't see any pictures of other friends or girlfriends, including Jessica. Hopefully we find that in his room at school."

"The detective in charge of Jessica Chandler's missing

persons case is downstairs," Liam said. "She confirmed it's Jessica."

Nikki followed Liam down the stairs. A slim, blonde woman knelt next to Jessica. She still wore her jacket, and beads of sweat shone on her forehead.

"This is Detective Brenner with MPD," Liam said. "Detective, this is Supervisory Special Agent Nikki Hunt."

Brenner didn't answer, her gaze transfixed on the victim.

Nikki crouched next to the young detective and put her hand on her shoulder. "First homicide as a detective?" Nikki asked.

Brenner's chin trembled. "How could you tell?" She rubbed her sleeve against the tears building in her eyes, her cheeks growing red. "I worked patrol for six years. This isn't my first dead body, but I've never seen anything like this."

Nikki looked around at the horrifying scene, wondering if anything could truly surprise her anymore. Luckily, few detectives ever had to attend such scenes. Hers was a rare line of work. "Jessica was reported missing a couple of days ago, right?"

"Thirty-eight hours ago, to be exact. But no one's seen or spoken to her since Saturday morning," Brenner answered. "She went home for the long weekend, but she was able to pick up some shifts at work on Sunday, so she came back early. Her parents received a text from her around two p.m. on Saturday, letting them know she'd made it back. They didn't hear from her again, but assumed she was just busy with work. The roommate didn't realize that Jessica hadn't come home until late Tuesday, when her parents called the dorm, asking for her. The roommate called Jessica's friends who live in another dorm, and they hadn't heard from her since Saturday, either. She was reported missing on Wednesday. We found her car, with her travel bag still in the back. Her wallet and cell phone weren't in the car."

"Was it an iPhone 13?" Nikki asked.

"No, it was an older model. A ten, I think," Brenner answered. "Since she'd taken her wallet and phone, my commander wasn't convinced that she'd actually been taken against her will."

"But her car was locked?" Liam asked.

"Yes," Brenner said. "We were able to get the spare key from her dorm room and checked the trunk right away. Everything appeared normal."

"Which dorm did Jessica live in?" Nikki asked.

"Centennial." Brenner opened the canvas bag sitting next to her. "She parked in the Oak Street ramp, which is where her parking contract designated." She handed Nikki a wrinkled campus map. The dorm and parking garage had been circled, along with a handful of small x's.

"What do the 'x's' represent?" Nikki studied the map, trying to remember the area. She'd graduated nearly two decades ago, and the campus had expanded since then.

"Locations of working cameras," Brenner said. "Apparently most of the lots have a camera or two that needs fixing, including the one on Jessica's normal route from the car to the dorm, which is where she likely would have gone first."

"But she didn't reach the dorm?" Nikki knew that residents had to sign in and out with the front desk at the dorms.

Brenner shook her head. "No record of her signing in, and everyone I spoke with yesterday said they hadn't seen her since she left Thursday afternoon. That's when she last signed out too."

"Did you find any connection to Bryce Weber in your investigation?"

"We're still waiting on her phone records." Brenner looked slightly flustered. "I got the warrant late yesterday, and I've been told I should receive them by tomorrow morning, but Verizon only keeps a few weeks' worth of text records."

"Those are the ones we're interested in," Miller said. "Please make sure we all get a copy as soon as possible."

Brenner flushed red. "I'm not sure my boss would appreciate that. He doesn't usually like working with the FBI."

"I'm happy to chat with your boss," Nikki said. "Believe it or not, we're all on the same team. You didn't answer the question about Bryce."

Brenner sighed. "I think they were in a relationship in the past. According to her friends, last year Jessica was involved in some kind of love triangle. Last fall, a senior named Kai Richardson volunteered with the freshman orientation week, which is how he met Jessica. They hit it off and stayed in touch. At the time, Kai shared a room with Bryce Weber and another member of the fraternity. Just a couple of weeks before winter break, Kai got into a fight with Bryce over Jessica. Kai had a crush she didn't reciprocate, and she got cozy with Bryce at a party."

So much for Nikki's theory that Jessica had somehow ended up in the Weber home by accident. "Did you speak to Kai, or is this all information from Jessica's friends?"

"Her friends, and then Bryce confirmed it when I spoke to him yesterday. Kai took time off at the end of the semester, citing mental health issues. His parents live across the river in Wisconsin, and they told me that Kai had been diagnosed with schizophrenia but refused to give me any other contact information. According to them, Kai had outpatient treatment and is working part-time at a small restaurant near his parents' home, trying to get back on track so he can finish school. He's supposedly living with them, but again, they refused to let me speak with him or get his contact information."

"Did you speak with the other frat brothers?"

"Briefly," said Brenner. "I haven't been able to get through them all, and I couldn't exactly force them all to talk to me."

"Did anyone you spoke with know if Jessica was still in contact with Kai?" Liam asked.

"According to her friends and parents, no," Brenner said. "I stopped by the Caribou Coffee shop near campus yesterday. Jessica studied there a lot, and one of the baristas confirmed she'd seen her talking with a man matching Kai's description a few times. They haven't seen either one of them since last week."

"Did you find any foreign prints in her car?" Liam asked.

"Just hers."

Most kids Jessica's age with cars wound up serving as the friend group's taxi, so Nikki was surprised at that.

"Apparently she's very meticulous about her car." Brenner looked down at the broken girl. "Look, I've only been a detective for three weeks. My superior had his doubts about her actually being taken against her will, and I followed his lead. Oh God, how am I going to tell her parents?" Brenner's eyes brimmed with tears. "How do you tell someone their child has been murdered? I saw some bad things as an officer but I never had to deal with the family."

"I'll go with you to tell them, if it helps." She looked at Miller. "Do you think your people can keep a lid on the details from today? I'd like to keep Jessica's name out of the media for as long as we can."

"I'll tell them," Miller said. "I can't promise someone won't leak to the media, especially from the medical examiner's office. We've had a problem with that lately."

"Why keep her name out of it?" Brenner asked.

"Because whoever's responsible, she is victim zero. The chain of events started with her disappearance," Nikki said. "Has Jessica's credit card been used since Saturday?"

Brenner shook her head. "She filled up with gas after she

left for the city, at a station about half an hour from her parents' house. That's the last time she used her credit card. We're still trying to get the warrant for her full financials, but the bank did confirm she hasn't withdrawn any money since she disappeared."

"And the gas station CCTV footage?" Nikki asked.

"Shows her leaving."

"What else did the security cameras pick up?" Liam asked. "Anyone following her in or out of the parking lot? Did she talk to anyone?"

"Just the cashier. She came in and paid for gas and coffee."

Nikki handed Brenner a business card. "My email address is on there. Would you mind emailing us copies?"

"Sure, but we've looked at it a hundred times."

"And you probably didn't miss anything," Nikki answered. "But we should look again. Liam, can you get everyone's financial records pulled? Pushing the warrant through for Jessica's shouldn't be an issue now that we can confirm she's dead." Nikki glanced at Brenner. "Detective, why weren't you able to get full access to her records?"

Brenner scowled. "She's an adult who went missing over a weekend, so my boss wanted to proceed with caution. He said girls her age usually turn up after a few days."

"Not all of them," Liam said grimly, writing in his notebook. "That's why you have to take every disappearance seriously."

"Do you have a list with everyone you've interviewed since she disappeared?" Nikki asked.

Brenner nodded. "I can email it to you."

"You're already the first point of contact. Can you call each person and tell them the FBI has been asked to help and I'd like to talk to them face to face? Start with her inner circle and work your way down the list. You have all of her social media accounts, right?"

"Not logins, but the addresses, yes," Brenner said. "She was more active on Instagram and Snapchat."

"Which means Instagram is our best option, since Snapchat deletes things. After we talk to the parents, I want to go to the frat. Liam, how long do you think it will take to get those security videos?"

"I'm not sure," he said. "I was thinking about going back to the sheriff's station and working with his computer guys to speed things along, while Miller goes to the hospital and talks to the family."

"That's fine," Nikki said. "Miller, you've got guys canvassing neighbors and checking the property, right?"

He nodded. "They're coming up empty so far. This location's pretty private and there's a lot of tree cover, especially in the ravine behind the house. We're looking for any sign that someone was hanging around trying to figure out the family's schedule."

"The woods back up to a fairly busy county road, don't they?" Nikki mused.

"I think so," Miller said.

"Have your guys walk from the house to the road on the other side of the woods, along with the road we came in on," Nikki said. "If Jessica and Bryce had a history, there's a chance she'd been to this house, and she might have recognized it and tried to escape. It's a long shot, but we need to rule it out."

Nikki left Liam with Miller and headed back toward the metro area. Brenner had asked the parents to meet them at the police station, so she'd gone ahead to make sure the parents didn't arrive early and find out about Jessica's death from someone else.

She called Rory, hoping that he would pick up. He'd been working extra hours the past couple of months since his major construction project had been halted when human remains had been found. They'd turned out to be those of Rory's ex-girlfriend, and the ensuing investigation into her murder had taken its toll on him. He didn't want to go to therapy, insisting that she and her daughter were his therapy, but Nikki worried about him. Rory was the type to bury his emotions and keep smiling until he snapped.

Her call went to voicemail, and even though she knew he was working, she still had a little flutter of nerves. He'd ignored her calls while he'd been dealing with the investigation into his ex's murder, and he'd gone on a couple of drinking binges. Even though she knew he was probably fine, old habits tended to die hard.

She left him a message letting him know that she would be late and asked him to pick Lacey up from his parents, who watched her after school for a couple of hours most days.

Nikki's heart ached for Jessica's parents. Brenner had told her she'd been their only child. They no longer had grandkids in their future because of some callous person who decided Jessica's life wasn't worth living. As much as she hated losing time with her daughter, Nikki did the job because of people like the Chandlers. Finding out who killed their daughter wouldn't bring her back, but it always helped the healing process, and Nikki would cross hell and high water to do that for them.

THREE

At the police station, Nikki found Brenner pacing in front of her cubicle, which was in the back corner away from the windows. "Are the parents here?"

Brenner nodded. "They're waiting in the conference room. I haven't actually seen them. They'll figure it out the moment they see my face. I can't hide my emotions."

"Do you want me to tell them?"

Brenner shook her head. "No, I'll do it."

She led Nikki out of the bullpen area to the back, which housed the meeting and interview rooms. Brenner stopped at the first door and took a deep breath, trying to compose herself. Nikki waited behind her, ready to jump in if she had to, but she understood why it was important for Brenner to do this. She'd spent time and energy with the parents already, forming some modicum of trust. Hearing it from her would likely help the parents accept the truth faster.

Brenner whispered something to herself and then opened the door. "Mr. and Mrs. Chandler, I'm sorry to keep you waiting." Her voice cracked on the last word.

Nikki immediately saw the resemblance between Jessica

and her mother. Her dark hair was streaked with gray, and she appeared exhausted. "Did you find her?"

Brenner didn't answer right away. Mrs. Chandler stared at the detective, tears building in her eyes. "Tell us where our daughter is."

Mr. Chandler dwarfed his wife, but right now he was as helpless as she was. He closed his eyes, as if waiting for an incoming blow.

Brenner cleared her throat. "I'm so sorry, Tina, Larry." Still standing by the door, she looked at each of them in turn. "But your daughter is dead. She was found at the scene of a triple homicide this morning. We're still working out how she got there—"

Nikki squeezed Brenner's arm, warning her not to share case details. It was an easy mistake to make when the family was informed.

Larry and Tina held each other and sobbed. Brenner looked like she was fighting tears. She sat down across from the couple. "This is Special Agent Nikki Hunt from the FBI. She's going to be helping with the investigation."

"Mr. and Mrs. Chandler, I can't imagine how difficult this must be," Nikki said, taking the chair beside Brenner.

"I don't understand," Mr. Chandler finally choked out. "She was killed? And with two other people?"

"Yes. We'll be investigating every possible angle to find your daughter's killer," Nikki said. "I'd like to ask you some questions, if I may. I know this news is hard to take, but the more information we have the better." Nikki waited while the couple composed themselves. Time was always a factor in murder cases, but the one thing Nikki refused to rush was interviews with the victim's family.

After a few minutes, Mr. Chandler motioned for her to go ahead. Nikki started with the easier questions. "Did Jessica talk about anything unusual when she visited for fall break? Did she seem worried about anything?"

"No," Larry replied. "She was happy and excited about her classes. She'd decided to major in child psychology. Wanted to be a therapist." He pressed his hand to his mouth. "Do you know how she died? How badly did she suffer?"

"We're still trying to piece together what happened at the scene," Nikki answered, trying not to picture the girl's broken body lying in the foyer. "Hopefully the medical examiner will be able to tell us more after the autopsy."

Mr. Chandler closed his eyes, no doubt imagining his child being cut open and dissected.

"I begged her not to take those extra shifts." Tina Chandler finally spoke. "But she's always been independent. She got as many scholarships as she could in order to attend school. Insisted on working for her own spending money. Working the weekend meant higher tips, especially with the football game Sunday. Everyone wants to work those shifts. She was over the moon about being asked."

"She worked at The Crooked Pint Ale House," Brenner clarified. "It's just blocks away from the stadium, and it's always packed on game days, home or away."

"I'm familiar with it." The brewery was always packed, especially during Vikings home games. Nikki could see why it was a coveted shift. "I probably would have done the same thing if I were in her shoes."

"I had a bad feeling," Tina said. "I watched her walk out the door and thought 'I'm never going to see her again.' I told myself I was being ridiculous."

"I know how hard this is and that you've already given Detective Brenner a lot of information. I just have a few more questions, I promise." Nikki slid the photocopied list of names from Brenner's file over to them. "We'll follow up with her friends and any other contacts on campus, but can you think of anyone else not on this list?"

Both parents glanced at the list and shook their heads. "She kept a small circle of friends," Tina said. "Her focus was really on school."

"What about a sorority or any extracurricular clubs?" Nikki asked.

"She wasn't interested in that," Tina said. "I know she and her friends went to frat parties and that sort of thing, but Jessica usually stayed sober to take care of everyone. That's the kind of person she was."

Brenner leaned across the table and grabbed Tina's hands. "I promise you we will find who did this and hold them accountable."

Nikki bit the inside of her cheek. She didn't want to chastise Brenner in front of the parents, but a promise like that was never a good idea. "I'm going to see if victim services has someone available to help you get through this. Detective Brenner, can you show me where they're located?"

Brenner nodded and followed Nikki out of the room. She closed the door, looking nervous. "Victim services has already been notified. Someone should be down here soon."

"I know," Nikki said. "I just wanted to talk to you quickly and caution you against promising anything else you may not be able to provide. I understand why you felt the urge to do it—and I've done the same thing myself. But we can't always deliver on those promises, and that isn't good for the families or the police department."

"Shit," Brenner hissed. "I didn't even think."

"It's okay," Nikki said. "This is a terrible case for any homicide detective, let alone a rookie. Why don't you go back inside with them and see if they need anything? I'm going to check in with Liam and Miller."

She clicked on Liam's name in her contacts, hoping he

didn't have his phone on silent. He tended to zone in on what he was doing and often didn't notice the phone vibrating.

"Hey," he answered. "I was just about to call you. We got into the laptop about five minutes ago. The last video from the front camera was recorded at 5:07 p.m. when UPS dropped off a box. Joan came out and grabbed it. Last thing on back door's camera was a bird triggering the sensor around 6:00 p.m."

"That's it?"

"Miller's deputies should have checked the security cameras first," Liam said, irritation in his voice. "Someone took the batteries out of them both. We're bagging them for prints. Miller verified with the office that Dave left at his usual time. There's no activity on his credit cards since late yesterday afternoon so it's likely he came straight home."

"We already thought this was probably a planned attack," Nikki said. "The killer knew where the security cameras were and disabled them. Did the camera not pick something up when the batteries were taken out? Isn't it motion activated?"

"It did, but they knew to stay out of frame. We've got about a second of blurry movement in front of the camera, and then it ends. They're searching the trash and garage but so far no sign of the can of spray paint."

"Well, I've just spoken to the parents," Nikki said. "They didn't have Bryce on their list of Jessica's contacts, and they're certain they can't think of anyone to add to the list. If Bryce and Jessica were still in a relationship, ever since that party, it was a secret."

"There's more to this," Liam said. "I just can't put my finger on it yet."

Nikki ended the call and stowed her phone. The only thing they knew for certain was that the killer either knew the family or spent enough time watching them to have their normal routines down, suggesting they likely had a specific plan of attack. But why put the taser in Bryce's car? Had he left it unlocked? And how did Jessica figure into this mess? Her presence made little sense at this point. The more Nikki thought about it, the more questions she had. A familiar sense of anxiety settled over her. No case was easily solved, but this one was going to be tough.

By the time she returned to the family, victim services had arrived and taken control of the situation while Brenner hung back.

"I'm going to campus," Nikki said. "You coming?"

"I want to," Brenner asked. "I just need you to convince my boss that this is still my case. He said that if the FBI is working on it, I need to move on to something else, but I want to see this through."

"I'll see what I can do," Nikki replied, walking off in the direction of the sergeant's desk.

She'd met Sergeant Gill a few years ago on a case, and he'd impressed her with his willingness to work with the FBI without any ego issues.

"Sergeant Gill, you have a moment?" she said as she reached his desk.

Gill swiveled around in his rolling chair, the back tilting dangerously. His head was considerably balder than the last time she'd seen him. He was never without a toothpick, obsessively chewing it in his bid to quit smoking.

"Agent Hunt, good to see you again. What brings you down here?"

Nikki didn't really understand why Brenner felt like she should check with her superior given that she'd been working Jessica's disappearance. But she'd forgotten what it was like to be a rookie, and police departments had varying policies when it came to working with the FBI. Not to mention that Brenner checking with her boss would probably give her some bonus points in his mind. "I'm working with Detective Brenner on a homicide case."

He looked past Nikki at Brenner. "A homicide, Detective? I thought you were working that college girl's missing persons case?"

"I am," Brenner said. "She was found dead this morning in Washington County. The sheriff asked Agent Hunt to help with the case."

"Sheriff Miller?" Gill stroked his graying goatee. "He asked the FBI for help on a single homicide?"

"I wish it were that simple." Nikki ran through the essentials of the case. "We're, of course, asking for discretion about Jessica Chandler's body being found at the scene. We're clearly dealing with a very dangerous individual. I've gone through Detective Brenner's very thorough and useful notes on Jessica's case, and I'd like her to assist in the investigation as well."

Gill worried his lower lip. "Our commander's stuck in a meeting with the chief, so I guess this one's my call. Brenner, your shield's brand new, and I know you've been stuck riding with some of the veterans. What other cases do you have right now?"

"Jessica's has been the priority," Brenner answered. "I've got a couple of petty thefts and a robbery, but the suspect was arrested yesterday for a separate incident. Detective Boston already had that case, so we decided it was best for him to take the lead on my robbery as well. We've got the guy on camera along with an eyewitness, so I'm confident it's the right person."

Gill nodded. "All right. Go ahead and assist Agent Hunt, but you're still on call if we get another big call."

"Yes, sir. Thank you."

"Don't thank me," he said. "Use the opportunity to gain the confidence you need to put the other guys in their place."

Nikki apologized to Brenner for the messy state of her jeep. A box of old case files that she wanted to go through for a presentation at a crime conference next month sat on the back seat, and she hadn't had a chance to clean the jeep since it rained the other day. Rory's gravel driveway meant the inside was always dusty.

Brenner didn't seem to notice, her focus on the case. "Why the Bible verse?" she asked. "Is this a serial killer trying to make a name for himself or something?"

"We can't rule it out," Nikki said, thinking about what Liam had said at the scene. The phrase was just ambiguous enough it could have been targeted at anyone, for any reason. It also could be a deeply personal dig at one of the Webers.

"Jessica's social media posting is kind of sporadic this last year." Brenner swiped her tablet screen. "There's no obvious photos of her at the frat or even at parties."

"What about the year prior?"

"Her freshman year she was more active, at least for the first few months. There's a couple of gaps in her posting time, but they also coincide with the winter holidays."

"That's interesting." Nikki made a mental note to dig into Jessica's social media later tonight. If she was anything like the rest of her generation, most aspects of her life would be broadcast online somewhere, and Nikki's team had learned more things from social media in some cases than from actual family members. "Once we get all the names of the fraternity members, we need to start cross referencing their social media for any sign of Jessica. We need to corroborate the story that Jessica and Bryce had shown interest in each other and find out how serious things really were, if at all."

"Her friends said they weren't," Brenner said.

"But maybe they didn't know everything," Nikki said. "Was she staying there for some reason and not telling her parents, and simply in the wrong place at the wrong time when the family was ambushed? Given Bryce's current condition, we can't count on getting those answers from him. Right now, the fraternity is our best bet."

Nikki didn't need directions to the Sigma Alpha Epsilon house. The largest fraternity at the University of Minnesota also had one of the nicest places on Greek Row. The four-story Gothic estate had been upgraded since she'd last been inside, including a dark-brown metal roof that complemented the hand-cut stone. The two gold lion statues that guarded the entrance had been painted orange and black for Halloween. With the holiday falling on a Saturday this year, Nikki had no doubt the brothers were preparing for a weekend of partying. The university had banned anything with more than 15% alcohol content a few years ago after a string of hazing incidents. The results had been positive, especially after SAE ended pledging, but she knew there would be plenty of beer and wine at the party, and Nikki had no doubt some of the brothers snuck in contraband.

"I just scanned SAE's social media posts from the past few months," Brenner said as Nikki parallel parked across from the frat house. "I don't see Jessica in any photos, but a lot of them are just the frat guys. They just canceled all events this weekend because of a tragedy involving one of their members. Asking for prayers for Bryce."

"Already?" Nikki asked, glancing at the clock. The family had only been found a few hours ago, and the story hadn't been on the news yet. "I'd like to know who leaked the information." She killed the engine and grabbed her bag out of the back seat, making sure her notebook and pencil were inside. "We also need to make sure we get a list of all the active brothers and recent alumni. Once we have the names, we cross reference social media looking for any connection to Jessica. Don't forget to bring the photos." She locked the jeep and double-checked that her badge was in her coat pocket. A curtain moved in the bay window that overlooked Greek Street.

She and Brenner jogged across the street. Halfway down the sidewalk, the front door opened, and an athletic-looking guy in his early twenties wearing sweats and a University of Minnesota track and field shirt stepped outside.

"You're the FBI," he said loudly as they approached. "I've seen you on television."

"Follow my lead and don't mention Jessica unless I do," Nikki whispered as they approached the front steps. She showed him her badge. "Special Agent Nikki Hunt. You've met Detective Brenner with the MPD."

"Did Bryce make it?" Fear laced his voice.

"As far as I know, he's still in surgery," Nikki answered. "What's your name?"

"Greg. I've known Bryce since we were freshmen."

"Mind if we come in?"

"Shit, yeah. Sorry." He opened the door and gestured for them to go inside. "Normally the house is pretty empty this time of day, but with what happened to Bryce, most brothers skipped class. We're planning a candlelight vigil tomorrow instead of the Halloween party."

"I'm sure his uncle will appreciate that," Nikki said, taking in the house. Unlike some frat houses, SAE's had carpeted floors, and the residence smelled relatively fresh. She wondered how much the cleaning bill was after a big party. A large bay window in the living area had a built-in seat, and much of the furniture reminded her of an executive's office. The dark leather chairs were filled with distraught-looking young men. "Did he call and let you know what happened?"

Greg shook his head. "One of our alumni was Bryce's emergency contact. Someone from the hospital called him."

"Greg is the other roommate I talked to." Brenner kept her voice low. "He, Kai, and Bryce shared a room until this year."

"The FBI's here," Greg said. "And the MPD."

Every pair of eyes turned to them.

"Holy shit." The dark-haired kid sitting closest to them looked more like a middle schooler to Nikki. "Guys, you know who this is, right? She caught that Frost killer and a bunch of other serial killers from those documentaries. I've seen you on the news a bunch of times."

"Who are the other officers?" Nikki asked.

"Right." Greg pointed toward the shuttered fireplace. "That's Adam, our president. Ishaan is the secretary—he's the one who recognized you."

Ishaan waved at her. "Criminal justice major. Bit of a fan. Sorry."

"It's okay," Nikki said. "Do most of the people in this room live in the house? I want to make sure we speak with everyone Bryce interacts with on a daily basis."

"Yeah, pretty much," Adam said. "Bryce was so busy with school and swimming, he wasn't close to some of the newer guys living in the dorms. He just doesn't have the time. How is he doing?"

Nikki realized every male in the room seemed transfixed on her, with the exception of the man sitting on the edge of the fireplace surround. Knees drawn to his chest, he kept his gaze down and fidgeted with the fraying strings on his Chuck Taylors. "Still in surgery. I'll get the worst part out of the way."

Nikki watched each man's expression as she spoke. "Even though Bryce had gone home for the weekend, we still need to alibi all of you. Is there a list of member names we could use for reference?"

"Sure, I can email you," Greg said. "You want every member or just the guys living in the house?"

"Everyone and their phone numbers." Nikki handed him a business card. "My email address is on there, but would you be able to print a copy as well?"

"Absolutely." Greg hurried out of the room, and Nikki

turned her attention back to the group. The man sitting on the fireplace surround still hadn't looked away from his shoes.

"Bryce left for home yesterday, correct?" Nikki asked. "Did he just decide to skip Friday classes?"

"He didn't have class on Fridays," Ishaan said. "He said he'd be back for the party tomorrow. He just wanted to get away for a couple nights to study. He's pre-law and there's a big test Monday."

"He should have come back for the dinner yesterday," one of the guys sitting on the window seat said. "Then he'd have been okay."

"Dinner?" Nikki asked.

"One of our alumni brought his son for a campus tour, and we all had dinner together last night here at the house," Adam said. "It was scheduled in advance, but Bryce decided to go home."

Nikki thought she detected an edge in Adam's voice. "What time was the dinner? Who else wasn't able to attend?"

"Six thirty. The dinner was only for the guys living in the house." Adam looked around the room. "Who else wasn't here last night?"

Only two raised their hands. "We had night class," the one sitting nearest Nikki said.

"The rest of you were here all night?"

"It was Thursday night," the same guy answered.

"What does that mean?" Nikki asked. "Is there a Thursday night ritual or something?"

Adam shook his head. "Pre-weekend party. We started after the alumni left. I went to bed early, but I don't know about the rest of these guys."

"I wasn't here, either." The shaggy-haired man sitting next to the fireplace finally made eye contact. His scruffy beard made him look older than the others but Nikki thought she'd seen him before.

"What's your name?"

"Gavin Boyd. I graduated a couple of years ago."

"You swam at trials with Bryce," Nikki said. "I saw the picture in his room. Were you two close?"

"Used to be," Gavin said. "We still talk, but I'm working full-time and he's in his last year. We've both been too busy." He looked down at his shoes again. "He still had me as his emergency contact."

Greg returned. "Here's a list of all members, both living in the house and in the residence hall on Seventeenth Street. That's where most of our freshmen and sophomores are. I put asterisks next to the guys living in the house. I assume you're more interested in talking to us than the dorm guys."

Nikki skimmed the list. "Anyone not in this house last night before ten p.m. needs to write down where they were next to their name along with a phone number of your alibi." She looked at the two who'd raised their hands. "That means your professor's name and number. Gavin, I don't see you on this list."

"Because I don't live here anymore."

Nikki dug a pencil out of her bag. "Then I need you to put your address and phone number on here. Since you and Bryce were close, I'd like to speak with you privately. Greg too, since you were his roommate until this year."

She handed Gavin the list of frat members. "I need you all to look at this and make sure your contact information is correct. If you were in the house last night, put an X by your name. I noticed a security camera at the front door. Is there one for the back entrance too?"

Adam nodded. "Do you need to see something? It's a simple system and we have it set to delete after seven days, I think."

"It would really help us to confirm no one slipped out the back door last night without someone knowing," Nikki said. "The faster we confirm who was actually here, the better.

Detective Brenner, would you mind looking through last night's videos with Adam while I speak to Greg and Gavin?"

"Of course," Brenner said, looking up at Adam. "Lead the way."

He smiled, pulling his phone out of his pocket. "I can access it all right here. It's motion activated , so it only records when something sets it off."

Nikki motioned for Greg and Gavin to follow her back to the entryway. Greg followed obediently, but Gavin took his time getting up, avoiding eye contact with everyone. Nikki wasn't sure if he had something to hide or just didn't want to show his emotions.

"What happened between Kai Richardson and Bryce?" Nikki asked. "I heard they got into it a while back."

Gavin shoved his hands in his pockets and shrugged. "That was months ago. What does it matter?"

"Everything matters right now," Nikki said.

"They were both drinking," Greg answered. "Bryce was flirting with someone—a girl called Jessica—and Kai got pissed off. I don't think they really spoke after that, and Jessica didn't stick around, she left pretty quickly."

"She walked home by herself?" Nikki said, pretending she didn't recognize the name. "I don't know of any female who'd walk home by themselves at night, especially on campus."

"I walked her home." Gavin leaned against the wall. "She was upset at the arguing."

Nikki nodded. Brenner had assumed this story indicated some sort of relationship between Jessica and Bryce, but it sounded like a short meeting. So why had they found Jessica in Bryce's clothes? Had they been in a relationship or not? she wondered. Did the issue between the frat brothers have something to do with the quote on the wall? Brenner hadn't been able to track Kai Richardson down, but it was crucial they found him.

"No one has spoken with Kai recently?" Nikki asked.

They shook their heads. Nikki's gaze landed on Gavin, who seemed to perpetually scowl.

"I thought you graduated two years ago," Nikki asked. "Why were you at that party?"

"I'm an alumnus, and I work for the school. I still visit the house pretty frequently." Gavin shrugged.

Things had probably changed, but when Nikki had been in school, the only time alumni came back to party was during homecoming week. But Gavin had only graduated a couple of years ago, and she had no idea what his personal life was like, so she reserved judgement for now. "And why did Kai decide to leave the school?"

"I have no idea," Greg answered. "We all knew Kai had mood swings, but his leaving was a shock. He just didn't come back after winter break."

Nikki nodded, more interested in the two men's body language than the answers. Gavin still leaned against the wall, one foot crossed in front of the other, seemingly staring off into space. Greg's constant glances at Gavin made her wonder exactly how much power the alumnus had over the members. Was Greg seeking Gavin's approval with his answers?

"Greg, you roomed with Bryce for two years," Nikki said. "What was he like?"

"Uh... intense is the best word. His life was swimming and school. Girls and friends came after that. I always kind of admired how he could put blinders on and just focus on the important stuff."

"He didn't have a choice," Gavin snapped. "He has a full ride for swimming and academics. Failing wasn't an option."

Greg nodded and looked down at the floor.

"But surely he had some social life?"

"I guess," Greg said. "He never had a serious girlfriend, at least not one that he brought back to the room. Not to say that he didn't bring girls back. He just didn't let them get too comfortable."

Gavin gave him a dirty look.

"You know what I mean," Greg snapped. "He didn't hide who he was. I heard him tell plenty of girls it was just sex, not to get attached. Never saw anything wrong with that."

"There isn't," Nikki said. "Were Kai and Bryce on speaking terms when Kai dropped out?"

"As far as I know," Greg said.

"What about rivalries on the swim team?"

"Friendly ones," Gavin said. "Bryce was a team player, though. He encouraged the younger guys. That's why he's a captain this year."

"How long have the two of you known Bryce?" Nikki asked.

"Since the 2016 Olympic trials. I kind of took him under my wing." Gavin looked down at the floor. "He came here because of me."

"I met him as a freshman, when we both joined," Greg said. "We got along so we decided to room together the next year. Kai too."

"But you weren't close?"

"Depends on how you define close. We lived together and did pretty much everything together unless he was in the pool, but it always seemed like Bryce kept everyone at arm's length."

"And Kai?" Nikki asked.

Greg grinned. "Kai's a blast. Or he was, before everything happened. We knew he had depression and anxiety, but he was always upbeat and ready to stand up for his frat brothers. It still makes me sick that he left."

Nikki asked Greg to go back into the living room and make sure all of the members were putting the right information on the printed list. She wanted to speak to Gavin with no distractions.

She hadn't noticed the fresh-looking splint on his middle

and index finger until now. He must have been covering it up earlier, but she wasn't sure if that was intentional or just coincidence. Nikki pointed to the splint. "What happened there?"

"Football." Gavin clenched his jaw, his arms wrapped around his chest. "I feel like this is my fault."

"Why?"

"We were supposed to get together yesterday after work. I wound up getting stuck at the rec center and by the time I was done, I didn't feel like driving to his parents' in Stillwater. Maybe if I had, he wouldn't be going through this right now."

"Don't get hung up on 'what if,'" she said. "Did you actually speak to Bryce yesterday or was everything done through texts?"

"Texts, why?"

"Just wondering if you got a sense of his mood," Nikki answered. Jessica had been reported missing Tuesday afternoon, and Brenner had spoken to Bryce about her yesterday morning. Sometime last night, the attack happened. She had a hard time believing that was coincidence, and any one of these boys could theoretically be involved. "Did he mention anything upsetting him? Any trouble he might be in?"

Gavin narrowed his eyes. "What kind of trouble?"

"The sort that might have gotten his family attacked." Nikki didn't flinch under his hard gaze, getting the sense that Gavin was used to intimidating people. "You said you work for the university?"

"Assistant recreational sports coordinator, and we had a rec game go into overtime. Then I got stuck having to stay and clean up because we're short staffed. Work will have my exact hours, but I'm pretty sure I clocked out around six last night."

"Where did you go after that?" Nikki asked, keeping her voice neutral. Six didn't seem too late to meet someone for drinks, but she understood not wanting to drive the forty-plus minutes to Stillwater and then back to the metro area.

"Home. My girlfriend lives with me. She can confirm for you."

Nikki typed the number into her notes app, still trying to get a read on Gavin. He was obviously upset about his friend and struggling not to let his emotions get the best of him. But his sharp, short answers gave the impression that he was ready to bolt, not to mention Greg's unease around the alumnus. Nikki waited a few seconds to see if he was going to say anything more, but Gavin looked down at his hands, picking at the white tape around the splint. "I'll be stopping by the hospital later, so we may bump into you there. Here's my card if you think of anything else."

"I'm not going to the hospital," Gavin said flatly. "I can't see him like that. Sorry if that makes me a jerk." He stowed the card in his coat pocket.

"It doesn't," Nikki said. "But I'm sure you know that friends and family are a vital part of the recovery process after something like this."

"You really think he has a chance?" Gavin asked.

"I hope so," Nikki said. "We need his help to find out who did this to him. And he doesn't have many people left in his life."

"I need to get to work." He tucked his hands into his pockets and walked out of the front door without saying anything to his fraternity brothers.

"We just finished going through the videos," Brenner said when Nikki rejoined the group. "Nothing other than those two"—she pointed to the guys who said they had night class—"coming in around nine forty-five p.m., after class finished."

"Where did Greg go?" Nikki asked.

"He said he needed air," Ishaan said. "Went for a walk."

Nikki scanned the group again, this time making sure to have eye contact with each member. Their grief appeared genuine, but the men also struck her as a united front that was going to be hard to penetrate. Even with all of the positive changes with the fraternity in the past few years, brotherhood was still everything.

"Adam, would you mind showing me Bryce's room?"

She expected to be asked why his room needed to be searched, but Adam nodded. "Sure, but my guess is it's locked."

"I don't suppose there's a master key around, is there?"

Adam shook his head. "No, but he might have given out a spare." He looked hopefully around the room, but all of the men shook their heads.

"I'll take you upstairs," Adam said. "Maybe he left it unlocked."

"Detective Brenner, would you make sure we have everyone's information? I'll be right back." Nikki had already started composing a group text to Liam and Miller, asking them to search Bryce's room for keys. His car had been outside, so his keys must be in the house. She couldn't remember ever being upstairs at the SAE house, but she hadn't been a big partier in her college days. She'd had enough of that in high school.

"How well do you know Bryce?" she asked as they climbed the stairs.

"As well as anyone in the frat," he said. "We pledged together, came up the ranks together." He stopped at the second-floor landing. "Do you think he's going to make it?"

"I haven't seen him yet, but his injuries are extensive," Nikki said. "I'll make sure to update you guys as soon as I hear anything."

"Thanks. President and Vice President's rooms are on the top floor. Perks of being elected."

Nikki wasn't sure if climbing three floors every day should be considered a perk, but she stayed silent, mostly to conserve oxygen. "I know that Bryce and Kai had issues before Kai left last year. What about the other guys? Did Bryce have any run-ins with other frat brothers?"

"Nothing serious," Adam said. "Sometimes arguments get out of hand, but it doesn't last. None of these guys would do anything to Bryce or anyone else."

They'd finally reached the top floor. Nikki tried to catch her breath without being obvious. "Even Kai? Guys can be pretty unhinged when a girl comes between them."

"I can't see Kai hurting anyone," Adam said. "He emailed me in the spring, apologizing for bringing the frat down, and said his leaving was the best thing for everyone." He walked to the door with the University of Minnesota swimming stickers and tried the doorknob. "Yep, locked. Do you want us to call a locksmith?"

"No," she said, wanting to avoid media attention. "If we have your permission, we'll take care of that. I'm sure you understand we need to get into his room as soon as possible." She was tempted to use the crowbar she kept in the jeep, but the locksmith was the better route. Fortunately, she had a couple of contacts who could probably be at the SAE within the hour.

"Of course," Adam said. "Bryce and I are usually the only people up here, anyway."

"Even during parties?"

Adam made a face. "Especially during parties. I don't need puke on my stuff. And Bryce rarely let anyone into his room, even when we were underclassmen and had roommates."

"Greg mentioned Bryce never had a serious relationship. Does that go for this year too? No girlfriends—or boyfriends?" She'd only heard female companions mentioned, but she didn't want to leave anything to assumption.

"I'm the one with the boyfriend." He grinned. "And no, not really. He's been mired in schoolwork. He's always been more studious than most of us, and sometimes I think he only joined the frat because his dad and uncle are both alumni."

"That does tend to happen." Nikki wasn't surprised to hear

that Adam was gay, but it wasn't that long ago that guys who joined frats had to hide their sexuality. She was happy to hear that things had changed for the better at the university since she'd attended in the late nineties.

"How many active members are there this year?"

"One hundred and eleven," Adam answered. "Thirty-seven living in the house. All of that's on the list Greg gave you."

"How well do you know Gavin?" she asked.

"Not that well," Adam said. "He usually hung out with the other athletes in the house. We partied together and all of that, but that's about it. He's always been uncomfortable around me."

"Because of your sexuality?"

Adam nodded. "Not all of my generation is as enlightened as the rest."

"I'm sorry to hear that," Nikki said. "Was Gavin as serious about swimming as Bryce?"

"I guess not, since he and Bryce always bickered about it. Gavin was kind of swimming's rebel, you know? He always had long hair until he absolutely had to shave it, he didn't obsess over practice and working out. Bryce used to tell him he was wasting his potential." Adam shook his head. "That's the only time I ever really saw them get into it."

"When was this?" Nikki asked.

"Freshman year—Gavin was a senior. I think he was probably over it all by then, but Bryce saying that really struck a chord. We had to physically separate them." Adam headed downstairs, and Nikki fell into step behind him.

Nikki debated asking her next question. She didn't want the frat to get the impression she blamed Bryce for anything. "Do you know how his relationship with his family was? Were they close at all?"

Adam hesitated. "I know his dad put a lot of pressure on him with swimming, and that caused some issues. But that's the limit of my knowledge. Gavin might know more."

Nikki nodded. "I plan on speaking with him again. How often did Bryce see his parents?"

"He probably spent a weekend a month there during school," Adam said. "But he talked to them at least once a week, especially his mom. They were close, I think."

"So his going home wasn't out of the ordinary?" she confirmed.

"Not at all, especially with an exam coming up. He liked to study there."

"Thank you for your time and willingness to help," Nikki said. "Please make sure the rest of the members understand all of this is procedure and important to finding out who did this. It's not a witch hunt. I'm going to contact the locksmith."

Right now, it felt more like throwing ideas at the wall and seeing which one stuck. The perpetrator had clearly stalked the Weber house, but nothing she'd heard so far sounded like any sort of motive. She shivered, the pebble of anxiety in her stomach growing larger by the minute. No motive tied to the family meant a planned home invasion, but no valuables had been taken, unless they couldn't track down Joan's wedding set. But even then, there had been much more expensive items in the Weber home. Were they dealing with someone who killed for the fun of it, dispensing judgement in his eyes? If that turned out to be the case, the murders were just beginning.

Detective Brenner met her at the bottom of the stairs, red-faced. "There's a lawyer here representing the Weber family. He says we can't get into Bryce's locked room without a warrant."

FOUR

Nikki strode outside, trying to mask her frustration. In her experience, the only time a victim's family did something like this was because they had something to hide. What did Vic Weber want to protect Bryce from? A shiny, black Tesla had been parked behind her jeep, a gray-haired man in a three-piece suit standing next to it. He nodded as she and Brenner approached.

"Agent Hunt, I presume?"

Nikki nodded. "And you are?"

"Walter Turnbell."

She stopped short. "Turnbell and Partners is a criminal defense practice."

"Among other things," he said. "I'm licensed in general practice, and I'm a family friend of the Webers. Vic asked me to handle this case. I presume you didn't try to breach Bryce Weber's room?"

"We didn't, but I need to get in there as soon as possible. We have very few leads right now, and every bit of information is crucial."

"Be that as it may," Turnbell said, "my client is now legal

next of kin, and he will not allow access to the room without a warrant."

Brenner's face was pinched with anger. "Bryce is the victim. How are we supposed to figure out what happened to him and his family without access to his room?"

"You'll have access as soon as you get your warrant," Turnbell said smoothly. "My client is just trying to protect his family."

"From what?" Nikki asked. "I'm sure you realize this makes Bryce and the family look like suspects."

"FBI agents who like to bulldoze their way through a case." Turnbell looked down his nose at her. "You've earned a reputation for going full-steam ahead over the last year, Agent Hunt. The Weber family wants everything done by the book."

Nikki fought to keep her anger in check. Arguing with the lawyer wasn't going to get her anywhere. The family had the right to ask for a warrant, and since Bryce was the sole occupant, Nikki didn't have any way to force the issue. "Fine, but we need your assurance that no one enters that room until after we've thoroughly investigated it."

"Of course," Turnbell said. "You have our word. Good day, Agent Hunt." He headed around the front of the car to the driver's door. "Thank you for your cooperation."

Nikki cursed him under her breath and looked at Brenner, who looked as flustered as she felt. It was starting to become clearer that Jessica could have been at the Weber house because of Bryce, and that meant he'd lied to Brenner when she'd questioned him the day before the murders. "I need to make sure that room is secure."

She jogged back to the house. Adam and Greg, along with a few other members, had watched the exchange from the porch. "We have to get a warrant to enter the room. I need you two to promise me that no one else will go in there until I come back with it, and that includes the Weber family."

Adam looked surprised. "Why can't they go inside?"

"Because we need to make sure we see the room as it was when Bryce last left it. The family means well, but they could inadvertently mess up the investigation." Nikki didn't want any of the men to figure out the family had essentially forced her to look at Bryce as a real suspect.

"That makes sense," Adam said. "I promise, no one gets through the door until you're back, Agent Hunt. We have a security camera at the end of the hallway. If anyone tries to get in, I'll get an alert about motion being detected."

"Thank you." Nikki handed Adam several business cards. "If that happens, call me immediately no matter the time of day." She reminded the brothers their alibis would have to be confirmed. Some of them had looked nervous but she imagined it was just because their alibis would reveal that they were drinking underage or God knows what else. She didn't care, she just needed confirmations so they could move on to real suspects.

"What in the hell?" Brenner asked when they were both back in the jeep. "Bryce is fighting for his life. Why would the family want to keep us out of that room?"

"I don't know," Nikki said. "But Vic Weber's going to have some explaining to do when I get the chance to talk to him." Had Bryce been into something illegal that would make the family name look bad? Vic Weber had just lost his brother and sister-in-law, and protecting Bryce was a natural instinct. But unless he had a stash of drugs, Nikki had no clue why the family would essentially delay the investigation.

"How do you feel about Gavin?" Brenner asked.

"As a suspect?" Nikki checked her messages to see if Liam had replied yet about the keys. "Damn. No sign of Bryce's keys. They're checking with the hospital to see if they came in with him in his pocket. As for Gavin, I'm not sure about him."

"I'm glad it's not just me," Brenner said. "The guy's just so deadpan about everything."

Nikki nodded. "He's tough to get a read on, but he might be really good at masking his emotions."

"And everyone grieves differently, I know," Brenner said, staring out of the passenger window. "And there's no motive for him to kill Bryce, Jessica or Bryce's parents, at least that we know of. I guess something about him just bugs me."

"Everyone's a suspect until we rule them out," Nikki said. "You have the list of the SAEs' alibis?"

Brenner flipped through the list. "I told them to keep it simple. A lot of them were right here in the house and vouch for each other. A few were working or at class and gave me contact information of employers and professors. Adam said they have security cameras at both entrances. He said he'll email it to you, and we can double-check all the guys who said they were in the house last night."

"Very helpful." Nikki was usually suspicious of any person who offered so much information, but she knew the SAE house had been embroiled in controversy over the past few years. It didn't surprise her they were willing to help. No one wanted to lose the chapter altogether. "We prioritize the guys living in the house," Nikki said. "Then move on to the other group."

Brenner nodded. "Adam sent out a mass email to those living in the dorms, telling them to expect a call."

Nikki grimaced. She couldn't expect to surprise the other frat members about interviewing them regarding Bryce. Jessica was a different story. "You didn't mention Jessica's name, right?"

"No," Brenner answered. "There are a few sophomores and a couple of juniors who don't live in the house staying in her dorm. Looks like the rest are in the freshman dorm on Seventeenth Street. The lack of motive of this is starting to worry me.

If this family was chosen at random, doesn't that increase the odds of this happening again? What if we have a serial killer on our hands?"

Nikki caught the hint of excitement in her voice. It was the second time she'd brought up the possibility of a serial killer. Brenner hadn't been on the job long enough to become jaded, and Nikki could still remember the excitement of her first serial case. They were the cases every new agent wanted to solve, cementing their relevance as a cop. "It's one possibility, but we can't get too far ahead of ourselves. Jessica's the first victim, and her connection to Bryce throws a bit of a wrench into the random attack theory, especially with the lawyer's involvement. That's why we need to know why she was at the house. You spoke to Bryce yesterday and he didn't mention her, but maybe he was covering for her. Maybe she didn't want to be found."

"I really hope that's not the case," Brenner said softly. "Being in the wrong place at the wrong time makes her death even more horrible. But none of the brothers mentioned her hanging around or said anything about Bryce being close to her."

"I don't think Bryce is very close to any of those guys," Nikki said. "That's why we need to talk to the frat brothers living in the dorms privately and find out where they were the last day she was seen and if they know anything about her and Bryce. Had Jessica declared a major? If you have her schedule, we can try to find out which classes she had with SAE guys, although privacy issues won't let us get very far without a warrant."

"I don't follow," Brenner said, looking for something in her oversized bag. "Why would any of the frat members hurt one of their own like that? I thought the brotherhood was supposed to be sacred."

"It is, until a woman comes between them, but this is

mostly just procedure," Nikki said. "We'll go to the residence halls and see if we can track down these other guys and alibi them."

"I'll email you her class schedule." Brenner was still focused on the list, looking through the names. "I should have fought harder to get Kai Richardson's contact information."

Nikki shook her head. "You didn't have any grounds to do that, and we don't even know that he and Jessica were in contact. But we need to know about his past and time in the house. What's the address of the Caribou Coffee shop Jessica frequented? We'll stop and see if he's been in before we go to the hospital."

Brenner rattled off the address and Nikki typed it into her GPS. "You also need to put out a BOLO. Be sure you communicate that he's a person of interest and is to be treated like we need him to help us, not that he's a suspect in a murder investigation," Nikki reminded her. "He'll try to run and close up on us if they don't."

"I will, but I can't promise the patrol guys will be very sensitive to his plight."

"Tell them you're working with the FBI and the request comes from me. Don't even tell them that he's a possible suspect. Just say he's a known associate of hers and I need to speak with him asap. Play to their egos and let them know the FBI will be very grateful for their help."

"Ugh," Brenner said. "I'd rather play nice with a criminal trying to get a confession than some of those guys. A few weren't too happy I moved up from officer to detective, even though they all said they wanted to stay on patrol."

"Typical pissing contest," Nikki said. "I know it's hard, but sweetness will take you farther with them than spice. Save that for when they really need it. And trust me, the time will come to put them in their place. It always does." She stopped at a red light. "What's Kai look like?"

Brenner held up her phone. "Here's an older photo from social media, before he started having issues."

Kai appeared to be of mixed race and had to be at least 6'2" and two hundred pounds. Nikki recognized a couple of the other SAEs in the photo, including Gavin. He and Kai held up their beers proudly, grinning like fools. "What caused the breakdown? Was he actually diagnosed with schizophrenia? Did we confirm that with a doctor? Schizophrenics have been known to kill people, but it's a lot rarer than television wants you to think. I'm more interested in what he knows about Jessica. If he did have some kind of interest in her, he might have information that can help us."

"His parents said it was schizophrenia," Brenner said. "Do you think this will be enough to get his medical information?"

"I doubt it," Nikki said. "HIPAA laws are hard to penetrate, and there's enough evidence that Bryce could have done this that I can't see a judge signing off. You have his parents' number?"

"Yeah, should I call them?" Brenner asked.

"I'd like to, if you don't mind," Nikki said. She didn't want to sound cocky, but her name was well recognized in the media. "Getting a call from an FBI agent about your son tends to scare people." She unlocked her phone and asked Brenner to type in the number while she navigated traffic.

"It's ringing," Brenner said.

"Put it on speaker."

The call went to voicemail after four rings. "Hello," Nikki said. "My name is Agent Nicole Hunt with the FBI, and we are looking for your son, Kai. It's very important that we speak to him as soon as possible, for his own safety." She left her cell and office numbers before ending the call.

"Caribou's on the next block. Good luck finding a place to park," Brenner said.

The University of Minnesota's Minneapolis campus had

grown so much since Nikki had attended that it was essentially its own small city, with various coffee shops and other businesses that catered to students. Jessica had studied at the coffee shop located a couple of blocks off campus, and its proximity to the university meant parking was a nightmare.

Nikki circled the block four times without any luck. "Damn. I'll stop in front of the shop and you go in and ask if they've seen Kai. Ask if he's been in any altercations with staff or done anything to send up red flags. And give them this." Nikki handed Brenner her card. "I'll keep circling and pick you back up."

"Got it." Brenner hopped out as soon as Nikki stopped, drawing angry horns from the people behind her. She waited until Brenner had gone inside before putting her foot back on the gas.

As Nikki circled the area, she kicked herself for not reminding Brenner to lay low if she spotted Kai in the shop. Surely Brenner had enough experience and common sense to realize that without Nikki telling her. She turned back onto the street, but Brenner was still inside. Nikki accelerated, planning to circle again.

Caribou's door suddenly opened, and a tall man wearing grimy-looking clothes raced out of the coffee shop, right into the street. Nikki slammed on the brakes, her tires squealed, and she could hear her brakes grinding with the effort to stop. Kai froze in the middle of the street, his eyes locking with hers as the jeep's front fender rammed into his chest.

FIVE

Nikki jumped out of her vehicle and ran around to the front, her stomach in knots. She'd only been going a few miles an hour when they'd connected, but Kai could have still hit the street hard enough to do serious damage, especially to his head.

"Are you all right?" She dropped to her knees next to him. He'd rolled into a ball, his hands wrapped around his head. She could see that the backs of his hands had road burn. "Don't move. I'll call an ambulance."

Kai groaned and rolled onto his back, breathing hard. Shock and confusion registered on his face as he stared at Nikki.

"I'm so sorry." Brenner had hurried outside, holding up her badge to stop traffic. "I didn't realize he was inside."

Nikki held up her hand, trying to warn Brenner not to give her away as a cop, but Nikki saw it register in his eyes. He reared up, catching her chin with his fist, and rolled over on all fours, trying to get up. Nikki's head spun and the bright fall colors all merged into a blur, but she managed to grab his ankle and hang on.

"Calm down," she choked out. "I'm not the enemy."

He kicked her hard, his boot landing squarely in her chest. Nikki doubled over in pain.

"Stop or I'll have to tase you," Brenner yelled.

"Don't," Nikki gasped, trying to stand. "He's injured already."

Kai was on his feet now, backing away and clutching his ribs. "I didn't do anything."

"No one said you did," Nikki answered. "I just want to make sure you're okay."

Kai pointed to Brenner, who stood less than two feet away, her taser ready to deploy. "You're with her, and she's a cop. I heard her ask about me."

"If you didn't do anything, then why did you run?" Brenner asked.

Nikki waved her off. "Listen, Kai. I know you've had issues and you probably don't trust us. But we really need to talk to you about Jessica Chandler."

His eyebrows furrowed together. "Jessi? Is she okay?"

Finally on her feet, Nikki shook her head. "I'm afraid she isn't."

He seemed to freeze in shock, his eyes glazing over. Horns had started to blare, and the sound of sirens blasted down the street. Kai's head snapped in the direction of the sirens, panic all over his face. He backed up, his gaze flashing between Nikki and Brenner.

"Please sit down and let the paramedics look at you," Nikki said. She showed him her badge. "You know who I am. You were waiting for me at the lake this morning." She'd thought he looked familiar in the photo Brenner had showed her, but Nikki had recognized him the second she spotted him running from the coffee shop in the same clothes she'd seen him in earlier at the lake.

Kai nodded, still looking uncertain. He clutched his left

side, wincing with every breath. The sirens grew closer, demanding traffic move out of the way.

"Please, Kai," Nikki said. "I swear to you that you have nothing to worry about." She prayed she didn't have to break that promise. "We don't even have to talk about anything right now."

"Paramedics are here." Brenner still held the taser high, her arm shaking.

"Let them check you out," Nikki said. "We can talk after they're finished."

Kai stared past her. "I'm not going to the hospital. I'm taking my meds and going to work."

"You don't have to go to the hospital if you don't want to," Nikki said. "Just let them check you out."

Breathing hard, Kai nodded. Two medics approached. "Go slowly," Nikki told them. "He doesn't trust us."

"Understood." One of the paramedics walked past Nikki and approached Kai.

"Can you walk, man? We can get out of the street so people will stop honking."

Kai nodded, still looking at Nikki. "Only if she comes with me."

"That's fine. Brenner, the keys are in my bag." She lowered her voice. "Go ahead and find a place to park so you still have eyes."

Brenner flushed, obviously frustrated that she hadn't handled the situation inside correctly. "He ran. Isn't that enough to warrant holding him?" she whispered.

"If we do that, he's not going to talk."

Nikki walked with Kai and the paramedics to the ambulance, which had managed to maneuver out of the way enough that traffic could start going again after Brenner moved the jeep.

Kai didn't appear to have any internal injuries, but the paramedics thought he should get an X-ray to make sure no ribs had been fractured. "How fast were you going at impact?" the paramedic asked Nikki.

"Skidding to a stop," Nikki said. "A few miles per hour at the most."

"Then it's probably just bruised ribs," the paramedic answered. "But you should get an X-ray."

"I'm not going to the hospital," he said flatly.

"Your choice." The woman turned to Nikki. "You've got a nice bruise on your jaw. Did you smack the steering wheel?"

Kai's eyes widened, and she could tell he was terrified of being arrested for assaulting an officer. "Yeah, but I'm okay."

"We should check you out for a concussion."

She wanted to refuse, but since she'd insisted on Kai getting checked out, she did the same.

"Doesn't look like you have a concussion," the paramedic told her. "But keep an eye out for symptoms."

"I will." Nikki focused on Kai sitting on the sidewalk in front of Caribou. "Are you able to talk with me now?"

He nodded. "Long as we do it here."

"How about inside? I could use some caffeine after this." Kai would also be on familiar turf, and she hoped that would help him relax enough to answer her questions.

Kai nodded. Nikki followed him into the shop, the rich smell of coffee overpowering her senses. "Why don't you choose a table, and I'll get the coffee. What would you like?"

He shook his head. "I had my limit for today. Too much makes me so wired I can't think straight."

"Got it." Nikki walked to the counter, keeping an eye on Kai's reflection in the front window. He'd chosen the table closest to the door, positioning himself for an easy exit. She messaged Brenner and told her to come back to the shop after she'd parked and be ready to intervene if Kai bolted again.

She ordered a large coffee with two espresso shots, along with plenty of cream and sugar.

"That looks more like chocolate milk," Kai said when she sat down.

"I hate the taste of coffee," Nikki confessed. "But I need it so a pound of cream and sugar it is."

He finally smiled a little bit. "Makes sense, I guess. I love everything about coffee. The smell, taste, texture. All the different drinks they can make. Crazy to me." Kai rolled his eyes and snickered. "But I'm the crazy one, I guess."

"Don't say that about yourself," Nikki said.

He shrugged. "It's true."

"No, it isn't. Crazy is outdated and offensive. Would you say that to another person you knew had mental health issues?" She didn't wait for an answer. "I don't think you would, and you shouldn't say that about yourself."

"I'll try not to." Curiosity burned in his dark eyes. "How come you're being so nice and not accusing me? Cops always think the mental patient did it."

"Good ones don't, and I happen to be pretty damn good." Nikki unlocked her phone and went to the voice memo app. "Mind if I record? I don't really feel like taking notes right now."

"I guess." He looked down at the scuffed table. "Is Jessi hurt bad?"

"I'm afraid she's dead," Nikki said softly, crossing her fingers that he wouldn't try to flee again.

Kai's head dropped into his hands. "I told her to let it go."

"Let what go?" Nikki asked. A text from Brenner came through, confirming she was in position outside if Nikki needed her.

"She was going to file a grievance with the university. She was assaulted last year and pressured to keep it quiet. I think they paid her off." He snickered. "I know they did. His family has money, and he's too important to the university to get kicked out."

Nikki's head spun. Jessica's friends hadn't mentioned that to Brenner. Was Kai making it up? "Did she tell you who assaulted her?"

Kai didn't answer, so she tried a different question. "When did you meet her?"

"At orientation last year. I volunteered to help incoming freshmen. Jessi and I clicked right away. I wanted to ask her out, but I chickened out. Figured I'd let her settle in and then maybe ask."

"Did you?"

"I didn't get the chance," he said. "Everything went to hell a few weeks later. My life's basically ruined."

"No, it isn't," Nikki said firmly. She could tell that Kai was innocent, that what his parents had said about his issues with mental health were legitimate. The way he panicked told her everything she needed to know about him. "I know it's really hard, but if you're able to consistently stay on your medication, you can live a relatively normal life. You're working."

He looked disgusted. "Bussing tables. My IQ is almost one hundred and forty, and I can't use it."

"It's only been a year, right?" Nikki asked. "You're still adjusting. Stop beating yourself up. There are dozens of support groups around that might help you, Kai. So many people live with similar issues, and you'd be surprised how much it helps just to talk with someone who truly understands. Frankly, I'm amazed that you're able work at this point. It takes some people years."

"That's what my counselor says."

"I'm glad to hear you're seeing a therapist."

Kai shrugged. "I'm not sure if it helps."

"It does, I promise."

He snorted. "What would you know? Someone like you doesn't need therapy."

Nikki laughed out loud. "Come on now, you were waiting

for me at the lake, which means you know at least some of my history."

"I wanted to go into criminal justice," he said. "The Frost case fascinated me. I'm sorry about how everything played out, by the way."

"Me too," Nikki said.

"Is your little girl okay?" Kai asked, sincerity in his eyes. "She was taken by that guy this spring, right?"

"She's doing pretty good, thanks to therapy. I guess I am too, most days." She smiled at him, hoping to set him at ease. "Why were you waiting for me at the lake? Normally I'd be pretty upset knowing that someone had my routine down well enough to wait on my jogging route."

"I don't know what you're talking about." Kai clammed up again.

Nikki sipped her coffee, trying to think of the best way to frame her question. "We'll circle back to the lake later. Why did you run from Brenner?"

"I don't know," he said. "She sounded so serious and businesslike. Like she didn't want my help or information, she just wanted to arrest me."

"I think you might have read into that a little bit, but she is a new detective. We just need to talk to you about Jessica."

"Can I ask you a personal question?" His dark eyes bored into her, full of pain.

"Sure."

"Do you ever blame yourself for what happened to your ex-husband and daughter?"

"All the time," Nikki confessed. "I know there are things I could have done differently that might have changed the outcome. That eats at me every day."

"Me too," he said quietly.

Nikki leaned forward, her hands on the table near Kai's but not touching him. "Kai, talk to me, please. I can help you."

Kai closed his eyes, tears rolling down his cheeks. "I led him to Jessi. I introduced her to him and didn't tell her what a possessive, cruel piece of crap he was."

Nikki's heard pounded from the adrenaline rush, but she tried to stay calm. "Who did you introduce to her?"

Kai shook his head, his hands over his ears. "I can't. I can't go to that place again."

"What place?"

"The past. All the things that put me here." He'd started to sweat, shifting in his chair so quickly that Nikki reacted, her hand reflexively going to her hip even though her weapon was locked in the jeep.

"I saw that." Kai's voice dropped half an octave, his eyes glittering, his pupils wide. "I see everything."

"I'm sorry," she said. "I was afraid you were going to run again." Nikki shifted and pulled up her sweater. "I don't even have my gun. Just a reflex. I know it's really hard, but if you can tell us anything that might help us find out who did this to Jessica. I know something happened between you and Bryce, and she was at the center of it."

Kai stared at her. "Did you go to the frat house? Do they know you're looking for me?" Before Nikki could respond, Kai hopped to his feet like he'd just been given a dose of adrenaline. "I can't stay here. They're going to come looking for me."

"Who?" Nikki asked.

"Doesn't matter. I have to go."

"Kai, you need to stay here and talk to me." Nikki noticed Brenner outside, out of Kai's eyeshot. "If you run again, Detective Brenner will have to bring you in."

He swiveled, looking toward the entrance. "What the hell? You said we were just going to talk."

"That's all I want to do," she told him. "Kai, who assaulted Jessica?"

"I can't tell you," Kai said. "They'll come after me."

Nikki couldn't tell if he was experiencing paranoia or speaking from a genuine fear. "Who?"

"Piranhas," he whispered, sitting back down. "That's what they are, you know? They swim in and attack so fast you don't know what's happening."

"Who are the piranhas?" Nikki pressed.

"They're everywhere around here," he said. "They probably already know you found me."

He put his head in his hands and rocked back and forth. "I don't want to talk to you anymore, Agent."

Nikki weighed her options. She could bring Kai in for hitting her and hope that he'd talk once he was safe in the police station, assuming he wasn't in the middle of an episode. But she would lose his trust by bringing him in, and she wasn't sure that she'd be able to earn it back.

Kai's head shot up, and he tensed with anger. Nikki followed his gaze, seeing Brenner leaning against the crosswalk sign, her eyes on the door.

"Why is she waiting out there?" he asked angrily.

"Because I asked her to," Nikki said. "I thought you'd feel better about that than her being in here with us."

"What about that guy?" He slammed his hand against the window.

A uniformed officer had stopped to talk to Brenner, his hand on his gun belt. Brenner said something to him, and the officer's head swiveled in their direction.

"See," Kai fumed. "They're waiting to take me away."

"No, they aren't," Nikki insisted. "Just relax."

Kai stood, his chest heaving. "I know how it works. I'm the crazy guy who had a thing for Jessi, and I'm black. You think I don't know what the MPD is thinking?"

"I think you shouldn't care about that, because it's my opinion that matters."

He dragged his hands over his face, tears brimming in his

eyes. "I'm not going back to the mental ward. If I tell you anything else, that's what will happen. They'll make sure of it."

"The piranhas?" Nikki asked. "I promise you, I have more pull than they do."

He looked down at her, biting his lip so hard he drew blood. "I'm sorry, Agent."

"You don't have to be sorry, Kai—"

He moved too fast for her to protect her face, his fist landing squarely on her jaw. He didn't hit her hard enough she saw stars, but the blow still hurt like hell.

Nikki clutched her jaw, staring up at him in shock. "Why?"

"I'm sorry."

The bell over the door sounded, and Brenner rushed in, followed by the uniform. Kai didn't struggle as the officer read him his rights and cuffed him. He kept his head down, limp as a rag doll.

"Are you okay?" Brenner asked.

Nikki nodded, rubbing her sore jaw. "I'm not pressing charges. Don't take him in."

Kai stiffened, his cuffed hands trembling. He'd just been worried about going back to the psychiatric hospital, and then he'd done something that just might land him there.

"Kai, who are you afraid of?"

He shook his head.

"I realize you don't want to press charges," the uniformed officer said. "But I'm a witness. So is Detective Brenner. We have to take him in."

"Brenner, please go get the jeep." Nikki stood, trying to hide how off-kilter she felt after the punch. "You and I will bring him in."

SIX

Kai refused to say anything else on the ride to the station, sitting in the back of the jeep with his arms crossed over his chest. The anxiety that gripped him earlier seemed to ease, and Nikki's mind raced trying to figure out why. She replayed the last hour in her head, thinking about his body language and the cryptic things he'd said. This morning, he'd thought Jessica was alive. Now he knew she was dead, but Nikki was almost positive Kai was innocent. His behavior and reactions reminded her of other suspects with mental illness she'd interviewed who'd been accused essentially because they were perceived as dangerous, including the man wrongfully arrested in the Ivy League case. What did Kai have to gain by getting arrested?

"Are you taking him to the MPD?" Brenner asked quietly. "Or the jail?"

"We'll go back to the precinct," Nikki said firmly. "You're in the first precinct, right?" The third precinct had been burned during protests last summer, and most of the staff was now operating in a temporary space while the city argued over the cost of rebuilding the third precinct.

Brenner nodded. "I've always been out of the first. Last year, during the pro—"

Nikki cleared her throat, glancing at Brenner. She discreetly shook her head. Kai already had reason not to trust them and bringing up last summer could make things worse. Brenner flushed and looked down at her hands.

"When we get there, we'll find a quiet interview room and then Kai can tell us the truth." She glanced in the rearview mirror. "Brenner will have to call your parents. You really want to put them through that, Kai?"

He didn't answer.

Nikki sighed. "Suit yourself."

When they arrived at the precinct, Nikki asked Brenner to find a holding cell while she checked in with Liam, who was still at the Webers' home.

"Hey, boss," he answered. "I'm still slogging through stuff over here. It's not looking very promising."

"What do you mean?" Nikki asked.

"Courtney's collected a ton of prints, but she's comparing them as she goes, and she's pretty certain most of the prints are the family's. Same ridge patterns."

"I'm not surprised," Nikki said. "Most criminals are smart enough to wear gloves. I've got one of Jessica's friends at the MPD." She gave him the CliffsNotes version of what had happened between her, Brenner and Kai. "Kai's clearly afraid of someone," Nikki said. "That's why he hit me."

"Piranhas," Liam mused. "Swimmers?"

"Maybe," Nikki said. "He's in such a state it's hard to know what's real and what's in his head. Brenner's contacting his parents and his psychiatrist. I'm hoping they will be able to help get a better read on him."

"You think he's good for this?"

"My gut says no," Nikki said. "I don't think he's mentally capable of pulling off an organized attack. But I think he might be able to tell us why Vic Weber doesn't want us in his nephew's room at the fraternity."

Every pair of eyes in the bullpen followed Nikki as she looked for Brenner's cubicle. Cops were suspicious by nature, and detectives were always on edge when an FBI agent arrived, like Nikki was going to swoop in and steal their active cases. A small-town police chief had once told her that her celebrity meant she could do whatever she wanted, even though the law was clear about which cases the FBI had automatic jurisdiction over.

Nikki found Brenner crammed into a corner cubicle in the back of the bullpen, an honor usually bestowed on rookies. It never ceased to amaze Nikki how little police departments changed. Detectives had to earn a good cubicle by solving cases. "I'm jealous of how organized you are in this tiny space."

Brenner laughed. "I lived in a tiny studio for several years. I learned to adapt." She leaned back in her chair. "I spoke with his psychiatrist. She said that Kai was pretty even for a few months, but in the last several weeks, he's had some episodes of paranoia and anger. They're trying to work on what triggered it."

"Perhaps Jessica reaching out to him?" Nikki guessed.

"Probably," Brenner said. "But here's the kicker: Kai has been seeing the psychiatrist twice a week, and they had an appointment last night at seven p.m. Kai stayed for ninety minutes, and then his parents picked him up. I just got off the phone with his dad, who confirmed the timing. He's also on his way in to pick Kai up and pay his bail."

"Let's not tell him that just yet," Nikki said. "I want to see if he tells us the truth about last night."

"What does it matter?" Brenner asked. "He's not good for it."

Nikki told her about Jessica's accusation of sexual assault. "I never got past that part, and I want to see if we can get to the bottom of this before his dad arrives."

Nikki hadn't been to the first precinct in a while, but it was still as dingy and crowded as she remembered. The station was housed in a renovated, one-hundred-year-old firehouse on Fourth Street, in the heart of the downtown entertainment district. Nikki had heard plans were underway to move locations, but for now, they were confined to one of the poorly lit, windowless interview rooms.

"Sorry about the room," Brenner said. "I know it's not very welcoming."

Kai shrugged and sat down at the small table, folding his hands across his chest, his jaw tight. Nikki and Brenner took the seats opposite.

"Can we get you anything?" Brenner asked. "Water, soda, stale coffee?"

"No, thank you."

Nikki decided to plunge ahead. "Before things went off the rails in the coffee shop, we were talking about you being at the lake this morning while I was out running. You said that you couldn't go back to that place, you talked about the piranhas that would come after you."

"What lake?" Brenner looked between them. "He followed you?"

Kai's gaze cut sharply to Nikki, watching her reaction.

"We never established exactly how he found me there."

Brenner looked up at the camera mounted in the corner. "Well, he punched you earlier, and now I'm hearing that he followed you." She pointed to the camera. "So is Sergeant Gill. He's not going to let that go."

Nikki tensed, afraid mentioning the camera would set Kai off, but he said nothing, staring down at the table.

"Kai, she's not wrong about that. Sergeant Gill can't just pretend he hasn't heard, and while I believe you weren't trying to harm me, the police might see it differently. You knew something had happened to Jessi and wanted my help, right?"

Kai closed his eyes, tears rolling down his cheeks. "I told you that I followed your career. You fight for the little guy, and you never take anything at face value. I thought if anyone could help her it would be you." He put his head in his hands. "But I kept chickening out. I tried to leave a message, but they sent me to some answering service and I got flustered. This morning, someone in your office actually answered and mentioned you'd gone out on a run and would be back. Since Palmer Lake is right there, I took a chance. And then I saw you, and you saw me, and I realized what it had to look like to you. I'm sorry if I freaked you out."

Nikki had her doubts that anyone in her office would have given him such detailed information, but she let it slide. "You didn't, but it's time to tell me everything. I might not be able to save Jessi, but I can figure out who did this with your help."

He raised his head, his gaze sharp. "How do you know I didn't do it? I knew her, we'd talked recently. Isn't that why you were looking for me?"

"Just because you're ill doesn't make you a murderer." She didn't mention the information Brenner had just received from the doctor and his father.

"That's what you said about the Ivy League Killer when you presented on campus my freshman year," he said. "The original suspect had severe mental health issues, and all the police had was circumstantial evidence. You said that mental illness is not a good indicator of serious crime."

"It's not," Nikki said. She knew the lecture Kai was talking about. It was the first time she'd been back on campus since she'd returned to the state after her years at Quantico. Nikki glanced at Detective Brenner. She hadn't given her the details of the conversation with him at the shop because she'd feared Brenner wouldn't be able to keep from interrogating him during the drive, and Kai would have undoubtedly clammed up. "Kai said that Jessica was assaulted last year, and she'd finally decided to file a grievance with the university. He blames himself because he introduced the person to her and didn't warn her about him."

Brenner's eyebrows knitted together. She looked between them in confusion. "Kai, her friends never told me that."

"Maybe they didn't know," he said. "You'd have to ask them."

"Are you sure that something bad didn't happen between you and Jessi, that you might have twisted around in your head?" Brenner asked gently.

"No." Kai's hands clenched into fists. He smacked them on the table. "No!" He shouted at Brenner. "That's why I didn't want to talk to you. I knew the police would just assume that I'd done it and make the rest up."

Nikki jumped in before Brenner could say anything else. She didn't want to boot the detective out of the interview with her boss watching, but Brenner was also skating on thin ice. If Kai clammed up again, Nikki might not get another chance. "I don't think that, and Detective Brenner is new to the job. She's probably not had a lot of experience talking to someone dealing with as much as you've had to endure, so please give her some leeway. We all have the same goal—finding out what happened to Jessica."

He hesitated, gnawing the inside of cheek. "I'd never hurt her," Kai finally said. "But my inactions were just as bad. When things went south, I just tucked my tail between my legs and ran off instead of sticking by her when I knew she was messed up."

Nikki was pretty certain she knew the answer, but she needed him to tell her the story. "Who assaulted her last year, Kai? The piranhas?"

He ground his teeth. "I don't want to talk about them."

"I get that," Nikki said. "If you've followed my career, then you know I have a background in psychology. I'm pretty good at figuring people out, and I think I've figured you out."

His gaze flashed to hers, and instead of anger or fear in his eyes, they shined with curiosity. "You profiled me?"

She didn't miss the whisper of excitement in his voice. "You could say that."

Kai relaxed a little, sitting back in his chair. "I want to hear it."

Nikki hoped she wasn't making a mistake. "You're very intelligent, and before your mental health issues started, outgoing and fun to be around. I bet you were the life of the party with or without alcohol."

He grinned a little. "Maybe."

"You come from working-class parents, and nothing was handed to you. Being black sometimes meant you had to work twice as hard, and it certainly shaped your view of law enforcement. That's why you wanted to go into criminal justice, right? To help reform things?"

Kai nodded. "Yes, yes I did."

"For what it's worth, you can still do that," Nikki said. "You volunteered to help with freshman orientation because some upperclassmen helped you, and you wanted to pay it forward. You were interested in Jessica from the start, but too much of a gentleman—and too shy—to do anything about it."

"I wanted her to get settled into the dorm and school before asking her out," he said eagerly.

"Exactly. And the SAE party came at the right time: a few weeks into the school year, she's learned the ropes and is excited to hang out with you at the party." Nikki threw the last one in for good measure. "You were so happy she was there that you didn't think twice about introducing her to Bryce. After all, even if he was interested in her, you saw her first, and there's a code between brothers."

His face darkened. "There's supposed to be. I didn't want to introduce him, but he saw her and wouldn't stop talking about her. I knew as soon as he talked about the Olympic trials and bragged about his records she was hooked."

"You drank too much and got into it with Bryce, and another fraternity brother, Gavin, broke off the fight and walked her home. That's what we were told by the fraternity. Is that accurate?"

Kai nodded. "If I hadn't gotten jealous, maybe Bryce wouldn't have set his sights on her."

"Because you're a loyal guy, you stepped aside."

"I thought I'd just be patient. Bryce is never serious about girls, he's just into the physical stuff. I thought she might realize that, and I'd have a chance."

"But that didn't happen?" Brenner asked.

He shook his head. "I didn't see her for a couple of weeks, but I finally managed to track her down after class to apologize. She looked awful. I kept asking her what was wrong, and I even said my feelings weren't hurt if she wanted to date him. That's when she told me they'd gone out the night after the party. Her roommate was still out when he walked her back to the dorm, so they fooled around. He refused to stop."

Until this point, his story gelled with what they'd been told at the fraternity and by Jessica's friends. Kai and Bryce got into a pissing match over the girl, but Gavin had walked her home. "Is that what Jessica said?"

"She begged me not to say anything, and I said that I wouldn't, but then I got back to the house and saw him acting all cocky and perfect, and I couldn't take it. I called him out right in front of half the house."

Nikki had a terrible gut feeling about what happened next, but she let him continue.

"He laughed. Wasn't even fazed by it, because he knew that he could get away with it. Then he called her, right in front of everyone, and put her on speaker. She denied it, said I was crazy and jealous. She wasn't wrong about that, but I didn't imagine the conversation with her."

"Did you speak with her again?"

He shook his head. "I tried. She told me to leave her alone or she'd get a restraining order. I think that was the last straw."

"I'm sure it was devastating," Nikki said. "Have you spoken to her since?"

"She found me at the coffee shop after the semester started. She'd heard about my dropping out and all, and she wanted to apologize."

"For what?" Nikki asked.

"Dragging me into it," he said. "I was so happy to see her that I just accepted her apology and said I was getting better. She didn't bring up the rape and neither did I."

"She never spoke of it?" Brenner asked.

"Not until a couple of weeks ago. She finally admitted that she'd panicked when Bryce called her on my phone that day. He'd already told her that the school wouldn't believe her, that he'd get her thrown out of school because of his status, so she called his father's law firm and told him that his son was a rapist."

Kai finally cracked a half-smile. "She was so proud of herself. I was too. Bryce's dad claimed that he didn't believe her, but he wrote her a check for ten thousand dollars. She still had it in her wallet. Never deposited. She told me that she'd gone to the hospital the night he raped her and had the exam done. I know they keep those kits for a long time, so I convinced her to at least think about reporting him. It wasn't too late, and having the check in her wallet as evidence didn't hurt, either. She promised that she'd think about it the last time I saw her. And now she's dead. He'll get to keep on bulldozing through people's lives."

Nikki was certain that Kai didn't know what happened to the Webers. "When was that?" Nikki asked.

"Last Wednesday. I hugged her goodbye, said I was proud of her." He slammed both fists against his legs. "I should have just kept my mouth shut. He's killed her, hasn't he?"

Nikki didn't answer. So much of the scene at the house still didn't make sense. "You didn't talk to either of them after that?"

He shook his head. "I tried to call her from work Tuesday, because she'd promised to let me know when she was back in town. She'd planned on telling her parents about Bryce."

The Chandlers hadn't mentioned that, and Nikki was fairly certain they would have if Jessica had gotten the opportunity to say anything. Still, she would have to confirm Kai's information. "Did you work all weekend, then?"

Kai drew his knees under his chin and wrapped his arms around his legs. "That's all I do unless I take the bus and meet Jessi for coffee."

"You don't drive?" Brenner asked.

He shook his head. "My parents had to sell my car to pay hospital bills. I take the bus everywhere, unless they drive me, which I try to avoid."

"Bryce and his father are the piranhas, right?" Nikki asked softly, hoping she'd earned enough trust for him to answer honestly.

"Bryce and Gavin," he whispered.

"Why are you afraid of them?" Nikki asked.

"Because Bryce gets what he wants," Kai said. "Everyone knows that. His dad gave Jessica money to stay quiet. He's not just going to roll over when she comes forward."

"But she hadn't yet," Brenner clarified. "Did she say anything about talking to Bryce first?"

He shook his head. "Doesn't mean she didn't, though."

Brenner's phone vibrated with a text, and she showed it to Nikki.

"Your dad's here to take you home," Nikki said. "I'll see to it that you aren't charged for hitting me."

"Really?"

She nodded. "I just want to know why you're so frightened of these guys that you hit an FBI agent so you could get arrested."

Kai hesitated, his teeth digging into his lower lip.

"We'll arrange to have a car near your parents' house while we're working the case," Nikki said. "You and your parents will be safe."

"During winter break last year, Bryce called me, saying he wanted to make amends. I fell for it. I met him at a bar near campus, and we got drunk. He called Gavin to bring us home, and they drove out to the river and beat the hell out of me. Left me bleeding in the freezing cold."

Nausea rolled through her. "How did you survive?"

"They didn't take my phone. I called my parents for help, told them I got jumped by a driver. They wanted the taxi's number and all that, but I said I couldn't remember. I was too much of a coward to press charges. That's the night things really changed up here." He tapped the side of his head. "If they find out I talked to you—"

"They won't," Nikki said firmly. "I'm so sorry for all you've gone through, Kai. Thank you for trusting me."

"Thanks for believing me."

"No problem. We'll handle the paperwork and get you out of here."

Brenner followed her out of the room, closing the door behind her. She stared at Nikki in awe. "How did you do that?"

"Years of experience," Nikki said. "A lot of it was information given to me by other people. In this case, it was all in how I framed it. He just needed to feel safe."

"This has to be why Vic Weber doesn't want us in Bryce's room at the frat," Brenner said. "He must be afraid that he's done this to other girls—"

"Let not get ahead of ourselves," Nikki cut in. "That's one possibility, but Vic Weber may not even know about the accusation or the hush money. He may just be acting on emotion and trying to control an uncontrollable situation by using the legal system." She checked her phone. "Liam's headed to the hospital," Nikki said. "I'm going to meet him there. Can you handle things here?"

Brenner fell into step next to her. "Keep me updated." She jammed a stick of gum in her mouth. "God, I could really use a cigarette right now."

"Don't give into the craving," Nikki warned. "All it takes is one puff, and you're starting all over again."

"I wouldn't have pegged you for a smoker."

Nikki laughed. "I started in college, and I didn't quit until I found out I was pregnant. My lungs are still healing."

"How old is your daughter?" Brenner asked.

"She'll be six next month," Nikki said. "Time flies. Do you have kids?"

Brenner touched her stomach. "I'm eight weeks along, and I haven't told my boss yet. I just made detective, you know?"

Nikki did know. She'd found out that she was pregnant with Lacey shortly after agreeing to move back to Minnesota and take over the major crimes unit. Tyler had always joked that Lacey had been a jetsetter even before she was born, since she'd been conceived when they both still worked at Quantico. "Surprise pregnancy or planned?"

"Big surprise," Brenner said. "My ex-boyfriend and I are completely incompatible. I know he'll be a great father, but a husband? No way."

"I take it he's supportive?"

"Thank God." Brenner nodded. "I trust him to pay child support and do the right things, but I don't want to be kicked back to patrol for being pregnant. I know that's technically against the law, but pregnant cops seem to disappear behind a desk or go back to patrol."

"If you really want to be a detective, then my advice is to keep your head down and work as many cases as possible before you start to show. I assume that's what you want?"

"It pays better," she said.

"So do a lot of other jobs," Nikki answered. "Patrol is dangerous, and being a detective is just as exhausting as being an FBI agent, especially when you're a good one. Work never stops."

Brenner stopped and looked at Nikki. "What are you saying?"

"I'm just telling you that it's okay to change your mind because of your child," Nikki said. "I think it was too late for me, because after seeing my parents dead, I vowed to take as many scumbags off the streets as possible. That's so ingrained in me that I'm incapable of functioning without it. And sometimes I really wish that wasn't the case." She put on her jacket and zipped it up to her chin. "We know Jessica didn't file a complaint, but can you go back through last school year and check police records for any reports against Bryce or anyone else from the frat?" Nikki asked. "Even if charges were eventually dropped."

Brenner nodded. "I'll let you know if anything comes up in the search. I'm going to track down the SAE members living in the dorms before I head home."

"Don't mention Jessica," Nikki reminded her. "Or Kai's being questioned."

"Why?" Brenner asked.

"This case is extremely sensitive. Bryce is a star swimmer,

and his father runs a prestigious law firm that's helped a lot of people in the area with personal injury issues. If word gets out that Kai could have been behind this, we'll never get control of the narrative. His guilt or innocence won't matter at that point, because patients with mental illness don't get a fair break in the media when it comes to murder, especially if the victims are prominent citizens.

"I'm going to meet Miller and Liam at the hospital in Stillwater, where Bryce is, and see what they've found out. I'll let you know if anything changes for tonight, but plan on meeting bright and early at the Washington County Sheriff's Office in the morning if you still want to work the case."

SEVEN

On the drive to the hospital, Nikki called Courtney. "How's it going over there?"

"We're going through the parents' cars to see if there's evidence of Jessica being in one of them," Courtney said. "Right now, we have a bunch of weird things that don't add up and not a lot of trace evidence. They must have worn protective gear. And before you ask, we've searched for that too. No sign of any discarded clothes."

"Keep working on it," Nikki said. "You've got the partial footprint, plus plenty of fingerprints to compare. There's still no sign of forced entry, I assume?"

"Not a one," Courtney said. "It's honestly like someone walked in here and did this just for the thrill of it."

"That's what scares me," Nikki said. "Let me know as soon as you compare Kai's prints to the ones on the scene."

"I will," Courtney answered. "There's no sign of the mother's wedding rings yet, either."

Nikki ended the call and moved over into the express lane, hoping that she'd remembered to renew her vehicle pass. If not, she'd have some healthy fees to deal with, but it wouldn't be the first year she'd spaced off the renewal, and she had a better excuse this year than any prior. Between her ex-husband's murder and worrying about Lacey, she'd barely managed to take care of the important things over the last six months.

A knot formed in the pit of her stomach at the thought of her daughter. Her attorney had assured her that Tyler's parents wouldn't be able to get custody of Lacey, but he'd also admitted that Nikki's job brought extenuating circumstances to the table. There was a slight chance they could convince the judge they deserved joint custody, but Nikki knew that Lacey's testimony would also be a powerful weapon. She didn't want to live with her grandparents, and since Tyler's death, she had trouble spending time with them. Her therapist said that was normal, as they were a direct tie to Tyler, but Lacey had also come home upset more than once. Her grandparents had talked about her daddy a lot, which was hard enough, but a month later, Nikki had drawn the line. Lacey had gone to stay with Tyler's parents for the weekend, but she'd called crying the first night. Her grandparents had told her that Nikki was at fault for her daddy's death.

Nikki's hands gripped the wheel, her muscles tight. Anger coursed through her every time she thought about that phone call. She didn't blame Tyler's parents for feeling that way, and some days, she even agreed with them. But to tell Lacey crossed a line. She'd already gone through more trauma than most people experience in a lifetime, and she was too young to really understand why terrible things had happened to her daddy. Accepting his loss was hard enough.

Moisture built in her eyes, and she impatiently wiped the tears away. "Focus on the case," she said to herself.

Her thoughts immediately went to Vic Weber's stonewalling them from investigating his nephew's room. As much as she wanted to march into the hospital and be hard-nosed with Vic, that approach had zero chance of working. She had to put herself in his shoes, show empathy. Nikki knew first-hand how grief clouded a person's judgement.

Rory's number flashed on the jeep's touch screen.

"Hey," she answered. "Perfect timing. I really need to hear your voice right now."

Some days, Nikki still couldn't believe the direction her personal life had taken. Rory Todd was kind, hard-working and nearly as damaged as her. She loved him more than she thought possible, and that scared the hell out of her.

"That bad?" he asked.

"Triple homicide, one survivor in surgery. Pretty much nothing adds up."

"Sounds about right," he said. "Mom's picking Lacey up from school, and I'll be done around six. We'll figure out dinner."

"I'll pick up a pizza or something," Nikki said. "Even if I can only come home for a couple of hours, I need to spend time with her. And you," she added.

"Don't worry about me, and don't worry about that custody stuff," he said. "You have family to back you up, and Lacey is doing well. No judge is going to shake that up."

A lump formed in her throat. It had been a long time since Nikki had any family other than Tyler and Lacey. She was so lucky the Todds had forgiven the past. They were also extremely attached to their honorary granddaughter, as they called Lacey, and she had them wrapped around her finger, Rory included.

"I love you," she said.

"I love you too," he answered. "We'll be all right, babe."

By the time Nikki arrived at Lakeview Hospital in Stillwater, the aspirin she'd taken earlier had kicked in, and her headache had started to subside. A nice bruise had formed on the side of her jaw. She dreaded Lacey seeing it. Despite how well she'd been doing after Tyler's murder, she was still traumatized and worried every time Nikki left for work.

She found Liam waiting outside of the intensive care unit. "Bryce is in recovery. He's septic from the cut and his brain was bleeding. The doctors put him in a medically induced coma. We won't know much for a day or two. That's the earliest they might wake him up, and that's only if enough of his brain swelling has gone down."

"That seems excessive from falling and hitting your head, but I guess those tiles are pure stone. And he's a big guy."

Liam touched her chin. "What happened?"

"The man with schizophrenia that Brenner asked about this morning was an SAE member before he left school and the frat. We stopped at the coffee shop he works at, and he got spooked." She told Liam about Kai's arrest and what he'd told her at the station.

"Jessica accused Bryce of rape? So he has a motive for her murder..." Liam said, shocked.

"Going by Kai's version, yes," Nikki said. "But we don't have anyone else to corroborate that part of his story. I've ruled him out as a suspect, at least. And I believe his story about Gavin and Bryce beating him up and leaving him out in the cold."

"Do you believe Bryce might have raped Jessica?"

She shrugged. "I'd have to see Kai's health records and his official diagnosis to have a clue about how his mind works, but given the timing of his mental break, it's possible Jessica actually liking Bryce was the catalyst, and he created the rest on his own. Brenner's going to talk with Jessica's friends and see if she can find anything to back up the accusation. Jessica's wallet hasn't turned up, has it? Kai claimed she kept the check in there."

Liam shook his head. "Assuming Brenner doesn't get information from Jessica's friends, we still don't know why she was there," he said. "Did her parents have any idea?"

Nikki shook her head. "They didn't think she kept secrets from them, but she was twenty years old, and in college. Of course she had secrets."

"It's possible she had a thing with Bryce she was trying to hide from them," Liam mused. "But then why make it seem like she'd gone missing? Why not just have a friend cover?"

"I don't know," Nikki said. "That's why this case is so confusing. If Jessica hadn't been on the scene, we'd probably be talking about the possibility of a serial murderer right now."

"Right." Liam leaned against the wall. "We need to check the tri-state area for any similar crimes in the last year, but it's really looking like Bryce or someone else in his family had it in for Jessica. If he pulled that stunt with Kai, kidnapping Jessica isn't a stretch. Did Kai's parents confirm they hadn't seen Jessica?"

"That's what they told Brenner," Nikki said. "I truly don't think Kai had anything to do with the murders."

Liam nodded. "We'll keep looking, but there's no evidence that she was held at the Weber home when she first disappeared, and we haven't turned up any family property he could have taken her to. You think Gavin could have helped him with her too?"

"That's one of my theories," Nikki answered. "We also need to get into the Webers' personal lives. If they were targeted for a specific reason, the legal practice could be at the center of this. That means the brother and his family could be in danger. Did you get the background checks back on Dave and Vic Weber?"

"No prior convictions, nothing on the system. No additional properties owned by Dave or Joan, like I said," Liam said. "Vic's the older brother and the founder of the firm. He has a lake house about an hour from here. I called the local police and had them check it out. It's locked up tight with no sign of anyone having been there lately."

"What about his alibi?" Family and close associates had to be ruled out, and Vic had access to the house. Since he knew the security code, he could have slipped in and out easily.

"Vic told Miller that he was working late at the office and didn't get home until past nine. His assistant and his wife confirmed his story. I'm hoping he will give us access to his office CCTV so we can confirm that way too."

Nikki checked her watch. It was already after five p.m. "Where's Miller? Is he talking with the family?"

"He got called into court. I told him we'd handle it."

"Have you spoken with any of them yet?"

Liam shook his head. "I thought I'd wait for you."

"Might as well get to it." She tapped the glass window and raised her badge. The charge nurse at the front desk nodded, and the door buzzed open.

"I assume you're here for the Weber kid," the nurse asked quietly. "What an awful situation."

"It is," Nikki said. "Do you know which family members are here?"

"Aunt, uncle, a cousin. Sounds like the grandparents are too devastated to come in right now. They're still dealing with the murders. Only one visitor allowed in the ICU room with him, per the sheriff's orders. His uncle is in there with him now."

Nikki thanked the charge nurse, and they followed her directions to the closed ICU room door.

"Figures." She knocked softly and then cracked the door a couple of inches. A tall, broad man sat next to the bed, head in his hands.

Bryce's red hair was a stark contrast to the sterile hospital room. His pale face had bruising around the eyes, but the ventilator he'd been intubated with prevented Nikki from seeing much more of his face. His right knuckles were bruised, and his fingers twitched occasionally. Nikki had always heard that coma patients, especially those in an induced coma, could likely hear, and many described vivid dreams. But the movement was probably involuntary. Bryce had a long road ahead of him—if he woke up.

"Mr. Weber?" Nikki spoke quietly. "I'm sorry for your loss and to disturb you, but we're with the FBI."

Vic Weber raised his head. He stared at them in confusion for a few seconds before nodding. "I guess they told you that he was in a coma?"

Nikki and Liam entered the small, warm room. "Yes. We're very sorry for everything that's happened to your family."

"I already answered the sheriff's questions this morning. My brother didn't have enemies, and neither did Joan. Bryce is just a kid," Vic stated. It was clear he was still in shock.

"I understand it's frustrating," Nikki said, cuing up the image of Jessica on her cell phone. "We'll try to keep this short. Do you recognize this girl?"

Dave glanced at the picture. "I don't think so. Is she the one who... the other one in the house?"

"Yes," Liam answered. "Her name is Jessica Chandler. Does that name ring a bell?"

"No, I'm afraid not. I already had my assistant check the business at your sheriff's request," Vic said. "We don't have any clients with that name."

"Were... are you and Bryce close?" Nikki asked.

"What do you mean?" Vic sat up a little straighter.

"We're trying to get a good picture of him," Nikki said, hoping her poker face was convincing enough. Vic Weber certainly had the legal knowledge to make sure his nephew was protected from a rape allegation, assuming Kai had been telling the truth, and he'd prevented them from searching Bryce's room. Even if Bryce had caught wind about Jessica's plans, and taken steps to silence her, the attack on his parents made no sense.

"Sheriff Miller's people are working through Mr. and Mrs. Weber's friends and contacts, but I want to make sure we don't miss anyone in Bryce's life."

Vic sighed. "I really don't know much other than the usual stuff. He's an incredible swimmer, works hard in school, doesn't blow through his college fund like some kids do. Works in the off-season, usually doing some kind of landscaping. And he swims year round."

"His friends at the frat said he saw his parents regularly," Nikki said. "They mentioned he was closer to his mother." She deliberately left out Bryce's father, but Vic didn't seem to notice.

"They were," he said. "She was the Zen force in his life, you know?"

"Did Bryce have a lot of anxiety?" Liam asked.

"Not necessarily anxiety," Vic said. "But he was under a lot of pressure from his coach, the school, himself. Joan was always able to get him focused on the right things." Vic coughed, unable to mask the catch in his voice. "Did the sheriff tell you what Bryce said when he was being loaded into the ambulance?"

"He mumbled 'look out,'" Nikki clarified.

"That means he saw his parents die, right?" Vic's deep voice cracked again. "If he makes it, he's going to have to live with that image the rest of his life."

Nikki knew that people in extreme duress often said things that didn't make sense. Bryce could have been remembering what happened, but he could also be caught in a memory loop that had nothing to do with the attacks. "I wouldn't worry too much about that right now," Nikki said. "Our brains have ways of protecting us. Bryce may not remember anything. We just won't know until he wakes up."

"Do you know any friends we should contact?" Liam asked.

"Swim team and his frat brothers," Vic said. "Talk to my daughter, Wren. She's a freshman, and she may be able to help you out. I think she's still here. My wife left to go check on my parents. They went to the morgue... I told them not to."

"One of his fraternity brothers mentioned that Bryce's father was pretty hard on him regarding swimming."

"He had high expectations," Vic snapped. "No more than any parent would with a kid who had that sort of God-given talent."

"Mr. Weber," Nikki said, choosing her tone carefully. "We're all working toward the same goal, and that's catching the person responsible for this. I have to ask why you sent a lawyer to prevent us from searching Bryce's room at the SAE house? I'm sure I don't have to tell you how important it is that we have access as soon as possible."

A muscle in Vic's jaw twitched. "It's what Dave would have wanted. He was protective of Bryce."

"Bryce is the victim," Nikki said. "Wouldn't your brother—"

"Look, Bryce is trying to get into law school," Vic said. "He's going through a lot of stress. His senior season was just getting started, and he's been coming back from an injury..."

Liam and Nikki glanced at each other. Was Vic worried about finding illegal drugs in Bryce's room? "Mr. Weber." Nikki tried another tactic. "Were you aware of the issues between Bryce and his friend Kai? They had a spat last fall over a girl." Nikki was careful to avoid the word "rape." Vic Weber would shut down if he had even an inkling they thought Bryce might have done something illegal, especially if he'd heard about the allegations.

"No, I don't know anything about that," Vic said.

"We aren't worried about illegal substances," Liam said. "We're just trying to find out who did this to your family."

Vic shook his head. "I'm not going to let you in without a

search warrant. That's just good police work. I'd think the FBI would understand that."

Nikki asked him about his alibi the night of the murders, expecting more pushback, but he reiterated the same thing he'd told Sheriff Miller.

"Just so we've covered all of our bases, would you allow us access to your office's security footage from yesterday?" Nikki asked, bracing for an argument.

"Yeah, sure," Vic said. "Talk to the office administrator. She can get you all of that. She's not in the office today. We're closed." He rubbed his temples, his voice cracking. "Let me give you her cell number."

Liam wrote the number down in his notebook. "I'll call her as soon as we're done."

They weren't going to get anything else from him right now. "We'll get in touch with her today, then. Thank you for your time," Nikki said. "We may have follow-up questions tomorrow, and we'll be pushing the warrant through. Your attorney assured me the room would be locked until we open it, and I trust the frat brothers to make sure that happens." She let the words linger, hoping he understood her meaning. If he was trying to recover something from Bryce's room before they were allowed to search, Vic Weber was going to have a bigger problem on his hands. "Try to get some rest."

They left him silently staring at his nephew, anguish etched into the lines on his face.

"What do you think?" Nikki asked Liam as they headed out of the intensive care unit.

"I don't know," he said. "It's possible Vic knows about the allegations, but if he believed Bryce was innocent, why is he trying to keep us out of his room? And surely Vic's not foolish enough to think that he can somehow get contraband out of there—if there even is any. And Bryce is an athletic star—"

"Who just came back from an injury that prevented him

from attending the Olympic trials this year," Nikki reminded him. "If he's using some kind of performance-enhancing drug and it comes out, his legacy will be tarnished at the very least."

"Don't they test the swimmers?"

"I assume so, but this wouldn't be the first time an athlete was protected by a school. The hospital must have done a full blood panel before surgery," she said. "Have them do a tox test, too, and tell them to rush. And call the swim coach and see about talking with him and the team tomorrow," Nikki said. "Make sure you get the CCTV footage from the office administrator at Weber Legal, and you've got the firm's client list, so start going through it looking for red flags. And get Jessica's financials asap. Kai said she had the check in her wallet, but she might have deposited it—if it existed at all. He also said Jessica went to the hospital and did a rape exam but didn't follow through."

Liam nodded, typing notes into his phone. "But he didn't say which hospital?"

Nikki shook her head. "We might be able to get a warrant given the situation."

"I'll work on it, but unless we get an open-minded judge, it might be tough. HIPAA privacy laws make our jobs a lot more difficult. I'll get warrants for Dave and Joan's financial records too. Miller's finished with court and heading back to the station. I'll stop by and brief him."

"I'll just be a few minutes behind you," Nikki said. "I want to strategize for tomorrow, but I'm going to talk to Bryce's cousin first."

A heavier-set girl sat alone in the waiting area, her hands in her pockets. She looked nothing like Bryce or his uncle. They were both red haired, but this girl had light brown skin and thick, dark hair that hung almost to her waist. A darker-skinned woman wearing pink scrubs sat beside Wren, her arm wrapped tightly around the young woman's shoulders.

"I'm looking for Wren Weber?"

"That's me," the girl answered. "Who are you?"

"Agent Nikki Hunt with the FBI. Can I ask you a few questions about Bryce?"

Wren shrugged. "Sure. We weren't close, though. This is my mom, Carla."

"Nice to meet you, Mrs. Weber," Nikki said.

"No longer Mrs.," she answered. "Vic and I divorced several years ago. Bryce and Wren were never all that close, but he'd taken her under his wing at school." She squeezed her daughter's shoulders. "It's nice to have a very popular senior on your side. God, poor kid. Have you figured out who did this to them? I haven't talked to Joan or Dave since the divorce, but they were good people."

"Not yet," Nikki said. "Wren, did you see Bryce on campus a lot this year?"

"Sometimes," she said. "But we don't have classes together and our schedules are different."

"What about at the frat house?" she asked.

"Yeah, I stopped over there a few times," Wren said. "Bryce was usually busy, so I never stayed long. I know some of the younger guys in the frat, though."

"They still live in the dorms?"

"Sophomores, yeah," she said. "They know Bryce better than me, really. You know people are always more comfortable around close friends than family. People open up more. Those guys all know each other's secrets."

"We spoke with the members earlier," Nikki said. "Who was Bryce close to in the house?"

"Greg was his roommate the past two years," Wren said. "He's a nice guy."

"What about his other roommate at the house last year? Kai?"

"I've heard his name mentioned, but I don't know anything about him. Just that he dropped out."

"He, Bryce and Greg shared a room at the frat house the past couple of years," Nikki told her. "I assume they were all pretty close given the living situation. Bryce had to be affected by Kai's leaving."

Wren shrugged. "If he was, I'm not the person he'd tell. I don't think Bryce is the confiding his feelings type, but if he did talk to someone, it would probably be Gavin."

Nikki caught the acidity that had crept into Wren's voice. "You don't like him?"

"He's never done anything to me," Wren said. "But it's just weird to see a dude who graduated two years ago hitting on freshman girls, you know?"

Nikki nodded. "Did Gavin's girlfriend ever come with him?"

"I never saw her."

"You have to understand that a lot of people thought Bryce was arrogant as hell, including me," Carla said. "But that's how he was raised. He was always more physically talented than everyone else, and he was encouraged to believe he was a little superior, especially by his swim coaches. Joan was always worried about his ego getting him into trouble, but Dave encouraged it, said it would make him more mentally tough in the pool." She dabbed at her eyes with a tissue. "I guess Joan might have been right."

"I know Dave was an Olympic swimmer," Nikki said. "I'm sure that put a lot of pressure on Bryce to make the team."

"It did," Wren said. "His dad was over the top, in my opinion. He was so pissed off that Bryce missed the Olympic team this year, even though he swims the 100 fly and his competition were some of the best swimmers the sport has ever seen. Most kids train in the hopes of getting an Olympic trials cut. They know the chances of making the team are slim. Bryce had hoped to just go and enjoy the trials, but his dad was so intense I think it put too much pressure on Bryce and affected his swims."

"I can't imagine," Nikki said. "What about Bryce's female relationships? Did he have any that ended poorly?"

"Not that I know of," Wren said. "He never dated seriously, I don't think. He liked no strings attached." She rolled her eyes. "Always his way or the highway."

"What do you mean?" Nikki asked.

"He's been a star athlete most of his life and catered to," Wren said. "He wanted things his way, and he didn't like it when that didn't pan out."

"Even in relationships?"

Wren shrugged. "I've heard him talk disrespectfully about women, I guess. Crude talk between guys, but it's still gross. Girls aren't just hanging around for his pleasure, you know?"

"Right," Nikki said. "I know this is a tough question, but given what you've just told me, I have to ask it. Did Bryce ever have trouble taking no for an answer in his physical relationships with women?"

Both women stared at her in surprise.

"I have no idea, but it wouldn't surprise me." Her mother started to shush her, but Wren waved her off. "He's always been coddled because of his talent. His coaches and his father treated him like he could do no wrong most of the time. He wouldn't be the first guy like that who wound up not being able to accept a no from a woman."

Her mother shook her head. "I just don't believe that. Joan taught him to respect women."

Wren rolled her eyes. "And everyone else taught him he could have whatever he wanted as long as he swam well." She stood and stretched her arms over her head. "Did you need anything else? I need to use the restroom."

"Actually, so do I," Nikki said. "I'll walk with you, if you don't mind."

Wren shrugged and started walking down the hall. Nikki gave Carla a copy of her business card and asked her to call if either of them remembered anything else. She hurried to catch up with Wren before she reached the bathroom.

"Wren, is there anything else you haven't mentioned?" Nikki smiled, hoping to set the girl at ease, but Wren stopped walking. Her eyebrows knitted together.

"What are you talking about?"

"Just that you must know more about Bryce than your mom," she said. "I know he's your cousin, but if there's anything else you didn't feel comfortable saying in front of your mom, now's a good time to share it."

"Like what?"

"Anything you can think of."

Nikki waited, hoping the girl would take the bait, but Wren shook her head. "I'm not the person to ask about his personal life. His frat buddies are, especially Gavin." She stopped at the restroom door. "This is a single person bathroom."

"Of course," Nikki said. "I'll wait my turn." She moved back a few steps and leaned against the wall. She checked her messages and email, hoping to see a new development from Courtney, but she was still slogging through the trace evidence. Blanchard hoped to have all of the autopsies finished by morning.

She heard the water running in the bathroom, and Wren emerged a few seconds later. "Uh, I guess it's all yours."

Nikki handed her a business card. "My cell's always on if you remember anything more."

Wren pocketed the card and headed back to the waiting area. In the tiny restroom, Nikki splashed cold water on her face and assessed the purple bruise continuing to spread on her jaw. She rolled her neck and shoulders, trying to ease some of the building soreness. Tomorrow was probably going to be even worse.

On her way to the elevator, Nikki spotted Gavin pacing outside the doors, his hands in his pockets and his head down. She thought about the fear in Kai's eyes when he talked about the older man. Nikki was positive he'd told the truth about Gavin and Bryce beating him and leaving him to freeze to death. If Bryce wanted to take care of Jessica, he would have called Gavin.

"Hey there," Nikki said. "I'm glad you decided to come see him."

She could have sworn Gavin scowled at the sound of her voice, but he recovered quickly. "Agent Hunt, we meet again. Did you find out who did this?"

"We're still working on it," Nikki said. "Do you mind if I ask you a couple of follow-up questions after you're done?"

"I don't know if I'm even going in. Not sure if I can see him like that." He stuffed his hands into his front pockets. "Ask away."

"Did Bryce have issues with women?"

He narrowed his eyes. "What kind of issues?"

Nikki was exhausted, and she needed to get something to eat and clear her head. "The not taking no for an answer kind. We've spoken to a few people—"

"Freaking Kai Richardson, right?" Gavin snapped, his voice loaded with disgust. "After all Bryce did for him, he goes around saying that shit."

"If you mean that a girl told Kai that Bryce raped her, then yes."

Gavin snorted. "Bryce called his bluff, did Kai tell you that? He called Jessica right then and there and she flat out denied it. I heard the whole thing. I know she was at the scene too. Vic told me about her when he called this morning. He described her, and I'd seen on the news she was missing. I knew it had to be her."

"I can't confirm anything."

"Well, I hope you're looking at Kai for this. He snapped when Jessica didn't play along, and now this happens."

Nikki tried to choose her words carefully. She couldn't flat out say Jessica had been at the scene, but Gavin had to know the details about the relationship between her and Bryce.

"What happened with Bryce and Jessica after the winter break?" Nikki asked.

"Nothing, as far as I know."

"Did she continue to come to parties and socialize with him?"

Gavin shrugged. "I never paid any attention, to be honest. And Bryce never talked about her."

"Why do you think Kai would make up something like that?" Nikki asked.

"Jealousy," Gavin said. "Kai and Bryce were in the same year, and Kai was always really shy about meeting girls. Bryce took him under his wing, helped him gain confidence. He's the one who encouraged him to do the freshman orientation thing. But all the girls still flocked to Bryce. He had a swagger that Kai just didn't."

"You don't think it's possible that Jessica panicked and lied? Bryce calling her had to have taken her off guard."

"I don't care. Bryce wouldn't risk his scholarship and his swim career because of some chick."

Nikki struggled to keep her voice neutral. "You're referring to the girl he allegedly raped or a different one?"

"He didn't rape her," Gavin retorted. "He didn't need to. Bryce got any girl he wanted. Jessica told him that she was a virgin and wanted Bryce to be her first. Then Kai finds out and makes up some bullshit story in his crazy head. Unless Jessica's just a lying bitch. Either way, Bryce didn't do anything."

"Stop right there," Nikki said. "I understand you're hurting and I'm not saying your friend is guilty, but I do not want to hear you call a woman who claimed to be sexually assaulted a lying bitch or refer to someone with a mental illness as being crazy, understand me?"

Gavin didn't answer, crossing his arms over his chest. "I guess you tracked Kai down. He have an alibi for last night?"

"I can't discuss details with you. But I would like to know why the rape accusation was left out of the conversation when I spoke to the fraternity this morning."

"I didn't mention it because it wasn't true."

"But Bryce did tell you that he and Jessica had sex?"

"After Kai stuck his nose in it, yes. Bryce didn't brag about it or anything, but he wasn't going to take Kai's bullshit lying down. He's probably got something to do with her being there too. Or she stalked him. You know how it is with girls and their first sex partners." He smirked.

The urge to cut him down a peg surged through her, but Nikki managed to rein in her emotions. In the end, Gavin's opinion wouldn't decide Bryce's role in all of this. "If you think of anything else, give me a call," she said. "Hopefully Bryce is able to wake up soon and we can sort all of this out." She'd debated asking him about what Vic Weber was trying to protect Bryce from, but she knew Gavin wouldn't tell her even if he did know the answer.

"Hopefully you do your job and find out who the hell did this."

"Oh, I plan to," Nikki said. "You can count on that. By the way, what were you doing last Saturday night?"

"Drinking at the bar with my girlfriend."

"Which bar? What time?"

"Why the hell are you asking me these questions?" he demanded.

Because I get a bad feeling every time I talk to you, Nikki thought, trying to make sense of the theory forming in her head. "It's my job. I'll be talking to you soon." She turned on her heel and headed for the elevators, the rage in Gavin's eyes haunting her. She stepped inside and turned around to see that Gavin was still glaring at her. Nikki locked eyes with him. "Kai Richardson has police protection. We don't want him left to freeze to death again."

She saw the anger flash across his face as the doors closed. Whatever his role might be in this case, Gavin was an all-around jerk. He deserved to have his chain rattled.

Gavin was clearly loyal to Bryce, but for him to be involved in Jessica's disappearance, that meant Bryce or someone else had advance notice of her plan to speak with the police. Kai wouldn't have ratted her out, but how well could Nikki trust the details of his story? Even if he'd told the truth, Jessica could have told Kai she planned on reporting Bryce and then changed her mind again, instead asking for more money. But that would mean she'd deposited the first check. Nikki swore under her breath and texted Brenner and Liam about Jessica's financial records. If the detective was still getting the run around, Nikki would send Liam to the courthouse to make sure the warrant came through. They needed to see if she'd cashed the damn check.

Her cell signal dropped in the elevator, so Nikki waited until she'd reached the main lobby to scroll through her notes for Gavin's girlfriend's phone number.

He'd probably already spoken to her today, but Nikki didn't want to give him any more time to create a cover story if he needed one. His loyalty to Bryce was evident, but if he'd been involved in the murders, then why was Bryce still fighting for his life? Nothing added up, Nikki thought as she keyed in the girlfriend's number. Like most of her calls today, it went to voicemail. Nikki left a message letting Gavin's girlfriend know that she'd spoken to him about last night, and Nikki just needed to clarify a few things.

"Story of my life," she grumbled, hoping the coffee shop on the bottom floor was still open.

She did a mental victory dance at the sight of the open shop with no one waiting in line. Hospital coffee wasn't usually at the top of her list, but she wasn't in the mood to be picky. Nikki ordered a large coffee with extra cream and sugar to cover up the bitter taste. A petite young woman sat alone at the far end of the counter, closest to the door, chewing on already short fingernails. A trio of small bruises on her left arm caught Nikki's attention, and she automatically started working through possible scenarios. Had the woman been mugged? A victim of domestic abuse?

"Is something wrong?" The girl's soft voice brought Nikki out of her head.

"What? No, was I staring?" Nikki laughed. "Just the cop in me refusing to stop thinking. That doesn't look like much fun."

The woman smiled, tucking her straight brown hair behind her ear. "It wasn't." She didn't look away, and Nikki could tell the girl thought she'd recognized her but couldn't place her name. "Sorry, have we met? You look so familiar."

"I don't think so," Nikki said. "My name is Nikki Hunt."

The young woman froze, her thin fingers on her good hand clutching the countertop. "You're here about Bryce Weber and his family, right?"

"I'm not really at liberty to answer—"

"Gavin's my boyfriend," she said. "You might have seen him upstairs."

"I did." Nikki sat down on the stool next to her. "Actually, I just tried to call you. Gavin gave me your number this morning."

"He's got my phone with him," she said. "His battery is low."

"I see," Nikki said, not mentioning the convenient timing of his phone's battery going down. "How long have you two been dating?"

"A little over a year," she said. "It's just terrible about Bryce and his parents."

"I know Gavin's really upset," Nikki said. "What's your name?"

"Ella," she said. "I hope Gavin wasn't too rude to you. He's really just upset with himself. He canceled plans with Bryce last night. If he hadn't, Bryce might still be okay."

"He told me that when we spoke this morning," Nikki said. "Hopefully he gets past blaming himself. He said he got stuck at work?"

"He got home around seven, still upset with the intermural guys." Ella sipped her coffee. "He can be a little intense when he's upset. I don't think he stopped talking about it all night."

"I got the impression he's not very good at letting things go," Nikki said.

Ella laughed. "Really? Why would you say that?"

"Just some things he told me about Bryce and an old room-mate of his. Sounds like Gavin's still angry." Nikki looked around the shop to make sure he hadn't come downstairs yet.

"Oh," Ella said knowingly. "Kai, right? Gavin said he's a piece of work."

Nikki waited for her to ask about Kai's involvement in the murders, but Ella continued to sip her coffee.

"Kai's working through some things," Nikki finally said. "Did you meet him before he left school?"

"A couple of times," she said. "It was early in our relation-ship, though, and I already knew Kai was struggling. Gavin told you about the stunt he tried to pull last year with some freshman girl, right?"

Nikki nodded, hoping that Ella hadn't heard about Jessica's body being found at the scene. The frat guys might have inferred as much, but Nikki and Brenner hadn't confirmed anything, and so far, the news hadn't mentioned the fourth victim's name.

"Gavin said she denied it when Bryce called her on the phone."

Ella nodded. "Gavin said later she felt terrible about Bryce being accused. I guess they hung out a few times but kept it from Kai."

Nikki nodded. "Are you attending the U as well?"

Ella nodded. "This is my last semester. I start student teaching next semester, and then I take my licensure exams. I want to teach grade school."

"Speaking as the mother of a first-grade girl, they'll love you." Ella's soft voice and quick smile would immediately endear her to most kids Lacey's age.

"Thank you so much," she said.

"You're welcome." Nikki thanked the barista for the coffee and put a few one-dollar bills into the tip jar. "By the way, do know the girl's name? The one Kai said accused Bryce?" Nikki asked. If Ella was a student, she had to have heard about Jessica Chandler going missing. "I'd like to talk to her."

"No, I don't," Ella said. "Gavin might know."

"Right, I'll check with him." He'd mentioned Jessica's name half a dozen times already to Nikki, but he hadn't said anything to his girlfriend? Even if they didn't have a great relationship, it made zero sense that he wouldn't have told her about Jessica, especially since he knew she'd been found at the scene. "This is your last semester of actual classes? I bet your weekends are busy."

"Yes, they are," she said. "Last weekend was nice because Gavin had to go out of town, and I caught up on a lot of things."

"All weekend?" Nikki asked, keeping her tone casual.

Ella's smile faltered just enough that Nikki noticed the switch. "Well, no. He's never gone more than a night."

"You live together? That's tough when you're still in school."

"It is, but it's worth it. Last Saturday he came back from his work conference with flowers and surprised me. Isn't that sweet?"

"It's very thoughtful," Nikki said.

"We went out for Italian, my favorite."

"Sounds like the perfect date," Nikki said. "Did you catch a movie after that?"

Ella's gaze flashed to hers, hesitation in her eyes. "We went out for a drink."

"Of course you're down here." Gavin glared at her briefly and then looked down at Ella. "I couldn't do it, babe."

Ella grabbed his hand. "That's okay. He'd understand. Are you ready to leave, then?"

"Hell, yes."

Ella hopped off the stool and put her coat on. "Nice to meet you, Agent Hunt."

"You too," Nikki said. "I gave Gavin my business card. If you guys need anything, call my cell, day or night."

Gavin grunted, but Ella nodded enthusiastically. "Take care, and good luck."

Nikki nodded and made a show of finishing her coffee as the couple headed toward the front doors. As soon as they were outside, she grabbed her bag in one hand and hot coffee in the other and speed-walked to the front doors, hoping Gavin and Ella were far enough ahead of her that she could observe them without being noticed.

She spotted Ella getting into an older Toyota pickup, while Gavin talked animatedly on the phone outside the driver's door. Inside the truck, Ella put on her seat belt and stared straight ahead, her expression carefully blank. As soon as Gavin opened the driver's door, her demeanor changed, flashing back to the bright, cheery girl Nikki had just spoken to. Gavin seemed to ignore her, tossing the phone onto the dash hard enough that Ella jumped and then reverted back to her previous state, still and expressionless.

"He's abusive," Nikki muttered. She'd seen the same type of behavior in countless other abused women, no matter the type of abuse. Words could do just as much damage as fists, and in Nikki's experience, the victim always presented similar telltale behaviors. Some were so good at concealing it that she'd missed the cues at first, but Ella wasn't one of them.

Nikki put a note in her phone to call Ella later and check on her, just in case Gavin decided to take his frustrations out on her.

EIGHT

Unlike the Minneapolis police station, the Washington County Sheriff's office had a modern design and was housed in the government complex, with easy access to city hall. After she found a space, Nikki fished out the parking pass Miller had given her and displayed it on her dash. She'd been here so many times over the past year that she was on a first-name basis with both day and night desk sergeants. "Hey, Kary." Nikki followed protocol and showed the sergeant her badge. "Is the sheriff in his office?"

Kary nodded. "He and your partner are waiting for you." She pointed to a dish of assorted sweet treats. "Take some of this Halloween candy before I eat all of it."

Nikki grabbed a couple of Snickers and headed down the hallway to Miller's office. He sat in his desk chair, looking exhausted. Liam slumped in one of the chairs in front of the desk, his eyes closed. "Hey, guys."

Liam grunted, and Miller didn't look up from his notes. "Hey, sorry I wound up dumping everything on you guys," he said. "We've got a child custody battle, and I'm a witness. Judge called an emergency hearing."

Nikki's stomach turned over at the mention of the custody hearing. She had one with Tyler's parents scheduled for Monday, and chances were she wasn't going to be able to make it. She'd already rescheduled once due to work, and that only helped his parents' case.

"Liam wanted to wait until you got here to go over everything, but he did tell me about Weber stonewalling and called in a favor. Hopefully we'll have a warrant tomorrow."

"How are you holding up?" Nikki asked, sitting down in front of Miller's desk.

He moved his notes aside, finally looking at her. "Christ, better than you, I'd guess. What happened to your face?"

Nikki sat down in the chair across from his desk and stretched her legs. "I hit a guy with the jeep, and he punched me."

"Sounds about right," Miller said, shaking his head. "What did you find out at the frat house?"

"According to all of the brothers, Bryce is a dedicated and intense swimmer and student, no serious girlfriends. According to an ex-member and friend of Jessica's, he also might have raped her last year."

Miller leaned back in his chair. "You're kidding."

"Nope." She went over everything Kai had said. "I think Gavin and Bryce did beat him up, and Brenner's going to try to corroborate with Jessica's friends. Of course, when I spoke to Gavin at the hospital a little bit ago, he adamantly denied the accusation. Liam, did you talk to the administrator at Weber Legal?"

"She's emailing me the video today," he answered. "She worked until six last night and confirmed Vic was still there when she went home."

"Good," Nikki said. "The sooner we get those videos, the quicker we can move on from Vic as a suspect. He's very protective of his nephew, which isn't surprising, but I also get the feeling Vic may know more about Bryce's private life than he's letting on."

"Bryce actually called her in front of Kai and the others and confronted her about the rape accusation? That's a ballsy move if he's guilty," Miller mused.

"It is, but it's also the move of a master manipulator." Nikki had been thinking about it on the drive back from the city. "It's Kai's word against his, and Bryce calls her when he's surrounded by his friends. She's on speaker. It's not hard to believe she would have been too intimidated to say anything other than what she did. I'm going to ask the brothers about it later when we search Bryce's room. I'm sure all of the frat guys would say the same thing Gavin did because they stick together. But it also seemed like Bryce wasn't close to many of the current members."

"Really?" Miller asked. "I had guys in my fraternity who didn't always see eye to eye, but I would call all of them my friends. Living that close together for a few years, there aren't a lot of secrets. Especially in a frat house."

"I wouldn't have pegged you for a frat boy," Liam said. "Which one?"

"Epsilon Tau," he said. "It's an all-black fraternity, party of Alpha Phi Alpha. I'm still close with those guys."

"But you all have a common bond that regular frats don't," Nikki said. "No matter where your members come from, you all have the experience of being black men in America. Seems like that's a stronger bond than a regular frat."

"Probably," he said. "Hazing used to be a huge part of bonding, until it got out of control. It's the old military thinking: you go through hell together, you bond for life. Isn't SAE one of the frats that got rid of hazing?"

"After their suspension ended in 2017." Nikki quickly did the math. "Which means none of the active members experienced it. I think they're still loyal to each other. The younger guys definitely look up to Bryce."

"What about this Gavin?" Miller asked. "He was one of Bryce's emergency contacts. I think the uncle is the one who called him. What's your impression of him?"

"He doesn't respect women," Nikki said. "And he's loyal to Bryce, which is why I believe that he helped beat Kai up to send a message. His background check is good, and there's no record of him being in trouble at the university."

"Why go after Kai, though?" Miller asked. "Jessica didn't come forward, Bryce's life goes on as planned."

"There had to be tension in the frat house after that," Liam said. "Maybe they decided to send a message. Or they waited until the right time to get their revenge. But Jessica's the odd one out here. Did she go to Bryce's parents' house to confront him and his father? Something went wrong and they wouldn't let her leave?"

Nikki shook her head. "If that's the case, they probably kept her somewhere else. Bryce wouldn't have left her in the house with his parents and then gone back to school. No way that happened." She rolled her neck, trying to ease some of the tension in her shoulders. "I initially thought Jessica might have been seeing Bryce and no one knew about it, but now I don't know. Gavin's girlfriend said that Jessica and Bryce supposedly went out a few times after the accusation," Nikki told them. "But she also claimed she didn't know Jessica's name, and it seems like Gavin would have mentioned that to her at some point, especially once he heard Jessica's body was found at the scene."

"There's also another option," Liam said. "What if someone used Jessica to get to the family?"

"What do you mean?" Miller asked. "The legal firm has had its share of threats, but the Webers had them all thoroughly investigated."

"They also live in the middle of nowhere, which is a prime location for a killer to attack. What if Jessica went out to talk to the Webers—confront them, ask for more money, and someone intercepted her?"

"How did she get to the house?" Nikki asked. "Her car was left at the university."

Liam shrugged. "She could have paid cash for a cab. Her parents have access to her accounts, and they would have seen a charge for a ride share and questioned her. She obviously didn't want them to know she was raped, and if she'd decided to ask for more money, she wouldn't have wanted any kind of paper trail they could question. She's a legal adult, so she could have opened an account without their knowledge."

"But she didn't," Miller reminded him.

"I know but hear me out." Liam sat up straighter. "This was planned. The killer knew the family routine because he'd probably staked out the house. He could have seen Jessica come by some time Saturday, intending to get more money, and snatched her. He could have wanted to use her for leverage to gain access to the house."

"That's so much coincidence," Nikki said. "Plus, the Webers were attacked after she had been missing for days."

"Not really," Liam said. "Whoever did this had to have been watching the house, and the woods provide that chance. If they usually aren't home during the day and she showed up, he could have taken her then and waited until he felt like the time was right."

"Where was the family last Saturday?" Nikki asked.

"Vic said that Dave and Joan flew to Chicago for the weekend," Miller said. "They didn't arrive home until Monday afternoon."

Nikki double-checked her notes. "All accounts have Bryce visible at the law library and the frat that weekend because there was an alumni function. He probably could have slipped away, but we don't have any evidence to support that."

"Then my scenario is plausible," Liam said. "And, in fact, probable. Why would Jessica give Bryce any kind of heads-up? That's the only way she could have been taken to his house against her will, and that makes no sense."

"It's one possibility," Nikki said. "Did you find any similar crimes in the database?"

He shook his head. "Plenty of B&E, but nothing like this within a hundred-mile radius. There were a few triple homicides, but they were gang and domestic related. If the family was chosen at random, and I'm right about Jessica's bad timing, we may be in store for more murders."

Nikki had her doubts about the family being chosen for their location and Jessica simply being in the wrong place at the wrong time, but they had to at least consider the idea. "Widen the search parameters," Nikki said. "Serial killers have been known to travel long distances to find new victims. I don't think that's what we're dealing with here, but we need to cover all of our bases."

"Between the Bible verse and everything we've found out today, I'm leaning to this being a personal attack on the family. It might have been planned, but I don't think they were chosen at random," Miller said.

"I agree with that," Liam said. "Someone wanted to make them pay for some perceived injustice. But I still think it's possible Jessica's timing got her killed."

"Maybe," Miller said. "We're investigating the legal firm as priority number one. It makes the most sense for a revenge scenario, except for Jessica's involvement."

"Exactly." Nikki felt like they were going in circles.

"But she could have come to confront Bryce," Liam insisted. "Stranger things have happened."

"You've checked the family's security videos from the day she went missing, right?" Nikki asked.

Liam nodded. "She doesn't show up at the door, but she could have been intercepted." He slumped down in his chair. "Maybe I'm grasping at straws. It just seems like this case is so odd that anything's possible, including coincidences."

"Let's call Courtney and see if she's made any headway." Nikki grabbed her phone and scrolled through her contacts. She put the call on speaker.

"Hola, my liege," Courtney answered.

Liam rolled his eyes. "Spanish and medieval English really?"

"Shut up," Courtney retorted. "We just finished processing the scene, so I don't have much for you. I took hair samples from the vehicles, and I can confirm the spray paint was a generic brand. You can buy it at any hardware store or big-box store," Courtney answered.

"What about the partial footprint in blood?" Liam asked.

"Do you think I just click my heels together and have answers?" Courtney demanded. "I asked Blanchard to get all three deceased prints to me so that I can rule some things out. Without those, it's really hard to figure out who belonged in the house and who didn't."

"Let's plan on reconvening here first thing in the morning," Nikki said. "Go home, rest, take care of anything that can't wait, and plan on long days until we get this thing solved."

NINE

Rory lived on the west side of Stillwater, in the same house he'd grown up in. His parents' farm bordered Nikki's parents' acreage, and she'd grown up hanging out with Rory's older brother, Mark. She'd snuck through the cornfields between their houses countless times, heading to Mark's to hang out and drink whenever his parents were out for the evening. The last time Nikki had run through a cornfield had been the night she found her parents dead and Mark Todd hiding in her house. That night had set off a chain of events that resulted in Mark's wrongful conviction and her parents' killer walking free for two decades. When she came back to Stillwater to work on a case, Mark's little brother had been the last person Nikki imagined spending time with, but he'd helped convince her to look at the case with fresh eyes, leading to Mark's exoneration.

Nikki smiled every time she pulled up to Rory's house. Since she and Lacey had unofficially moved in, Lacey had insisted on decorating for Halloween. Rory and Lacey had gone overboard, with the entire front yard full of tombstones and ghosts. A life-size Jack Skellington and Sally stood next to the front door, and Nikki could never decide if they were welcoming or creepy as hell.

Battery-operated candles glowed in the windows, and Rory had switched the porch light to an orange bulb. Nikki punched in the key code to unlock the front door, surprised at the quiet. This time of day, if Lacey had been picked up from Rory's parents, she was usually running around like a sugar fiend right about now.

"Hello?" Nikki called.

"It's Oogie's turn to boogie." Lacey burst out of the closet wearing the Oogie Boogie costume that Rory's mother had made for her. It had all the bells and whistles, including the dice he carried.

Nikki jumped back, her hand against her chest. "You scared me," she exaggerated for Lacey's benefit. "Very convincing."

Lacey whipped the top of her costume off her head, her black curls tousled. Her mouth hung open. "Mommy, what happened to your face?" Panic had crept into her voice.

"I'm a klutz," Nikki said. "Would you believe I marched into the police station today and tripped over my own feet?"

"No." Lacey's answer took Nikki by surprise. Had she already seen enough bad things in the world that she would be suspicious every time something happened?

"It's true." Rory had come in from the kitchen, worry in his eyes. "She texted me about it already."

"She did?"

"You think I'd lie about something like that?" he asked. "You know how disappointed I am that I wasn't there to see it and tease her?"

Lacey giggled. "Well, I guess that's true. Mommy, did everyone laugh?"

"Oh yes," Nikki said. "I'll be hearing about this one for a long time." She adjusted the top of Lacey's costume.

"Did you bring the pizza?" Lacey asked.

Nikki slapped her head. She'd completely forgotten promising Rory that she would pick up pizza for tonight. "I'm so sorry, baby. I got called into a case and completely forgot about it."

"Picked up a couple of frozen pizzas on the way home from Mom and Dad's," Rory said. "After you talked to me today, I figured you'd forget."

"I'll get the pizza out of the freezer." Lacey skipped into the kitchen.

Nikki dumped her purse and coat on the floor. She walked up to Rory and wrapped her arms around his waist, inhaling the scent of his skin. "Thank you."

He kissed her softly and brushed her hair off her face to examine the bruise. "You're welcome. How did that actually happen?" he demanded.

"A misunderstanding," she said.

His eyes flashed. "You're telling me that someone hit you?"

"A possible suspect, I'm fine, I promise."

Rory sighed. "Do I dare ask how the case is going?"

"Like brick walls going up around me," she said. "Nothing makes any sense, including why the victims were together in the first place." She jumped at the sound of something clattering to the floor in the kitchen.

"Nothing to see here," Lacey called.

They found her in the kitchen, standing on a chair, rinsing off the pizza pan. "It fell on the floor, but I'm washing it."

Rory laughed and preheated the oven while Nikki shooed her off the chair. "Go take your costume off before you get it dirty."

"Okay, but don't forget about this weekend," Lacey said in a serious tone. "You promised to go trick-or-treating with me like we do every year. And you're dressing up since Rory is." She flounced off singing Oogie Boogie's song from *The Nightmare*

Before Christmas. Nikki hadn't cared much about Halloween until Lacey was born, but it had been Tyler's favorite holiday, and he'd gone all out for Lacey's costume each year. She still couldn't believe it had been six months since her ex-husband's murder. The time flew by, even when it seemed to be crawling. She and Lacey were still going to therapy, and there were still nights Lacey cried herself to sleep over Tyler, but she'd adjusted better than Nikki had expected, mostly thanks to Rory's parents. His mother had held a grudge against Nikki for years because of her older son's wrongful imprisonment, but she stepped in when Lacey was taken and Tyler murdered at the hands of a serial killer.

Lacey had enjoyed the summer playing in the Todds' pool and taking care of the yard and flowers with Granny Ruth, and the experience had been good for her. She'd also made two new friends in Stillwater, and that made the decision about switching elementary schools easy for Lacey. Nikki got the sense her daughter wanted to put reminders of Tyler behind her, even if she was too little to realize it.

"If you can't make it, I'll still take her." Rory squeezed her shoulders.

"No, I'll figure it out." Downtown Stillwater's trick-or-treat night had been an annual event since Nikki was a kid. This would be the first year she'd attended since third or fourth grade, when her dad had dressed like Leatherface and scared the hell out of kids. "This year's too important."

After a heated game of checkers, Lacey's bath and two bedtime stories, Nikki settled down in the kitchen with her laptop and notes. She needed to take care of the mortgage and electric bill on her house in St. Paul before she wound up in collections; staying at Rory's so much made it hard to remember she also owned her own home. Rory had tried to talk to her about selling it, but Nikki wanted to keep it in case she worked late and needed to stay in the city.

Rory came into the kitchen, his damp hair pushed back off his forehead. He kissed her cheek, and her body immediately reacted. She loved the way he smelled after a shower, and she had to fight the urge to wrap herself around him for the rest of the night.

"You doing all right?" he asked, sitting down across from her with a beer.

She nodded, rubbing her temples. "I need to focus on this case, but I keep worrying about Lacey and Tyler's parents getting custody."

Rory made a disgusted face. Tyler had only been gone a month when Nikki introduced Rory to Tyler's parents. He'd become so involved in their lives that Nikki couldn't keep putting it off. Rory and his parents helped with Lacey when Nikki was swamped with work, and Tyler's parents needed to know that Lacey was safe. She'd hoped that meeting Rory and seeing how well he got along with Lacey would soften the blow, but they'd looked at him as though he were a homewrecker. Tyler's father made it clear he wouldn't deal with someone other than Nikki, because she was Lacey's parent, not "this substitute she was spending time with."

Nikki still burned every time she thought about that comment. She'd tried to be compassionate, but she also had to draw a line in the sand. She had told Tyler's parents that they were just going to have to deal with Rory's involvement in Lacey's life. The petition for custody had been filed the next week.

"They won't get custody," Rory said. "I get they are hurting, but the court will see that everything they've said and done is only doing harm to Lacey, and she's the only person who matters in this."

"I know," Nikki said. "I also know that they've kept track of how many times my work has interfered with spending time with Lacey, and I'm pretty sure they were doing it before Tyler died too."

Rory sipped his beer. "Seriously?"

"Lacey talked about her grandparents questioning things more than once after a visit to their house," Nikki said. "Tyler said he talked to them about it." Her voice caught.

Rory reached across the table to take her hand. "What happened is not your fault. You know this."

"Do I?" They'd had this exact conversation a dozen times, and Rory had to be getting frustrated, but he never showed it.

"Yes," he said. "Wouldn't Tyler tell you the same thing?"

Nikki swallowed the lump in her throat. "Yes, and he'd tell me to knock off the pity party."

Rory snickered. "I know it's hard, but for what it's worth, I think you've done an amazing job with her. The court will do the right thing."

"Thank you," she said shakily. "I forgot to ask earlier, how was therapy?"

Rory was still dealing with the aftermath of his high school girlfriend's murder and the toll the investigation had taken on him. He hadn't had anything to do with her murder, but he still felt like he should have been able to do something. The guilt had eaten at him until he'd broken down last month. Nikki thought he would balk at going to therapy, but he'd agreed with the idea, and he'd been trying to go every week despite running his successful construction company.

"Fine," he answered. "We talked about letting go of anger about the past. Apparently, I have an issue doing that, even with Mark's situation."

Nikki's original testimony had helped convict Mark, but she knew neither he nor Rory held it against her. But her presence in his life was a constant reminder of how a corrupt system had failed his family.

"Of course you do," she answered. "But you're working on it. That's what matters."

He finished his beer. "Right now, what matters is you finishing whatever work you need to so you can get some rest."

She laughed, knowing what he was about to say next. "Vikings game on TV? Go ahead."

"I'll be in the living room if you need me." He bent down to kiss her, his lips quickly moving to her neck. "For anything, by the way."

"Go watch the game before I cave and drag you to bed." Nikki laughed.

Rory winked at her and sauntered off, knowing the effect he had on her. Nikki rolled her eyes and pulled her legal pad out of her bag.

So much had happened today, Nikki felt like a week should have passed. She set her laptop aside and grabbed her legal pad and a pencil. She found a fresh page and started making a list of bullet points, in their current chronological order.

Last Thursday, Jessica left for long weekend. Arrived at parents'.

Saturday, leaves in afternoon to go back to Minneapolis to pick up a Sunday shift at The Crooked Pint. Stopped for gas, arrived on campus, parked in usual area. Didn't get back to room, doesn't show up for work or school.

Roommate didn't realize Jessica hadn't arrived back until late Tuesday, when her parents called the dorm, asking for her.

Report filed Wednesday.

Brenner speaks with Bryce Thursday morning/confirms alibi? Bryce leaves after practice to go to his parents. Murder occurred between Thursday afternoon and this morning.

Bryce had told Brenner that he'd been studying at the law library on Saturday well into Sunday morning, only leaving when the library closed. Brenner had confirmed that Bryce had signed in and out, but the law library was a big place. She opened her laptop and searched for pictures of it. It was an older building, and Nikki guessed most of the windows didn't open wide enough for anyone to squeeze through, much less anyone Bryce's size.

Nikki's phone vibrated with a text from Liam. He'd received Weber Legal's security footage and had been able to confirm Vic's alibi. At least they could scratch that off the list.

Nikki tried calling Ella, but the call went straight to voicemail. Hopefully she was just licking Gavin's wounds instead of dealing with her own. And how did Gavin fit into all of this? So far, he was the only person Bryce appeared to actually be close to, so if Bryce had gone to anyone for help about what to do about Jessica, it would have been him, but that would mean Bryce had some kind of advance warning. Had Jessica made the mistake of going to Bryce before the police? Doing that made sense only if she wanted more money—or trouble.

She glanced at her phone to see if any new information had come through, but Courtney was still processing the hundreds of prints that she'd taken from the Weber home and going over Bryce's car at the lab; Liam had a list of leads to follow up on, and the current information from the hospital was that Bryce was critical but stable, still in the induced coma.

Nikki rubbed the back of her neck. She should try to get a few hours of sleep, but her mind never really shut off when she worked a case like this one. The images of the three victims from this morning ran on a carousel in her head, but she kept coming back to Jessica's broken body.

She could imagine her as a shy freshman, desperate to come out of her shell but unsure how. Taking risks and trying to fit in, desperate to be noticed. All she wanted to do was fit in somewhere, and it had gotten her killed.

TEN

Nikki managed to get a few hours of sleep, but she woke up before dawn and started going over her notes again. She'd showered and dressed before Lacey got up. Work was urgent, but she wanted to take a few extra minutes with her daughter, so Nikki made Lacey pancakes for breakfast, which meant Lacey wound up a sticky mess. Nikki quickly scrubbed the syrup off Lacey's face and hands and quickly stuffed her notes back into her work bag.

Nikki kissed Lacey and Rory goodbye and had just pulled out of the driveway when her boss called.

"Good morning, sir," Nikki said. "I sent you an email last night about the Chandler/Weber case. We have a lot of questions still to be answered."

Hernandez was the Special Agent in Charge of the Minneapolis Field Office, and he usually gave Nikki free rein over her unit unless things started to go south. "I read it, and I trust you're heading in the right direction. But we need to do something about this serial killer narrative the media's pushing. Where are they getting that from?"

Nikki explained about the spray-painted message left inside

the Weber home. "Fortunately, that hasn't been leaked, but the Minneapolis detective handling Jessica Chandler's case asked me about this being a serial killer twice yesterday. I chalked it up to her first murder case and adrenaline."

"You think she's the one who spoke to the media?"

"My initial reaction was yes, but Brenner doesn't strike me as the attention-seeking type, which is exactly what the serial killer angle does. I think the idea of working a serial was exhilarating, but she's genuinely emotionally affected by this case. I can't see her leaking a tip for money. And she knows about the spray-painted message. I'd think she would have included that if she'd been the one to talk to the media."

"Well, someone did," Hernandez said. "One of the local stations is also going on about a black college student with mental illness being railroaded for this."

Nikki gritted her teeth. "I hadn't heard that. I can assure you it isn't the case." She told him about Kai Richardson's information and the time they'd spent with him yesterday. "We have already ruled him out as a suspect, and I assure you, both the FBI and the MNPD treated him with respect."

"I know you did," Hernandez said. "That's never in question. But with the state of things in this city, something like this in conjunction with law enforcement needs to be handled carefully. I'll have our media relations people draft a statement stating that he was interviewed—"

"Is his name out there?"

"No, but it's probably only a matter of time."

Nikki explained Kai's fear of retaliation by Gavin. "I only have his side of the story, but he genuinely believed that he might be in danger. He hit me just to get arrested. Even if the press doesn't have his name, it won't be hard for Gavin to put it together."

"Christ," Hernandez said. "Your email referenced Sergeant Gill—I've worked with him before. Good cop and a standup guy. I'll call him and coordinate security for Richardson. Hopefully a police presence will be enough to scare the guy off."

"Thank you," Nikki said. "Please make sure the press statement is clear that he's been cleared and things were handled professionally."

"I will, but I need a statement from you on the serial killer angle. Media knows you're working the case, and they're using that as evidence of a possible serial murder. Channel 9's morning news had an entire segment about whether or not killing three people in a home invasion would be a serial murder or a mass murder. The expert they had on was a former criminal justice professor who looked about a hundred years old, and he's leaning toward serial given the relatively low number. But the body count will certainly rise, according to the news experts. Idiots."

Nikki could almost hear him rolling his eyes. "Meanwhile, the Minneapolis homicide rate is higher than it's been in twenty years. They should do some reporting on that instead of speculating about something they don't know jack about." Her fingernails dug into the steering wheel. "That's my quote."

"Right," Hernandez said.

"I'm serious, sir," Nikki said. "All they're doing is stirring things up for ratings. I'm not going to play into it."

He sighed. "Fine, we'll find a way to word it so it's not completely abrasive. But I need something specific to the case too."

As much as Nikki wanted to tell the media they could stop talking about a serial killer, she couldn't act that irresponsibly. If it did turn out to be a serial and more people died, she and the FBI would be crucified in the press. "It's one of several possibilities. We're early into this investigation, and we are following every lead. Whether the classification is correct is irrelevant right now. The bottom line is that a murderer is out there, and that always means there's a chance for more attacks. People need to be smart and lock their doors, be alert in their surroundings, that sort of thing."

"We can work with that," Hernandez said. "Any of the autopsy reports back?"

"Blanchard actually called me into the medical examiner's office. I'm headed there now."

"Keep me in the loop, Agent."

Nikki promised she would and ended the call, her mind still on the media's obsession with serial killers. The idea had become romanticized over the years, with profilers built up on television and in books as some kind of macabre, yet glamorous profession. Private planes from the bureau, traveling all over the country and solving a case in a couple of days because they were just that good. It sounded ridiculous to Nikki, but it was no different than the CSI effect in courtrooms and made her job even harder. The media didn't care about the Webers or Jessica Chandler—they just wanted something sensational to talk about. Nikki would be damned if she'd give that to them.

When she arrived at the medical examiner's office, Nikki expected to be directed to the autopsy suite given Blanchard's notorious work ethic, but since Nikki had texted that she was stopping by, Blanchard was waiting in her office, looking only slightly less exhausted than she had yesterday. Nikki was always on guard with Blanchard, careful not to get on her bad side. She could be prickly at times, but Blanchard was the best pathologist Nikki had worked with in her career, including the ones at Quantico. The state was lucky to have her.

She knocked on the open door. "I think this is only the second time I've been in your office."

Blanchard looked up from her desk where she'd been narrating reports. "Trying to multi-task. And yes, I know the research shows that we really can't multitask, but I still try."

"Me too," Nikki said. "Thanks for rushing these. I didn't expect to have results until at least this evening."

"No problem," Blanchard answered. "There are so many weird things about these cases, I had to get started." She motioned for Nikki to sit in the empty chair in front of her desk. "Let's start with Joan Weber. I found migraine medication in her purse and in the medicine cabinet in the master bedroom. We won't know if she took them until the toxicology reports come back, but I'm not sure that's even relevant in this case. She was stabbed from behind, relatively efficiently and, as we thought, right into the lung, which collapsed instantly. She would have died within minutes, unable to yell for help."

"Can you tell me if she died around the same time as her husband?" Nikki found her small notebook in her bag and borrowed a pencil from the container on Blanchard's desk. She often took notes in the memo pad on her phone, but never with an autopsy. On the off chance her work cell was ever compromised, she didn't want personal details about autopsies getting out to the families of the deceased.

"That's where it gets interesting," Blanchard said. "One of my investigators checked with her colleagues at the library and confirmed Joan didn't eat lunch because she was dieting. That means if she'd been killed in the afternoon, before her husband got home, her stomach would have been relatively empty. However, both she and her husband had a meal before they were murdered, and neither had time to digest that meal."

"Meaning he probably came home from work, and they ate before the murders?"

Blanchard nodded. "I found a carryout pizza box in the fridge with leftovers. I called and confirmed Dave Weber picked up a family-sized pizza the night of the murders at approximately six forty-nine p.m."

"So Joan didn't feel well, he picks up a pizza for them. They both ate, so time of death couldn't have been much earlier than eight p.m. Thursday night?"

Blanchard nodded. "I checked with the hospital about

Bryce, because they likely would have done an abdominal ultrasound before surgery, to have an idea of internal bleeding and such. It showed a small amount of food in his stomach, which means he likely hadn't eaten before the family was attacked."

"What about Jessica? We're still trying to figure out why she was there. Could you tell if she'd eaten with them?" Nikki's mind felt cluttered with all the reasons Jessica could have been at the Webers'. If she'd really decided to come forward as Kai said, had she somehow tipped Bryce off? But bringing her to his house made little sense, and they hadn't found any motive for killing his parents.

"She hadn't eaten in several hours," Blanchard said. "Toxicology is rushing her tests, but you know how that goes. I can tell you that she doesn't present like someone held against her will for any amount of time, but there are some odd things."

"Such as?" Nikki asked.

"Her hands have several superficial scratches on them, and I found a few splinters embedded into one of the scratches. I also took dirt from beneath her nails." Blanchard typed something on her laptop and then turned it so that Nikki could see the image of Jessica's palms. "I took these this morning." She pointed to the fleshy part of Jessica's right palm. "See the bruise? It wasn't there last night, but it's not unusual for bruises sustained shortly before death to show up a day or two later. This is where the splinters were, and sure enough, the bruise appeared."

"That must have happened outside the house," Nikki surmised, a knot in her stomach. Could Liam have been right about Jessica being in the wrong place at the wrong time? If that turned out to be the case, her team was even farther behind the killer.

"Her leggings appeared unremarkable, but once I got her on the table I noticed a dark stain around the right knee, and initially thought it was blood since her right knee was skinned, but further testing confirmed the stain was actually mud, as though she'd fallen in a puddle. Given the state of her finger-nails and hands, I'd say she'd been outside before she was brought into the house, possibly running from someone. Unfor-tunately, her head was so damaged from the fall that I couldn't tell if she'd hit it prior to going into the house."

Nikki's mind raced. The day of the murders had been cloudy and rainy, with some areas getting more than an inch of much-needed moisture. Miller's team had searched the prop-erty for evidence someone had been watching the family and possible escape routes they might have used, but the heavy rain-fall the evening before had likely wiped away any signs of tres-passers. If Jessica had fallen down during a desperate sprint from her kidnapper, then whoever chased her had to have muddy shoes. They might have disposed of them, but if Bryce had something to do with the attacks, he might not have had time to dispose of his shoes before things went south on him. It was a long shot and one she normally wouldn't spend a lot of time on, but this case still had so many unanswered questions Nikki had to start thinking outside the box.

Why hadn't they thought to check Bryce's shoes and other personal effects at the hospital? She prayed that Vic Weber hadn't already disposed of them. "Did either Joan or Dave appear to have been outside? Could one of them have chased her?"

Blanchard shook her head. "Joan wore slippers, and Dave was still wearing loafers. We sent them to the lab, but I didn't see any debris indicating he'd gone anywhere outside of his normal routine, like the woods." She glanced down at the report she'd been working on. "The rest of Jessica's injuries appeared to have been sustained in the fall. There was no sign of sexual assault or recent sexual activity. She had no lesions around her ankles or wrists, either, and I'd definitely expect to see that in someone who'd been kidnapped and held. Unless her tox report shows significant paralytic drugs in her system—which is entirely possible—I can't tell you with any certainty that she wasn't there voluntarily. I can only tell you she had previously been in an area with wood and debris and fell in mud."

Nikki's jaw had started to throb from clenching it too hard. "Jessica told someone that Bryce had raped her last year and she'd planned to report it. His father had paid her to keep quiet, but we've been told that she never cashed the check. Did you find her wallet on her?"

Blanchard shook her head. "No personal effects, but what you're saying doesn't entirely surprise me." She turned her monitor around to face Nikki, revealing an evidence photo of a large diamond engagement ring and gold wedding band inlaid with diamonds. "I found these in Jessica's right hand. If you remember, the hand was basically crushed beneath her."

Nikki tried to reconcile the photo with everything she'd learned yesterday. "If she hadn't left her car at school, I would lean towards her confronting Bryce and things going really wrong." Unless someone else had been involved. Nikki's mind went to Gavin and Vic Weber. Both were protective of Bryce, and Vic had contacted Gavin about the attack. Could one of them have picked Jessica up and kept her hidden until bringing her to the house? Vic didn't strike her as the violent type. Gavin was another story. "Courtney's still working on all of the prints and trace evidence taken yesterday. I'm hoping she might be able to help us at least piece together the attacks."

Blanchard nodded. "My assistant and I found fingerprints on Jessica's watch that didn't match hers or the Webers'. I sent it over to the lab this morning. To my eye, it looks very fresh, but I'm not an expert. Hopefully Courtney will be able to figure out how fresh the print is, and she'll certainly be able to match it to the ones taken at the house."

"This just gets more confusing." Nikki rubbed her temples.

"It's going to be an around the clock thing, and that's going to make things even worse with Tyler's parents."

"How so?" Blanchard asked. "I wasn't aware there were issues."

Nikki hadn't realized she'd spoken out loud. She was tempted to blow off the comment, but then she remembered that Blanchard was a divorced mother of three. "Tyler's parents blame me for his death, and they've always had an issue with my work. Long hours and everything. They're suing for custody."

Blanchard snorted. "I'm sorry for their loss, but they're wasting their time and money. The state of Minnesota leans heavily toward the mother, and they aren't going to further traumatize a child by taking her away from her remaining parent."

Nikki felt tears building in her eyes. She didn't want to cry in front of a woman like Blanchard. "That's what my attorney says. Lacey's happy, she's in therapy and dealing with Tyler's death, she's got a support system. But I'm absent. That's what they will say."

Blanchard leaned across the desk and took Nikki's hand, an uncharacteristic move for the normally all-businesslike doctor. "You are not absent, Nikki. You provide for your daughter the best you can, and you've gone out of your way to make sure she is happy and safe when you're working. Do not let these people punish you for having a career, especially when that career is such a vital resource to law enforcement."

Nikki swallowed the lump in her throat. "Thank you, Doctor Blanchard."

"Call me Melissa." Blanchard released her hand and leaned back in the chair. "Now go do your job like the rock star you are."

· · ·

On the drive back to Stillwater, she called the hospital about Bryce's personal effects and was immediately deflated. He'd come in wearing slippers that appeared almost new. She thought about calling Courtney and asking her to send someone out to the house to look for the shoes, but she didn't want to slow down the process at the lab, and Nikki also wanted to get a second look around the home and property. Miller had put a lock on the door, similar to what real estate agents used when they were showing a house. He'd shared the code with her and Liam.

She hit the number she'd programmed into her phone yesterday.

"Agent Hunt," Brenner answered, a tremor in her voice. "I swear to you I did not talk to the media."

"I believe you," Nikki said. "My boss is putting out a statement today, but understand that we're now operating under the media's spotlight. Have you spoken to Jessica's friends yet?"

"I just finished speaking with the roommate, and I'm talking to her friends in a couple of hours. The roommate said she had no knowledge of Jessica being raped or having any issues with anyone at SAE. Jessica had just told her that she was tired of the frat scene and didn't want to go to the parties."

"What about Jessica's work?" Nikki asked. "Have you spoken with them since yesterday? I want to make sure we talk to her manager and as many co-workers as possible."

"The general manager is on today, along with at least two of the servers who've worked with her frequently," Brenner said. "I asked her friends to meet me there for an early lunch, but I planned on getting there early to talk with the staff before her friends arrive. It's right next to campus."

Nikki filled her in on the autopsy results. "Jessica fell outside not long before she was killed. She may have tried to escape from whoever kidnapped her and ended up at the

Weber house, which can't be a coincidence. I'd also like to know why she'd taken Joan's rings."

"Is it possible she showed up demanding more money and things went wrong?" Brenner asked.

"Maybe," Nikki answered. "But how did she get to the house? She left her car, and we know Kai doesn't drive. Brenner said there's no activity on her credit card since she filled up with gas, but she could have paid cash for a cab. We only know that someone else was in the house, and that person purposely left the taser in Bryce's car. And he tased Jessica after she was dead. Given everything we know, I just don't think she wound up at the house of her own accord."

"Right," Brenner said. "What about Bryce and Gavin? Could they have planned to silence her and things went wrong, like we discussed?"

"Maybe, but to kill his parents too? Even if they'd planned something and Gavin had snatched Jessica, I don't think Bryce would have put the plan into action when he realized his mother was home early." Nikki quickly explained Liam's theory about the killer using Jessica to get to the family. "Until I heard the autopsy reports, I didn't really think it was possible, but we know she ran through the woods and fell before she was killed. If she did go out to the house on Saturday, no one would have been home."

There hadn't been any sign of someone hiding in the woods surrounding the house, but they'd also had rain the night before the murders, which would have camouflaged a lot of evidence. "Liam's working on widening our net, searching for similar crimes along with enemies the Weber legal firm might have made. Given the way Vic Weber has tried to stonewall us, I want to have a second look at the crime scene, so I'm going to head over there before I meet up with Liam and Sheriff Miller." She told Brenner about questioning Gavin at the hospital yesterday. "Can you do some digging on him? Look for any unsolved assaults in the area during his high school and college years, including away meets. You can probably find information on previous swim seasons online."

Brenner promised to keep her updated, and after the call ended, Nikki put the Webers' address in the jeep's navigation system.

The ten-acre property was eerily quiet. Crime-scene tape still blocked the house, but no deputy was posted outside to make sure the house wasn't broken into by scavenging media or anyone else who might try to get inside. It was odd for Miller not to have posted someone, but between the murder and the flu making its way through the department, she knew his team had been stretched pretty thin.

Nikki pulled on latex gloves and made sure she had her phone before she ducked beneath the yellow tape and headed up the walk. She checked the front windows for any sign of tampering, and finding none, entered the code into the lock box attached to the front door.

She'd tried to brace herself for the lingering stench of death, but the heavy odor of dried blood and decay still made her gag. Miller had made sure to leave the heat off, but since he hadn't released the scene, the victims' dried blood remained, as did the painted Bible verse about revenge and betrayal.

Looking at the scene with fresh eyes and new information, Nikki rethought her original theory. She was still certain that it had been planned—the killer had too much familiarity with the family's schedule—but the difference in Joan's quick, likely silent killing, to her husband's bloody fight for survival told Nikki that something had gone wrong. Initially, she'd thought the killer must not have realized all three would be home, but after talking with Blanchard, that didn't quite make sense.

Nikki examined the shoes lined up near the entryway: a

pair of women's flats and sneakers, a pair of men's size ten rain boots, and a pair of size twelve, pristine Air Jordans. Dave Weber's feet weren't that big, so the Jordans likely belonged to Bryce. Nikki checked the soles, finding minimal evidence of wear. She sniffed the leather for any scent of cleaner but didn't smell anything.

She put the shoes down and walked to the kitchen, kneeling down next to the placard that marked where Joan's body had been. It was less than ten feet from the back door, and Joan had been attacked from behind. The cameras weren't working, something the killer probably knew, and Nikki was positive that Joan had let her killer into the house. Given the time of night, Joan had likely known the person. Had she been expecting them? Bryce might have told her Gavin was coming over... Nikki shook her head. That was hearsay, for now.

She went back into the big entryway. Dave hadn't been ambushed from behind, and he was strong and in good shape—whoever struggled with him had to have some bumps and bruises. And what about Bryce? Had he heard the fight, or was he a part of it? In either case, they were looking for more than one person. There had been at least two killers, if not more.

Nikki walked towards the big staircase. With Jessica's body gone, Nikki realized the girl had lost even more blood than she'd first thought. She prayed the fall had killed Jessica instantly.

Upstairs, she checked the master bedroom closet along with both guest rooms before going into Bryce's room. "What the hell?"

Courtney had a rule about not leaving a crime scene a complete mess. She always made sure things were put back into drawers and closets at the very least, but clothes had been tossed out of the drawers, shoes dug out of the closet, and storage boxes emptied. Nikki called Courtney at the lab.

"I'm working as fast as I can." Courtney rarely answered with a simple hello.

"I know," Nikki said, keeping her voice low. "Did you leave clothes and shoes and other stuff lying around Bryce's room?"

Courtney huffed. "I'm offended you would even ask that."

"That's what I thought," Nikki said.

"Wait, what's going on?"

"I'm not sure yet, but don't worry about it. I'll talk to you later." Nikki snapped several photos of the room before stowing her phone in her pocket. Miller's guys had left with Courtney's team last night, but a deputy had been left to guard the place. Where was he now?

Nikki went back to the master bedroom, heading straight for the window that provided such an amazing view of the property and the woods that surrounded it. Everything looked as she remembered it yesterday, but she needed to be sure something hadn't been missed. And whoever had ransacked Bryce's room could still be close by.

Her adrenaline had started to ramp up, and she shifted into defensive mode. Vic Weber surely knew the trouble he'd cause by walking through an active scene, but he also appeared desperate to protect his family.

Downstairs, she went to check Dave's office, but it had been locked, either by Miller's team or someone else.

The kitchen appeared secure, the back door to the patio locked, but cold air seeped in beneath the mudroom door that led to the garage. She eased it open, staying behind it in case someone was waiting to ambush her. Nikki peered around the door and scanned the garage. The Webers' vehicles were still inside, green tags attached to the windshields, indicating that Courtney's team had finished with them. Someone had broken into the garage window parallel to the mudroom door, and they'd been smart enough to remove all of the glass before climbing inside. They'd also chosen the window with nothing beneath it, meaning whoever had snuck into the house had some idea of the layout and had probably been there before.

Glass littered the floor beneath the window, but the glass was too damaged for any kind of shoe print or marks to be left.

"Damn it." Nikki locked the mudroom door and hurried back through the house, making sure the lockbox was in place before going around to the side of the garage to take photos. A partial footprint had been left, probably when the intruder hoisted themselves through the broken window. It probably wasn't enough to be of any use, but Nikki took several photos anyway.

Out of the corner of her eye, Nikki saw movement at the treeline. A twig snapped, followed by the rustling of bushes. Nikki reached for her gun, only to find the holster empty. She'd left it locked in the jeep.

Sweat dampened the back of her neck, and her heart raced. She yanked her phone out of her coat pocket. "Show yourself. I'm calling 911."

The wild growing bushes on the edge of the woods shuddered, as though someone were crashing through them. Before Nikki could turn and run, a large buck emerged from the woods, shaking the leaves off his enormous antlers. His dark eyes locked with Nikki's, his head lowering like he was ready to charge. A doe emerged a few feet away, staring at Nikki in fright.

It was mating season, and she'd probably interrupted sexy time. Since male deer were known to charge in these situations, Nikki needed to retreat before he had the chance.

Her phone blared, startling her and the deer. The doe turned and ran, but the buck hesitated for a few seconds, his gaze still trained on Nikki, before turning and racing after the female.

"Christ." Nikki retrieved her phone from her pocket. Liam's number flashed on the screen. "You'll never believe what just happened," Nikki started.

"Hold that thought," Liam interrupted. "Gavin and his girlfriend went to his dad's campsite on the St. Croix last night up by the bluffs in the park. They're missing."

Nikki felt like she'd just suffered whiplash. "He went camping the same day we found Bryce and his family?"

"According to his dad, Gavin goes there a lot," Liam said. "He likes the solitude. Ella's mom tried to reach her, and the Find My app showed she was still at the lake. She called Gavin's dad, and he went up there and found the campsite and Gavin's truck, but no sign of Gavin or Ella."

"Great," Nikki said. "There's got to be at least thirty miles of the trail in Washington County alone. And that's just running north to south."

"Miller's starting with a grid, and they're bringing out the K9."

"What about the river?" Nikki asked.

"Miller's putting that together too," Liam said. "Tent's right next to the water. He wants us to meet him out there. I can turn around and go talk to the swim team—"

"No, Gavin and Ella take precedence. If they're really missing, there's no way it's not connected to the Webers' attack. I'll see if Brenner can go to the pool. Text me the campsite's address."

Nikki quickly called Brenner. "Gavin and Ella are missing." She filled Brenner in on what little information she had. "I need Liam at the campsite. Can you go talk to the swim team? They're supposed to be available."

"No problem, I'll be on campus anyway, and Jessica's cell phone records just landed in my inbox. I don't see Bryce's number on there or Gavin's—he gave his contact information yesterday, at least. There are calls to Kai's number though."

"Let me know what you find out on campus," Nikki said. She promised to keep Brenner in the loop before hanging up and then put the campsite's address in the GPS.

She had a sick feeling things were about to get worse.

ELEVEN

Nikki parked alongside the other emergency vehicles that lined the Boyd property. She spotted a man that looked like an older version of Gavin talking animatedly to Miller. Nikki grabbed her coffee and phone before kicking the jeep door shut. As she jogged toward the two men, she was thankful Rory had convinced her to pick up a pair of hiking shoes since she and Lacey were spending so much time outdoors. They both loved taking long walks on Rory's property, and he worried that she'd sprain an ankle with only Lacey to help her.

"My son wouldn't have gone near that damn river." The man's voice had a desperate quality that sent a chill down Nikki's spine. "He's a collegiate swimmer. An Olympic trials swimmer, and he wouldn't do something so foolish. He knows how dangerous this thing is."

"Sheriff, what's going on?" Nikki asked.

"He says my son might have drowned," the man screamed at her. "That he was dumb enough to go swimming and take his girlfriend with him."

"I told him that we have to consider it as a possibility,"

Miller said. "Mr. Boyd believes we're wasting our time looking at the water."

"Gavin's not stupid. He doesn't have a boat, and he wouldn't fall off the dock. He sure as hell didn't go for a swim in this cesspool."

"I have to look at everything," Miller said, exasperation in his voice. "Agent Hunt, this is Don Boyd, by the way."

"Gavin told me about your conversation yesterday." Don turned his anger toward her. "He said you acted like Bryce was the bad guy, with his parents and that girl dead in the morgue. What's wrong with you?"

"I'm here trying to help find your son," she said. "Sheriff, do you have a moment?"

Miller nodded. "Boyd, excuse me while I brief Agent Hunt. I'll be right back."

He walked over to his SUV, out of the wind. "I've got good news." His tone dripped with sarcasm. "We're still waiting on the warrant for Bryce's room at the frat house, and Vic Weber is also stonewalling access to Bryce's cloud storage and his cell phone records."

"I'm not surprised." Nikki told him what she'd found at the Weber home this morning. "Someone was clearly looking for something. We'll have to talk to Vic and see if he has any information."

Miller scowled. "I knew I shouldn't have pulled the deputy to help search, but we're so short-handed."

"What time did the deputy leave?" Nikki asked.

"Less than an hour ago," he said. "You must have just missed whoever broke in."

"And they knew the house wasn't being watched," Nikki said, thinking of Gavin's disappearance. He'd likely been in the Weber home before, and the timing wasn't a coincidence. But what had he done to Ella?

"I've got a call into Dakota County for extra search volunteers," Miller said.

Dakota was the neighboring county and further down the river, and they had a strong diving unit. If Gavin or Ella were in the water, the Dakota County deputies would be the ones diving into the cold river. "Did you get a chance to speak with Weber Legal's employees or clients?"

"My chief deputy's going through the client list now and so far, nothing's come up. We're still working on tracking down all of the employees, including Dave's former administrative assistant that got canned a couple of weeks ago. Apparently, the termination was for 'misconduct,' whatever that means. Juicy part is that she was fired the day after Vic and Dave had a big blowup. No one knows what they fought about, but the rumor mill was that Vic caught Dave and the assistant in a compromising position."

"Gross, but not necessarily a motive for murder," Nikki said. "Vic's alibied, and I don't see him hiring someone to do his dirty work, especially since he didn't know Jessica, unless he knew about his brother paying her off. He seems more worried about Bryce's reputation than anything, which makes me wonder how much Vic Weber really knows about his nephew."

Miller nodded. "Any word from Brenner on Jessica's phone records?"

"She hasn't found anything yet, but she's going to be on campus talking to the swimmers and coach, along with Jessica's friends." She told him about the autopsy results. "It's possible that Jessica ran from someone in those woods. That's why I went back to the house, hoping to find muddy shoes that we missed yesterday. Now Gavin is missing, and someone with knowledge of the house broke into it."

"You think Gavin might be involved in the attack on his own friend?"

"Someone had to have taken Jessica, and Bryce had an alibi

for that time period. After what the two of them did to Kai Richardson, I can't rule it out, especially given the lengths Vic Weber has gone to in order to protect Bryce." Nikki glanced around his shoulder. "Mr. Boyd's getting agitated. You'd better get back to him. Where's the tent?"

Miller pointed toward the north. "Just around that big, wooded area. Liam's there."

Nikki left Miller to it and headed to find Liam. She spotted his red hair first, barely noticing the green tent sitting to her left. Liam stood on a floating dock, peering over the edge. Nikki stepped onto the dock without thinking, looking at her feet out of habit. She normally liked seeing the water peeking through the cracks, but this time, Nikki froze. Her chest constricted, her heart thudding against her ribcage. Her body felt like a lead weight. She was going to start sinking any second, and this time, no one would be able to save her.

"Nikki." Liam's hands closed around her shoulders, gently pushing her back off the dock. "Your feet are back on the ground."

She blinked, still struggling for air. She willed herself to focus on the Vikings logo on Liam's coat. Her mouth had gone so dry her lips felt sticky. "I'm sorry."

"Just breathe," he said. "It's okay."

She was grateful he didn't ask what was wrong. They both knew it was PTSD from nearly drowning in her battle with Frost. If Liam's girlfriend and investigative journalist Caitlin Newport hadn't been too nosy and stubborn to listen to Nikki about not following her several months ago, then Nikki would have died. Since then, Nikki had been so focused on Lacey's healing and navigating through her recovery that she'd buried those memories whenever they came up.

"I guess it's not always mind over matter," she joked.

"Don't ever talk smack about my bad jokes again." He

gently squeezed her shoulders before letting them go. "That was supremely bad."

"Yeah, I know," she said. "What are you doing standing over here? Did you find something on the shore?"

"Waiting for you," he answered. "Courtney here?"

"Not yet, but hopefully soon," Nikki said. "It's Saturday, so there's less traffic this time of morning. It is Saturday, right?" She'd been trying to keep the timeline of Jessica's disappearance straight, but right now the days all felt like a blur.

"What happened earlier?" he asked. "You had something to tell me."

"I almost got attacked by a buck for interrupting his time with a doe." Nikki told Liam what she'd found at the Weber home and her theories about Bryce, Gavin and a cover-up before briefing him on the autopsy results and Vic's latest efforts to block the investigation. "At the very least, he knows his nephew has something to hide."

"Curiouser and curiouser," Liam muttered.

"I wouldn't have pegged you as an *Alice in Wonderland* fan," Nikki said, slipping on a pair of knit gloves she kept in her jacket.

He grinned. "My favorite Disney movie."

"Please, *Aladdin* all the way." Nikki shivered in the wind. "I can't see Vic breaking into the house, though. He has the code and even though it's an active scene, he's smart enough to have a good excuse."

"The more we find out, the more bizarre this case gets. I guess we can rule out a serial killer, at least for now," Liam said. "I really thought Jessica might have been the victim of really bad timing." He yawned, and Nikki immediately did the same.

"Did you hear back from the university on Gavin's prints?" she asked.

"The rec program doesn't have his prints on file." Liam

motioned to the tent. "Guess Courtney will get them today, and she can compare to the ones in the Weber house."

So much for the possibility of his prints being matched as the reason he got spooked, Nikki thought. She turned her attention to the tent, hoping that the trembling in her stomach and the memories licking at her subconscious would go away if she ignored it long enough. "It's just a two-person tent."

"That's why I waited," Liam said. "Miller thought ahead and kept his deputies from doing anything more than opening it and looking inside. I thought you'd want to wait for Courtney to do her thing."

"Good thinking." Nikki opened one side of the tent. An electric light was still on, and both phones were charging on a portable battery. A small cooler that had probably been sitting at the head of the overturned cots had spilled ice everywhere, and Nikki could smell beer.

"Broken bottle?" She stood on her tiptoes, trying to see if anything was reflecting in the beam of Liam's flashlight.

"Maybe, or a spilled bottle. I can't tell from here. But something happened in this tent, and I don't think it was anything good," he said. "There's no sign of animals trying to get in, even with the snacks lying around." Liam shivered in the wind gusting off the lake. "It's windy now, but Miller said it was pretty calm when he got here. This tent is small, and Gavin's taller than me. He couldn't stand up straight."

"You're thinking the tent would be down?"

"Not down necessarily. I checked all of the stakes, and they're in solid. But we don't know what time things went sour. If they'd gone to bed and the problem escalated from there, I can see things getting turned over the way they are. Just seems like the tent itself would at least be askew. Am I the only one who thinks it's weird they came out here last night?"

Nikki shrugged. "Weird to you and me, but Gavin is known to come out here, especially when he's stressed. Ella tagging along is a little odd, but she's devoted, I guess. You have a map of the grid Miller established?"

Liam fished the paper out of his pocket. "Usual size, establishing a perimeter and working out from the center. You look awful by the way."

Nikki touched her sore jaw. "Yeah, I know. I probably should have made an effort to cover it, but I was too tired this morning. Blanchard called at the crack of dawn and asked me to come to her office. By the way, Jessica had Joan Weber's wedding rings in her hand." The entire case was so odd that she'd forgotten one of the more puzzling details.

"Jessica stole Mrs. Weber's rings?" Liam asked.

"Maybe," Nikki said. "Or maybe they were planted by someone to throw everything off. Blanchard sent them to the lab for Courtney to process. Miller did send someone to check Gavin's apartment, right?"

"First thing," Liam said. "They did a welfare check and confirmed that no one was home, but they stayed on in the property for a while in case Gavin or Ella showed up."

Liam ducked his head against the wind. "The warrant for the Webers' and Jessica's financials came through late last night. They both have million-dollar life insurance policies, and Bryce is the only beneficiary. No major credit card debt, and they have almost two million in their retirement account. I couldn't find any major debt for either one of them or Bryce, for that matter. He has a trust fund that he doesn't get until age twenty-eight, and his parents' death doesn't change that. His college is paid for, he's got several thousand saved in the bank. On paper, there's no urgent financial motive.

"What about Jessica Chandler? Did you find any deposits from the Webers to her?" Even though she'd told Kai that she didn't cash the check, Jessica could have been lying, but to what end? Had she been hoping to extort the Webers for more money?

"No," Liam said. "Regular paychecks from The Crooked Pint, some deposits from her parents and her student loan deposits are the only sources of income I found. Have her wallet or personal things been found yet?"

"They're probably at the bottom of a lake," Nikki said. "Warmer than usual temperatures this fall means none around here have even started to freeze. Any luck on the warrant for the rape exam?"

"I talked to two judges this morning who laughed at it. One said that if I knew the name of the hospital and had her next of kin's permission, he'd consider it."

"Damn." Nikki wasn't surprised, but she was still disappointed. "Did you mention the check to the judge?"

He nodded. "If we find record of it, then it might help our case. Until then, they don't care. It doesn't help that Vic Weber has some pull at the DA's office."

Nikki gritted her teeth. She knew privacy laws were vital, especially when so many rape victims were too scared to speak out, but Jessica was past that option now.

She spotted a familiar white, baggy Tyvek suit through the brush. Courtney rounded the bend, one of her investigators in tow.

"We haven't touched anything," Nikki said. "It's all yours."

"Sweet," Courtney said. "Miller asked me to send you his way. Ella's mother just got here. Liam, you stay here with me and help."

"You have the landlord's information for Gavin's apartment?" Nikki asked him.

Liam nodded, grumbling under his breath about Courtney not being his boss, even as he obediently began helping her and the assistant get their equipment ready.

"Call him and tell him we'll be coming to search within the hour. We need him to open the door for us."

Nikki jogged back toward the driveway. She heard the

shouting first, recognizing Don Boyd's deep cadence and picked up the pace.

Miller stood between Boyd and a small, gray-haired woman who looked like she'd rolled out of bed and went straight for her car keys. Nikki knew Ella's mother had probably done exactly that.

"Your lousy son did this," she shouted at Boyd. "He's a sorry excuse for a human being. I know what he did!" Her voice had risen to a shriek.

"My boy didn't do anything," Boyd shouted back. "He treated your daughter just fine."

"Is that why she was terrified of him?"

"What's going on?" Nikki asked.

The woman rounded on Nikki, her eyes red from crying. "That monster of his probably killed my daughter."

"This is Patty," Miller said. "Would you mind talking to her while I finish with Mr. Boyd?"

"Of course." Nikki extended her arm to the woman. "Agent Nikki Hunt, with the FBI. Why don't we go somewhere warmer and talk about everything? My jeep is just over there. If you want to sit inside while we talk—"

"My daughter isn't warm right now," Patty said, still glaring at Boyd.

"Fair enough," Nikki answered. She gently took the woman's elbow, guiding her away from Boyd. "Can we get you anything?"

"Is this a social call?" Patty snapped. "Why isn't every available body out looking for them?"

"Sheriff Miller has established a search grid," Nikki said. "He's limiting the amount of people in the immediate area right now, but he's got volunteers and deputies going up and down the trail, looking for any sign of them."

"I told her to leave him and come home." Patty's voice cracked. "I knew something like this would happen."

"Did Ella tell you that Gavin was abusing her?"

"Of course she didn't, but in just a few months of living with him, she went from bubbly and friendly to closed off. She stopped wearing makeup or doing anything with her hair other than brushing it. Said Gavin liked it that way."

"Do you think he was controlling from the beginning?" Nikki asked.

"I think so. She changed in a matter of months."

"They've been together around a year, right?"

Patty nodded. "He moved her in after three months. I begged her to stay in the dorms. It's her senior year, and I know most of the upperclassmen live off campus, but we couldn't afford rent for her and a car payment. At least she'd have a place to go if things got bad. But she moved out at the end of last semester to spend more time with Gavin."

Nikki knew the investigation—and Gavin's attitude—meant she was biased, but everything Patty was telling her gelled with the impression she'd gotten of Ella yesterday. "How did they meet?"

"They met at a mixer last fall." Patty rolled her eyes. "That's what Ella called it, but I'm not as country-stupid as she thinks. He's a frat boy, and she met him at one of their parties. Last year, mind you. He graduated two or three years ago, and he's still coming to frat parties, where he knows there will be throngs of younger girls."

"This sounds odd, but did Ella mention anything specific about the night she met him other than the mixer?"

"It was a costume party."

"Halloween, then?"

"No, before that. She was already with him during Halloween, because she canceled coming home and helping me hand out candy to be with him."

Nikki got the sense that Patty's attachment to Ella skewed her judgement. "Will Ella's father be joining the search?"

"He better not show up here," Patty said. "I haven't seen the sonofabitch since Ella was twelve. He was a mean drunk."

Meaning Ella's primary male role model in her formative years had been similar to Gavin, Nikki thought. She wished that she'd thought to grab the notepad and pen out of her purse, but she'd left them locked up in the jeep. Using her phone to take notes felt wrong given the urgency of the situation.

"When was the last time you spoke to your daughter, Patty?"

"Yesterday," she said. "She told me about Bryce. Ella was so worried about how Gavin was going to handle it if Bryce didn't recover, and I told her that he would take it out on her. She got mad, but guess what? Mom was right again."

"Patty, is there anywhere you can think of that Ella would go when she was in trouble?"

"Before he came into the picture, I'd say home. But now I don't think she has anywhere to go." She pointed a shaking finger at Nikki. "You mark my words, Agent. He'll show up again, with another perfectly crafted story that gets him out of hot water."

"What do you mean?"

"I didn't like that boy from the moment I laid eyes on him," Patty said. "He just looked dead inside—or high. I couldn't tell which it was, but I knew that he was bad. I did some digging, you know? I follow a lot of unsolved crime subreddits, so that's where I started. And sure enough, I found something."

Nikki had never ventured past Reddit's front page, but she knew cops who devoted hours every week going through the topics, hoping to find a nugget of information about a missing person or a murder case.

"The story was pretty much the same on each subreddit," Patty continued. "I searched through the news reports from the same time period, and what I read on the crime subreddits is similar to the news stories: the survivor said she cut across campus, walking past the pool because it was better lit than some of the other routes. She heard laughter and thought she recognized the voices, but didn't say anything. She was attacked by two males, who moved so quickly, dragged her into a big patch of foliage, and raped her. She said they were both wearing black, but then she said that she ripped one of their shirts and the one underneath had Seventeenth hall's dorm logo on it. The swimmers were questioned about it, and they all denied it, but there were reports of Gavin hanging around the area less than thirty minutes before the attack."

Nikki knew that each dorm, and often each floor, created their own logo or mascot every year. She'd have one of their research assistants look into the story, but Greg had roomed with Bryce that year. Hopefully she'd be able to catch him at the fraternity. She didn't want to add to Patty's stress, but other than the victim's statement, it sounded like most of what she'd been reading was hearsay.

"I told Ella the boy was going to hurt her," Patty said. "Why didn't she listen to me?"

"Do any of us listen to our moms when we're young?" Nikki asked. "I certainly didn't, and I've regretted that every day."

"At least you lived to regret it," Patty choked out. "I'm so afraid my Ella won't."

TWELVE

"There's definitely blood in the tent," Courtney said when Nikki returned. "Someone was hit with a broken bottle. There's blood and bits of skin on the glass." She glanced over Nikki's shoulder. "How'd that go? Sounded intense when I got here."

"It was," Nikki answered. "Ella's mother is certain Gavin did something to her."

"We searched the ground around the tent, trying to see if we could figure out which direction they went in, but there's no obvious blood trail. I'm assuming the wound had been bandaged or at least the bleeding had stopped." She motioned for Nikki to follow her into the tent, where she'd set up a lower wattage Klieg light.

"Is that blood on the cot frame?" Nikki asked.

Courtney nodded. "It looks like someone made contact with the cot, like they tripped and fell, rather than blood dripping from an injury. In other news, I think it's safe to say that I've got Gavin's fingerprints to compare to the ones taken from the Weber house." Courtney pointed to a sneaker lying on its side. "I found the other one in the corner. Looks like Ella might have cut her foot on the glass and then tried to put her shoes on before leaving the tent."

Liam stowed his phone in his coat pocket. "Gavin's landlord is not happy about coming back to let us in after Miller's guys already did a welfare check. He said if we don't show up in the next hour, he's not going to be there. They live near the campus."

Nikki checked her watch. "Damnit, that's cutting it close with traffic. I guess that means I'm driving. Court, work your magic and keep us updated."

"Why can't I drive?" Liam demanded.

Courtney snickered. "'Cause you drive like a grandpa."

Nikki grabbed Liam's arm. "Let's go."

Dinkytown was so close to the University of Minnesota's Twin Cities campus that some people thought it was actually part of campus. When Nikki attended the school in the mid-90s, the area was safe and low-key. It was still considered safe, especially compared to some of the other areas of the city, but driving through always left Nikki in a daze. Countless secondhand clothing and bike shops, used bookstores and dive bars lined the streets, and cheap eateries seemed to multiply with each block.

"Caitlin likes coming down here for the live music," Liam said. "There are so many little live music venues and a lot of talented artists. It's a cool vibe. She keeps asking me to get you and Rory to meet us down here one night."

Nikki smiled. "Maybe after this case is solved, we can do that." It was still strange to think of Caitlin as a friend. When Nikki had returned to Stillwater less than a year ago, Caitlin was in the middle of an investigative piece about the murder of Nikki's parents. She'd believed Mark Todd was innocent, and her pushiness helped Nikki put the real killer in prison. She'd started dating Liam not long after that, and Nikki had initially been suspicious of her motives, but Caitlin had gradually earned her trust and friendship. She also made Liam happy, which benefited the entire team. Before Caitlin, he was often negative about work and life in general, but being with her had softened him.

"My friends and I lived in an apartment in Dinkytown during grad school," Nikki said. "It's always been commercially convenient for students, but it's exploded since I went here."

"How'd it get its name?" Liam asked.

"I've heard several different theories over the years, and the most prevalent was always that it came from the street cars. They were small and called Dinkys a long time ago. There was also a businessman who owned a haberdashery where the Loring Pasta Bar is now. His last name was Grodnik, which means small or tiny. Anyway, his brother always said that Grodnik named the area because it was going to be a real small, dinky place," Nikki said.

"What the hell is a haberdashery?" Liam asked.

Nikki laughed. "It's a place that carries men's clothing and accessories, plus sewing items like buttons and stuff. It's not used much anymore, obviously."

"Loring Pasta Bar's a good place to eat," Liam said. "You know Bob Dylan lived in the apartment above that place in the early days?"

Nikki nodded. "Dinkytown's demographics are right in his wheelhouse. Folk music was the big thing at that time, and Dinkytown was the epicenter in Minnesota."

Liam snickered. "Is that ironic or an oxymoron? Dinkytown being the epicenter, I mean?"

"Pretty sure it's you making yet another bad joke." Nikki glanced out of the window as they crossed the Mississippi River. The fall colors had faded significantly over the past week, and the absence of the rowing clubs on the water gave the river a cold, lonely look, as though it were already bracing for the incoming winter.

Many of Dinkytown's apartments had a modern, gentrified look, but Gavin lived on the western edge of the area, near Saint Anthony Park, which had a different vibe.

"Old school," Liam remarked.

The three-story apartment building resembled the one Nikki had lived in during graduate school, its light-colored bricks the only appealing aesthetic.

"I'm guessing that's the landlord." Nikki pointed to the portly, bald man pacing in front of the entrance, the full key ring bouncing against his leg. "He didn't sound too pleased about having to come back from his other property and let us in again."

"Too bad," Liam said.

The man stopped pacing as they approached. "Agent Hunt?"

"James?" Nikki nodded, holding up her badge. "Thanks for coming back on such short notice."

He grunted. "I've kept an eye for Gavin like I said I would. He's not home. His girlfriend isn't, either. And you just made it. I've got to be somewhere else soon."

"We just need to look for a couple of things," Nikki answered.

James bypassed the secure entrance. The dueling scents of laundry softener and burnt popcorn filled the first-floor hallway. Unlike a lot of the newer apartment buildings in the area, the hallway was painted a dingy white and its track lighting barely did its job. "Gavin's got the one-bedroom on the end."

"How long has he lived here?" Nikki asked.

"Three years, I think."

"Has he been a good renter? No big parties or other issues?"

James shook his head. "Never had a single complaint about him." He unlocked the door and checked his watch. "I only have about ten minutes before I have to get back to my office."

"No problem," Nikki said. "You can head out and we'll make sure it's locked when we're done."

Gavin's apartment had the standard taupe carpet and white walls. The kitchen floor tiles had seen better days, but its white cabinets and subway-tiled counter looked well cared for. A clean coffee pot sat in the drying rack next to the sink, and other than a knife block and a blender, the kitchen had very little personality.

"Bachelor pad," Liam remarked. "I used to have this same leather sectional."

"I think it's a male rite of passage," Nikki said. "Along with the television that's nicer than everything else he owns."

"Plus the third-generation Xbox with the requisite beat-up controller." Liam checked the balcony. "Small charcoal grill and a couple of cheap plastic chairs. Nothing unusual."

Unless Ella was a lot more into swimming and the outdoors than Nikki realized, this apartment was entirely Gavin's. He controlled the decorations, the colors, everything. Ella was either his guest or his prisoner.

"Are you sure Ella actually lives here?" Liam asked, reading her mind.

"She told me that she did, and so did her mother," Nikki said. "But it's definitely Gavin's world."

They covered the small living area, checking through books and the end table for any sign of where Gavin and Ella might have gone. She found the junk drawer that every kitchen has no matter how small it is, but found nothing beyond pens, batteries and a sewing kit.

"Wow," Liam said as soon as he opened the bedroom door. "I might get high from the reek alone."

Nikki pointed to the dirty glass bongs sitting on the night stand. "More like sick to your stomach. Old bong water is as bad as sulfur." She pulled open the drawer. "Condoms, a couple of pipes, and a bag of weed. I'm guessing this is Gavin's side of the bed."

Liam held up an overstuffed bookbag with a floral print. "Looks like most of Ella's life's in here."

While he checked the bag, Nikki searched under the bed and in the small closet. Gavin and Bryce might be close friends, but they had very different tastes. Gavin lived in athletic pants and hoodies, and Bryce's room at home had been full of business casual clothes. She expected to find similar attire in his room at the frat. Bryce's poster was center stage outside the natatorium, along with a couple of the swimmers. Bryce was the current face of the school when it came to competitive swimming, so he probably felt like he had to present himself a specific way. He'd also grown up in relative financial comfort, and Nikki wasn't sure Gavin could say the same thing.

The place wasn't large, and it was possible Ella kept a lot of clothing and personal belongings at her mother's for now, but she barely had a presence anywhere except for the single drawer on one side of the bathroom sink filled with feminine products and makeup samples.

"Double bed. Not much fun with two people, especially with someone as tall as him."

Nikki stood on her tiptoes to reach the back of the shelf of the closet, which, like everything else in the apartment, appeared to belong solely to Gavin. She felt around the shelf, hoping to find Jessica's wallet or cell phone, but her fingers closed around a set of keys. Her pulse started to race as she examined them. House key, what appeared to be a room key, and a key fob for a Toyota Camry. She held them up for Liam to see. "What are Bryce's keys doing in Gavin's apartment? Bryce's car is a Camry, right?"

Liam nodded. "Well, I guess we can search Bryce's room now," Liam said. "Given that Gavin is an active missing person and a suspect in the murders. That should get us past the warrant, right?"

Nikki slid the keys into an evidence bag. "We'll call Hernandez on the way to the SAE house."

THIRTEEN

Nikki drove while Liam spoke with their boss, who immediately got on the phone with a judge who owed him a favor. Minnesota's electronic warrant system, implemented in 2017, made requesting and receiving a warrant a much faster process. Nikki always preferred to have the printed warrant in hand, but as long as it had been signed by a judge, she would be able to search the house.

"Warrant's signed and a copy's being rushed to the SAE house," Liam said. "I told the runner to look for your jeep."

"Okay," Nikki said. "Remember we need these guys on our side, and even if they aren't particularly fond of Bryce or Gavin, they're probably loyal. I don't think the underclassmen know much, but Adam and Greg are a different story." She told him about the information that Ella's mother had dug up from Bryce's freshman year. "It's circumstantial, I know. But it also lines up with other things we've learned, namely the attack on Kai."

"It would explain why Bryce was so brazen when Kai told him about the accusation. They'd gotten away with it before, and they knew they could do it again."

Nikki reminded herself that they didn't have concrete proof that Bryce had raped Jessica, and she knew Kai's word wouldn't be enough. Hopefully Bryce's room would give them some answers.

Nikki knocked on the SAEs' front door, surprised at how much life the fraternity house appeared to have in the wake of Bryce's attack. The house was almost as full of members as it had been yesterday, and louder. A large cauldron of candy took up part of the entry, and more decorations had been strewn along the bannister.

"Hi, Agent Hunt." Adam answered the door, looking considerably more tired than yesterday. "Is there an update on Bryce?"

"Critical but stable, induced coma," she answered. "This is my partner, Agent Wilson. We're here to search Bryce's room." She held up the keys. She'd stowed them in a clear evidence bag, and she'd need to use new gloves when she opened the door. Courtney might be able to get prints, and Nikki didn't want to make that process any more difficult. "We have a digital copy of the warrant, and someone's on their way with the paper copy."

Adam waved them inside. "Come in."

"I thought you guys canceled your Halloween plans?" Nikki asked.

"The party, yes," Adam said. "But we're doing a haunted house/trick-or-treat thing for underprivileged kids in the area. For some of them, this is the only chance they'll have at Halloween."

"Has anyone talked with Gavin since yesterday?" Nikki asked, watching for any reaction.

"I definitely haven't, but Greg or Ishaan might have."

"Are they both here? I'd like to talk with them before we leave."

"I think so," he said, looking uncomfortable. "That attorney yesterday said we can't let you look at Bryce's room without a physical copy of the warrant."

Nikki showed him the digital copy from the clerk's office. "This is as good as paper. We've recovered his keys, and we have someone on the way with the printed copy for you to keep, but this is enough for us to search without issue."

"That's good enough for me," Adam said. "I'll take you upstairs and then see if I can track down Greg and Ishaan."

"Cripes," Liam groaned when they finally reached the top floor. "I thought I was in good shape."

Adam laughed. "These stairs get me every time." He hovered near Bryce's door, obviously waiting for them to unlock it.

"If you don't mind, we like to go through the room on our own. It really helps to get a feel for the person."

Adam blushed. "Sure. I'll see if I can track Ishaan and Greg down for you."

"Thank you." Nikki snapped on a pair of new latex gloves, and Liam did the same. She made sure Adam was out of sight before slipping the keys out and unlocking Bryce's door. She put them back into the evidence bag and stowed it in her coat pocket. As she'd expected, Bryce's room was neat and clean, with a wall dedicated to his collegiate swimming awards. Nikki opened the closet door, and as she'd expected, it was full of Abercrombie, Urban Outfitters and Banana Republic.

"No laptop or school bag," Liam noted, lifting the mattress. "A lot of athletic shoes and Speedos. God, how do they wear these things?"

"Don't ask me," Nikki said.

"If Bryce did assault Jessica and it was eventually reported"—Liam spoke quietly as he sorted through a storage container—"do you think the school would have believed her?"

"Given that they're legally mandated to report to the police, they should have. But he's their star, and there's a lot of donor money involved. I wouldn't be shocked if they did ignore it." Nikki liked to think her alma mater was above something like that, but she was also jaded. Money talked, and no public university was immune to the pressure of a major athletic program. "It certainly wouldn't be the first time. Look at Penn State or USA Gymnastics."

Liam shuddered. "Penn State's bad enough, but at least those guys were close to being adults—they didn't have parental supervision, unlike USA Gymnastics. I still don't know how that pig managed to get away with touching those girls for so long when so many of them tried to tell their parents and others."

Nikki studied the law textbooks on the built-in shelves. "Think about the money that elite athletes can make. Add that to parents living vicariously through their kids and lack of oversight, and you've got a recipe for disaster. No one wants to believe that happened to their child. Bryce has a copy of current case law on Minnesota violent crime." She flipped through the heavy book, noting various sticky notes and handwritten ideas. "Interestingly enough, the section on rape and its statute of limitations doesn't have many annotations."

Nikki checked his nightstand, finding a pack of condoms and lubricant, along with an extra cell battery and various sugary snacks. His chest of drawers had been organized, his socks and underwear neatly folded in the top drawer. Shirts and athletic shorts were in the next drawer, and the bottom drawer had sweats and other odds and ends. Nikki checked the tags on his clothes in search of his initials, and sure enough, Bryce had labeled most of his clothes. "More labels," she told Liam. It wasn't unusual for a college student to do so given the shared laundry.

"That bugs the hell out of me," he said. "If Bryce has gotten away with rape, especially more than once, it's because he plans and does well under pressure. If Jessica confronted him and he did something to her, why would he make her wear a shirt that he knew he'd labeled?"

"He wouldn't," Nikki said. "Unless he wanted to get caught. And I keep circling back to his parents. He had no reason to kill them." She thought back to the Bible verse spray-painted on the wall. *The righteous hate what is false, but the wicked make themselves a stench and bring shame on themselves.* "I did some research into the Bible verse. It's generally about revenge or betrayal."

Liam sat back on his heels. "Gavin had the keys. What sort of betrayal could Bryce have made for him to go that far?"

"I have no clue, but according to Kai, they did some bad stuff together. Even if Jessica's rape allegation isn't true, I absolutely believe they beat Kai up and left him to freeze to death."

"Who knows what other secrets they might have," Liam said.

Nikki examined the printed photos that lined his closet door. Most of them involved swimming, but there were several drunken frat party pictures, showing Bryce inebriated. Nikki couldn't remember seeing any of those when she searched various social media sites. A group photo caught her attention. Nikki carefully plucked the photo off the door in order to get a better look at it. It was at least a couple of years old, featuring a smiling Greg, Kai and Bryce in what appeared to be a moving day. A younger Gavin sulked in the background, the logo on his shirt just big enough for Nikki to make out.

"Gavin was an RA," she said. She couldn't remember if Gavin had told her he'd lived in the house or not, but if he'd been a senior when Bryce was a freshman, then this had to be a photo of the younger guys moving in or out of the residence hall.

"Can you tell which dorm?" Liam asked.

"No, but I can probably find out," she said. "He and Bryce were besties from the start. Having an RA in your pocket can have a lot of perks."

"Like pretending your friend isn't a rapist?"

"Or not caring."

"Prescription pain medication." Liam dropped the bottle into an evidence bag. "Looks like generic Lortab."

"He's an elite athlete, so that's not surprising. They put their bodies through hell." Nikki got down on all fours to check under the bed. She saw that a couple of storage bins with mostly summer clothes had been stored beneath the bed, along with an old whiskey tin that contained several odds and ends like flash drives, broken goggles, and Band-Aids. She pulled the external hard drive out and carefully slipped it into an evidence bag, along with the flash drives. They hadn't found anything that incriminated Bryce, but the flash drives could be the smoking gun.

A soft knock on the partially open door startled her. She turned, expecting to see Adam checking in. "Greg, I'm glad you're here. I had a few follow-up questions."

"That's what Adam said."

"Liam, there are few items in there I'll need your help with." She slid it towards him and gave him a pointed look. He peeked in the box and nodded.

"Is it true that Kai was arrested?" Greg's voice shook. "I talked to Vic this morning, and he said if Kai's the one who did this, he'll make sure—"

"That is not what happened," Nikki said, trying not to lose her temper. "He was brought in for questioning and cleared. He had nothing to do with any of the murders."

Nikki's gut told her that Bryce's family might be controlling the narrative in the news given Vic's attitude about the investigation. How much did he really know about his nephew?

Greg looked visibly relieved. "Did he tell you everything?"

"What do you mean by everything?"

"What Jessica said Bryce did to her," Greg said.

Nikki nodded. "You guys made it sound like it was a little scuffle and nothing happened after it. I assume not everyone in the house knows about what happened? Or are they that loyal?"

"They don't," Greg said. "The three of us shared a room—me, Bryce and Kai. I was there when it all happened. I swear the light just went out in Kai's eyes when Jessica denied it. I knew he wasn't going to recover from that."

"And Bryce?"

"I never had any doubt that he'd raped her," Greg said softly.

"I'm out of evidence bags. I'll meet you outside," Liam said, leaving the room with the evidence box tucked under his arm.

"I'll be out in a few minutes." Nikki closed the door behind him. "Why do you believe that Bryce raped Jessica?"

"I told you, we roomed together since we were freshmen. I knew he had a lot of weird kinks, and rape porn—like real, violent snuff—is one of those kinks. He even talked about what it would be like to role-play a few times."

"That doesn't mean he'd actually rape someone." She didn't mention the information about the incident their freshman year that Ella's mother had uncovered or that it basically lined up with what Kai had said. She needed Greg to back up the story on his own.

"Bryce always got everything he wanted," Greg said. "His father rode the hell out of him about swimming, but Bryce also knew how to manipulate him into getting everything he wanted."

"Greg, I get the feeling there's more you aren't telling me."

He sighed. "I overheard him talking on the phone the day

after Kai confronted him. He said something about ten thousand dollars. I don't know for sure, but I think he was trying to get someone—probably his dad—to pay Jessica for her silence."

"And you're the only person who knows about this?" Nikki asked.

"Gavin has to know," Greg said. "He and Bryce did everything together back then. Gavin was an RA when we were freshmen, so they got by with a lot of rule breaking."

"Really?" Nikki feigned surprise. "Which dorm?"

"Seventeenth," he said.

"Do you happen to know if Bryce was really at the law library last Saturday, when Jessica went missing?"

"I wish I knew," he said. "I went to see my family that weekend."

"What about Ella?" Nikki asked.

"Gavin's girl? I've only met her a few times. She's very quiet. Seems his type."

"What's his type?"

"The kind who's too afraid to fight back." Greg looked down at the floor. "I'm biased, but I've seen how they both treat women. I wouldn't put anything past either of them."

"Why have you stayed silent all this time?"

"Cowardice," he said. "There was a guy our freshman year who lived across the hall from us. One weekend, Kai and I both went home. Bryce stayed to train with Gavin. I came home Sunday night, and campus is lit up with the news about a girl being assaulted within walking distance of the pool."

"This is a huge campus," she said, pretending she hadn't heard the same story earlier today from Ella's mother. "Proximity to the pool—"

"I know," Greg said. "But this guy who lived across from us was kind of a hermit. We didn't know if he was around half the time or not. He's the one who found her. She was unconscious and bleeding. He called campus security and told them that he saw a tall guy running down the hill behind the pool, towards the street."

"I'm not familiar with the case," Nikki said. "I might be able to track the girl down, though."

"Good luck," he said. "Word is she moved overseas. But that's not my point. My point is that he told this to campus security, and he reiterated it the night I came home when the police stopped by. Bryce wasn't home yet, but he saw the police leaving and got all worked up. He said it was because Kai had weed in the room, but I never believed him. We had our door open a lot—people were always running in and out. Samir—that was our neighbor—came out and saw Bryce. I don't think anyone else noticed, but it was like one of those movie moments to me, where it all clicks together."

"You had your suspicions about Bryce, then?"

"Not really," Greg said. "I knew he didn't respect women, but the way he and Samir looked at each other made my blood run cold. Samir moved within the week. I was never certain until the thing with Jessica happened. I should have defended Kai." He looked down at the floor, ashamed.

"Before I forget, has Gavin been around yet today?"

Greg shook his head. "I'll let him know you're looking for him if I see him."

"Please do," Nikki said. She'd already let Miller know there was no sign of Gavin at the frat house, but she'd see if Brenner could have someone from the MPD keep an eye on it until Gavin and Ella were found.

Greg walked her downstairs, his teeth digging into his lower lip.

"Greg, I get the sense you want to ask me something, so why don't you just do it before your lip starts bleeding?"

His cheeks reddened. "How's Kai doing?"

"He could use a friend. I'm sure he'd love to hear from you," Nikki said, fishing in her bag for a pen.

"You don't think I'd make his situation worse?" Greg asked.

"I think he needs to hear that he's believed," she answered, jotting Kai's phone number down on her business card. She handed it to Greg. "It's never too late to make amends with the people you care about."

She thought of Tyler's parents and realized she'd probably been colder toward them than she should have been. It hadn't been intentional, but she'd focused all of her energy on Lacey. She headed outside, resolved to call them as soon as she got the chance and apologize, see if they could start afresh.

Liam was pacing outside the jeep, the box still under his arm, his phone balanced between his ear and shoulder.

"No problem," Liam said to the person on the other end of the phone. "We'll track Vic down before we come back to the search area."

"What's up?" Nikki asked eagerly.

"Dave Weber was embezzling from his clients, and Vic found out." Liam grinned like the Cheshire Cat. "That's what the big fight was about."

"How much are we talking?"

"According to Miller's people, hundreds of thousands over a period of five or six years. Sounds like he was smart about it. Vic got suspicious when a couple of things didn't add up and confronted his brother last week. Dave begged him to let him get his affairs in order before he went to the authorities, and he promised to take full responsibility."

Nikki snorted. "Scout's honor, huh?"

"Right? Anyway, the assistant was fired by Dave because he realized that she was the one who went to Vic in the first place."

"So the rumor mill was wrong about Dave and his assistant?"

"Sounds like it," Liam said. "I told Miller we'd deal with Vic so he could keep searching for Gavin."

FOURTEEN

Nikki found Brenner waiting for them at the coffee shop they'd tracked Kai down in yesterday. She joined the detective in line while Liam secured a table. "Please tell me you're not being told to keep her phone records from me."

"No, of course not," Brenner said, confused. "Why would I?"

Nikki gave her the short version of Vic's latest efforts to stall the case. "We found Bryce's keys at Gavin's, so we did manage to search his room. Nothing stood out, but we've still got stuff to look through."

Brenner raised an eyebrow. "Interesting time for Gavin to disappear."

"Exactly," Nikki said. "I'm just hoping that we can find them before it's too late for Ella. What'd you find out about Jessica?"

"She had a lot of social media contacts, most of them tied to Snapchat and TikTok. I've been wading through them, but so far, I can't find anything connected to Bryce. She definitely hasn't spoken to him through phone or text, but Snapchat is a question mark."

Nikki was familiar with the app's issues. One of its so-called features was that Snapchat never saved photos or other data, making it difficult and sometimes flat out impossible for the police to find any useful information in an investigation. "How broad is the warrant?"

"Phone and text only," Brenner said. "I spoke with Jessica's manager and three employees who've worked with her before. They couldn't think of anyone she'd had trouble with, but when I showed one of the servers a picture of Gavin and Bryce, he remembered Jessica asking him to take their table the night before she left to visit her parents—Wednesday. It was a slow night, and she was due to leave anyway, so he agreed."

"Was she scared of them?"

"The server said it was weird. Not scared, exactly, but like she'd do anything to avoid them."

"Did he remember if they stayed for the entire meal, or did they leave early?"

"He said they ate and stayed about the same time as most people."

"And she'd never done that before?"

"No, but he didn't know if Bryce and Gavin came in prior to that, either."

Bryce may not have known Jessica worked at the restaurant, but they were both cocky enough to seize the opportunity to rattle her. Seeing them together might have been what spurred Jessica to come forward. Nikki took the coffees Brenner had ordered for her and Liam and followed her to the table.

"Black, like your soul," Nikki said, sitting the cup in front of him.

"Yum."

She repeated what Brenner had just told her about Jessica's work. "What about your interviews with the team and her friends?"

"No one on the boys' team had anything negative to say,"

Brenner said. "The coach talked about Bryce like he was God, and that without him their season is essentially over."

"Nice way to keep up morale," Nikki said, adding more sugar to her coffee.

Brenner sipped her water. "As I was leaving the pool, one of the women swimmers caught up with me. She'd been told by the men's coach that they shouldn't bother the investigators because they didn't know a thing about Bryce." Brenner looked disgusted. "The misogyny made me half sick. This girl's a senior and a backstroker." She unlocked her phone. "I recorded it with her permission, and I think it's better if you just listen, because I can't relate the pain in her voice." Brenner tapped her phone, and a soft female voice that sounded clouded with tears spoke.

"Bryce raped me our freshman year," the girl said shakily. "He knew I had a crush on him, so he gained my trust. Wasn't hard since he was kind of a celebrity in my world, you know? Anyway, we had a practice that went late. Bryce was working out, so he offered to walk me home. My roommate was gone, and he made his move. The first time was fine, even though I was a virgin. He was nice about everything and said he wanted to see me again, but he made it clear things would have to be casual because he didn't want a girlfriend. Swimming came first. I was secretly crushed, but I was so enamored with him that I was content just to be a booty call. Each time, the sex got a little rougher. And then he asked me to watch porn with him. I thought no biggie, this is what people do. But what he played was so demeaning to women that I got up to leave. He wouldn't let me." The girl's voice broke, followed by Brenner's gentle reassurance that she was safe and to take her time.

"He kept telling me to relax." The girl started talking again. "That I'd get used to it and realize I liked it rough. He even said something about making his own videos. I finally gave in and just let him finish. He laughed when I told him I never wanted to talk to him again."

Brenner ended the playback. "She's absolutely telling the truth. The sadness and anger in her voice, in her eyes. I asked her if she thought Bryce might have done it to other girls, and she's positive he did, because he got away with it."

"Did she ever think about going to the police?" Liam asked.

"He told her that his dad would make sure she lost her scholarship. She couldn't afford college without it."

Nikki pushed her mostly full coffee cup out of the way. "This is like the Stanford rapist all over again, only worse. He at least served some paltry jail time and was kicked off the swim team. Bryce has been treated like he's untouchable."

"Jessica's friends didn't want to talk about anything at first, and they were all pretty upset over her death. Two of the friends joined a sorority last year, but Jessica didn't, even though she'd talked about it endlessly at summer orientation. When rush started a couple of months after school started, her tone completely changed. She hated everything about Greek life all of a sudden."

Nikki went over the timeline in her head. "This would have been after Jessica told Kai that Bryce raped her."

Brenner nodded. "I asked about him, and they said she'd clam up if he was mentioned. She wouldn't talk about it, really. But she stuck to the story that Kai got drunk and jealous. The girls admitted that Jessica did go out on a couple of dates with Bryce after that, but nothing came of it." She scowled. "That's when the other friend started bawling and admitted she'd been the one to take Jessica to the hospital the night Bryce raped her. After Jessica decided not to come forward, she swore her friend to secrecy."

"It's a hard position to be in," Liam said. "And if Jessica never talked about Bryce or saw him again, at least to her knowl-edge, then she wouldn't have necessarily thought about him when Jessica disappeared."

Brenner still looked frustrated. "I know, and I'd told them

that Jessica's wallet and phone were missing with her, so they were certain she'd show up. But they did both reiterate that she would never, in a million years, go to Bryce's house. She was afraid of him."

"Which hospital did she take her to?" Nikki asked. They might be able to get a warrant now, as long as they had the name.

"The friend took her to Mercy, and they explicitly told Jessica that samples are kept for nine years. She told the nurse that Bryce used protection and made her wash after, but she scratched him."

"Did the friend tell you why Jessica decided not to go through with it?"

"Just that since he wore a condom, it would come down to his word against hers. Between his status at school and his family's legal firm, she thought her life would be ruined if the truth came out. Basically the same thing he told the swimmer."

"That's to our advantage," Liam said. "Assuming the swimmer and these girls don't know each other?" He looked at Brenner for confirmation.

"They don't. I did confirm with her roommate that she never talked about Bryce."

Nikki asked Brenner to make sure the MPD had eyes on the frat house in case Gavin showed up and to keep her posted on any new developments.

"Same to you, please," Brenner said. "I want to get this guy."

"What do you think?" Nikki asked as she peeled out of the parking spot and cut into traffic, ignoring the horn behind her.

"I believe that he's a rapist," Liam said. "Too many similar stories by unrelated people not to think that. Proving it's another story."

"Try to get the warrant for Mercy's records," Nikki said. "If

Jessica really did scratch him, then there's likely DNA in the kit. But even if the warrant comes through quickly, results will take weeks. And that still doesn't tell us what happened to Gavin and Ella."

"Bryce's keys at Gavin's apartment doesn't look good," Liam said. "If they were both involved in the rapes—or if Gavin just covered for him—they aren't as close as they used to be. A falling out might have led to Gavin attacking Bryce, but we're back to the same two questions: why was Jessica there and why did he kill the parents?"

Nikki merged onto the interstate, cursing at the traffic. "We've got two men from the same fraternity who appear to be controlling and abusive, and at least one is likely a rapist. I have to wonder just how much influence they've had on the other frat brothers. Adam and Greg are seniors, focused on graduating, but the younger ones clearly adore Bryce. They strike me as the type to feed Bryce's ego, reinforcing his belief that he can do what he wants. And Gavin has always been there to back him up." She drummed her fingers on the steering wheel, trying to articulate the theory forming in her head. "Think about what Brenner found out today and how it lines up with Kai's chain of events. Seeing them in the restaurant might have been the catalyst for Jessica. We already know she'd been thinking about coming forward because she'd told Kai. What if she said something to them and no one saw it? Or one of the frat brothers at the dorms got wind of her talking about the accusation?"

"I thought Brenner cleared them. They had alibis."

"Doesn't mean they didn't report something back to Bryce or Gavin. Either way, assume they somehow got a heads-up. Gavin's on campus most of the time, and he's the one who takes Jessica. He eventually brings her to the Weber house, where Bryce is waiting. Remember, Joan came home early. At some point, Jessica gets free and runs into the muddy woods, but she ends up back at the house."

"But Blanchard doesn't think the murders happened until after they ate the pizza," Liam reminded her.

"What if that's because Bryce and Gavin were panicked? It's not a stretch to think they had a disagreement about how to handle it and things went south fast. One of them feels like the parents have to be killed simply because they'd heard something, like finding out Jessica was in the house. Bryce might have hedged on killing his parents, Gavin forces the issue. He feels betrayed, so he leaves the message on the wall. That would also explain why Bryce was left alive."

"It's not implausible," Liam said. "But everything you're saying hedges on Gavin and Bryce finding out about Jessica's plan."

"Fair point," Nikki answered. "Let's see if Vic Weber can fill in some of the blanks when he gets to the sheriff's station."

Liam cleared his throat. "What time is the custody hearing on Monday?"

"Ten a.m.," Nikki said. "I need to call my lawyer and have him reschedule it."

"No, don't," Liam said. "Miller and I can handle things for half a day."

"I know, but Gavin and Ella are missing," Nikki said.

Liam didn't respond right away, and Nikki could tell he was working up to something. "Can I be frank?" he finally asked.

Nikki laughed. "We spend way too much time together for you to be anything else. What is it?"

"I'm just wondering if part of the reason you want to postpone the hearing is because you don't want to deal with the possibility of losing any time with Lacey."

Nikki's hands tightened on the wheel. "You're probably right."

"Would it help if I told you that I had dirt on Tyler's parents?"

Nikki was so surprised she jerked the wheel and nearly drifted into the other lane. "You what?"

"Caitlin and I were talking about it, and she wished that she could do something to help, so she did some digging. Did you know that Tyler got his father out of two drunk driving convictions?"

"No way," Nikki said. "Tyler was by the book."

"It's true," Liam reiterated. "It wasn't too long after your divorce. He was dating someone in the prosecutor's office and used his influence to make a deal. Both people he hit received compensation for dropping the charges."

Nikki couldn't fathom Tyler doing something illegal, but he'd been close to his father. "Is that why they sold their big house and moved into a condo? They said they wanted to downsize, but the timing would be right. It was about eighteen months after the divorce."

"Probably," Liam said. "I talked to both people he hit, and they confirmed it was true. Fortunately, neither suffered severe injuries. One was a college student desperate for money, and the other a senior living on fixed income."

Nikki was silent for a few minutes, trying to digest everything Liam had said. She turned into the police station's parking lot, looking for an open space.

"I don't know what to say," Nikki finally said. "Obviously this could really influence the hearing, but I don't know if I could do that."

"I know," Liam said. "I'm not saying you should, either. I think you should have a face-to-face talk with both of them. Get a mediator and talk things out."

"Then why did you tell me?" Nikki asked, squeezing the jeep into a space that pretty much guaranteed fresh door-dings.

"So you would know you had the option, on the off-chance things didn't go the way your attorney says they should." He flushed. "I thought it might bring you some peace of mind."

A lump swelled in her throat, and tears started to well in Nikki's eyes. "Thank you."

"You're welcome," he said. "I know you won't use the information unless you're backed into a corner, but if you get backed into that corner, I want you to use it."

Nikki wiped the tears off her cheeks. "Deal. Tell Caitlin thanks for being a nosy ass again."

Liam laughed. "That'll make her day."

Still fighting emotion, Nikki struggled to compose herself before they spoke with Vic. As sneaky and underhanded as it seemed, the motive behind Caitlin and Liam's actions overwhelmed her. Tyler's malfeasance would sour his legacy at the FBI, and she didn't want to do that to his family. But Liam was right: just knowing she had fresh ammunition if she had to use it eased some of her anxiety over losing Lacey.

"Don't think too badly of Tyler," Liam said gently. "People do crazy shit for their family sometimes."

Nikki nodded. "Speaking of doing stuff for your family, let's see what Vic Weber has to say."

FIFTEEN

Vic Weber looked even more wrung out than he had the last time Nikki saw him. "Agent Hunt, I'd hoped Sheriff Miller would be here too. He said you were running point on the murder investigation, but he was actively involved."

"He is," Nikki assured him. "When we assist a sheriff or police department, we normally try to chase down the leads in locations they can't, be it online or in person. That's been the case with your family's case as well, but unfortunately, Gavin Boyd is missing."

"Gavin?" Vic sat in stunned silence for a few seconds. "I saw him at the hospital yesterday."

"So did I," Nikki asked. "He and Ella, his girlfriend, camped out on his father's property on the St. Croix last night. Gavin wanted to clear his head."

"How does that lead to him going missing?" Vic asked. "Is Ella all right?" Worry lined his features.

Nikki hesitated, working through her options. Normally she'd never talk about a case to someone not directly involved, but there were multiple extenuating circumstances in the

Weber murders. And Nikki still believed he knew more than what he was telling them.

"We don't know," Nikki said. "It appears there was some kind of a struggle inside the tent."

She waited, expecting him to ask about the couple being robbed or attacked by a stranger, but Vic hung his head. "Damn him."

"Who?" Liam asked.

Vic ignored the question. "How does someone just go missing?" he asked. "He probably went for a drive and got temporarily lost, you know? They're young."

"His car was left at the scene." Nikki sat down across from him. "What do you think of Gavin?"

Vic shrugged. "I've met him plenty of times. But I know more about him through Bryce than my own experiences."

"Right, but you're an attorney," Nikki said. "Personal injury primarily, right?"

"Mostly."

"I know some people would say that the ability to read a person isn't as vital to an attorney in your field than say a prosecutor, or cop. But a good attorney is just like any other good public servant: gut instinct and experience."

"I think that's a compliment, but I'm not sure what you're getting at, Agent."

"Sorry," Nikki said. "I'm sure you're as exhausted as I am. What I'm trying to say is that you didn't get to your level of success without knowing how to read people. It's got to be a big part of how you argue your cases."

"It is," he said. "You watch the other person, mirror their cues—or don't, depending on the scenario."

"Exactly. So, again, what do you think of Gavin?"

Vic sighed. "He's damaged and unhappy. He's smart and in the position to really be a good influence on the young people coming through the university, but he just spends too much time talking about... well, hate. And Bryce fed right into that."

"Explain," Nikki said.

"Every time Bryce talks about him, every situation they found themselves in, Gavin's actions are negative. He's angry, arguing, depressed. Always ready to get in a fight, although calls it standing up for himself." Vic rolled his eyes. "He's got to get his point across, I guess."

"Have you ever gotten the impression Gavin could be violent?"

"From Bryce's stories, yes, I've thought about the possibility that he could be provoked."

"Provoked enough he was abusive?" she asked. "I don't mean to make you psychoanalyze him. It's just that Gavin doesn't seem to be close to anyone other than Ella, and we need to find them before something bad happens."

Vic looked down at his fidgeting hands. "It wouldn't surprise me, but I've never witnessed anything."

Liam glanced at his notes. "You said Bryce fed into the negativity. How much did he change after he and Gavin became friends?"

"It's hard to say," Vic said. "Bryce has always been cocky, but I really never noticed the spoiled brat in him until he went to college. I don't know if that's Gavin's influence or not."

"Spoiled brat how?" Liam prodded.

"He got his way about everything," Vic said. "He always did, but it got worse when he went to college. Being a star swimmer inflated his ego, and he just... changed, even towards his mother. He wasn't mean to her, but he really didn't like it when she disagreed with him or mentioned how she thought he was changing. Dave defended his attitude as stress, and nothing really changed." He looked down at his hands, and Nikki could tell he still had something to share.

"What is it, Mr. Weber?"

He shook his head. "I'd honestly forgotten it until now, but during Bryce's freshman year, at one of the home meets, I waited near the locker rooms to let him know I thought he looked great, that sort of thing. He was always the last one out of the locker room, even when he was a kid. I heard him and Gavin talking about a girl, and the things coming out of Gavin's mouth... he definitely believed women were just around to serve him, and he was encouraging Bryce to take what was his, because he was an athletic star, and the girls would throw themselves at him. I tried to chalk it up to macho locker room talk, but something about Gavin always left me uneasy. That's all I can tell you because I tried to avoid being around the guy as much as possible after that. It was difficult because they were always together, and I saw less and less of Bryce."

"Did you feel like Gavin had some kind of hold over him?" Nikki asked.

Vic shrugged. "I always assumed he did. Bryce idolized the guy from the minute he met him at trials."

"Thanks for sharing the information," Nikki said. "I'm sure it's not easy to speak negatively about your nephew."

Vic's eyes shined with unshed tears. He pulled a handkerchief out of his pocket and dabbed at his eyes. "I'm still in shock over all of this."

"That's completely normal," Nikki said. "And we appreciate your time. Back to Sheriff Miller's reason for wanting us to speak with you, when did you find out your brother was embezzling from clients?"

"A few months ago." Vic slumped in the chair. "I couldn't believe it. Still can't, really. He's always been a little shifty, but I took it in my stride. Growing up being told you're better than everyone because of your athletic talent has that effect on you."

And Dave had done the same thing to his son, Nikki wanted to say. "How did you find out?" Nikki already knew the answer from her earlier conversation with Miller, but she wanted to hear the story from Vic.

"Dave's assistant found some anomalies when he asked her to help him catch up on paperwork. She came to me, and I started looking into things."

"She came to you because you were sleeping together, correct?" Nikki couldn't think of any other reason for the assistant to risk her job.

He narrowed his eyes. "I don't have to answer that question."

"I don't care about your marital issues, Mr. Weber. I just need to know the facts."

He sighed. "Yes, we've been having an affair. My wife—I guess she's on her way to be yet another ex—knows now too."

"But she's still willing to alibi you for the night of the murders?"

"She's willing to do that because I was home, just like I said, and I have nothing to hide," Vic snapped.

"I'm glad to hear that," Nikki said. "Were you at the hospital this morning, or at home?"

"Why?"

"Someone broke into your brother's house, looking for something in Bryce's room."

Vic looked dumbfounded. "Uh... yeah, I got home last night around midnight, left for the hospital by seven, I think. Came straight here from the hospital."

Nikki jotted the alibi down in her notes. Vic's surprise about the intruder seemed genuine, but she wasn't finished with him just yet. "What happened when you finally confronted Dave?"

"I expected a screaming match, but he broke down. And broke into a bottle of Scotch he kept in his office." Vic dragged his hands over his face. "We argued about Bryce too."

Nikki could tell he wanted to say more, that whatever he'd

been trying to protect his nephew's reputation from weighed heavily on Vic's shoulders. "I'm not sure if you're aware, but we did obtain the search warrant for Bryce's room. We're still going over evidence." Nikki waited, hoping he would take the opportunity to tell the truth. "You have to realize that it's not a stretch for us to believe you had someone break into the home in search of something you didn't want found in his room."

"I didn't." Vic stared at the wall, grinding his jaw.

"Mr. Weber," Liam said, irritation creeping into his voice, "you know as well as we do that eventually everything's going to come out. I understand wanting to protect your nephew, but he may have done some bad things, which led to his attack. We need to hear the truth."

Nikki saw the shift in Vic: the inner turmoil in his eyes, the sudden slack jaw and finally, the head dropping into his shaking hands.

"My brother told me that he'd paid off some girl who'd accused Bryce of assaulting her. I didn't believe him at first, but he showed me the copy of the check. When I pressed him on whether or not he believed the girl, he said it didn't matter if she were telling the truth. Her accusation would sully Bryce enough, especially in this 'new pro-women environment.' His words, not mine." Vic's voice trembled with anger. "I think that's what pissed me off more than anything. Bryce had so much potential as a human being, but my brother ruined him a long time ago."

Nikki and Liam both sat up straight. "Just to confirm, you're telling us that Bryce assaulted a woman?"

"I'm telling you what my brother said. I didn't ask Bryce because I didn't want to know the answer. But he was accused, and she was paid off. Dave tried to blame Gavin, for the same reasons I mentioned, but I told him he's primarily responsible for ruining Bryce."

Liam scribbled into his notebook. "How do you think your

brother ruined Bryce? Did he treat Joan the same way Bryce treated women, or did he have some modicum of respect for the sanctity of marriage?" Liam's question had a sarcastic edge. His father had been a serial cheater, and that had led to his mother's battle with addiction. To Liam, cheating was as bad as any other form of abuse.

Vic glared at him, clearly catching his underlying meaning. "I treat women just fine, Agent. Just because I have affairs doesn't mean I'm a total louse."

"But Bryce is?"

Vic sighed. "I told you, he's coddled. My kid is too, I guess. We spoil them with material things because we don't know how to show love any other way. Dave had Bryce in the pool before the kid started crawling. Scared the hell out of Joan, but he took right to the water. I don't think he was ever scared of it, even then. Dave taught Bryce how to swim—I was always jealous of that, I guess." Vic motioned to his belly. "I didn't get the athletic gene. My daughter didn't either, so I guess we've got that in common. Anyway, Dave got Bryce into club swimming as soon as he was eligible, which is five years old, I think."

"That's my daughter's age," Nikki said. "Club swimming is through what, the YMCA?"

Vic shook his head. "No, that's a separate league or whatever they call it. Club swimming refers to USA Swimming. It's a massive program that spans the country, obviously. A lot of the elite swimmers come up through the ranks there before they even make it to high school. Dave missed a medal at the Olympic Games by less than a hundredth of a second. He came in fourth in the world in the breaststroke, but no medal equaled failure to him, especially when he was expected to earn at least the bronze. He went into those games ranked second in the world in the breaststroke."

"I can't imagine coming in fourth at the Olympics and

feeling like a loser," Nikki said. "I understand it, but I can't fathom it, if that makes any sense."

"It does, actually," Vic said. "I felt the same way. I kept telling him that he was an Olympian. He had a world record at that time. Out of the thousands of kids swimming at the elite levels in this country, Dave's in an even more elite group."

"But he couldn't see it that way."

"Never," Vic said. "I always thought Bryce was supposed to be his redemption, at least in Dave's eyes. When Bryce got his trial cut for the last Olympics, I thought that might be enough for Dave. He got Bryce to that point, and the competition is just ridiculous."

"But Bryce didn't make it on the team?" Nikki asked.

"He's a flyer," Vic said. "Bryce swam in the same heat as Michael Phelps, the most decorated Olympian in history, when he was still in high school. Bryce didn't make the team, but so what? He was good enough to be in the same heat as the best ever."

"Your brother didn't see it that way?"

Vic shook his head. "If it weren't for Joan, I think Bryce would have quit swimming after that. He was so devastated about disappointing his father. But he didn't quit because the scholarship offers poured in, and she wanted him to get a good education."

Nikki hadn't watched much of the 2016 Olympics because she'd been mired down with work. This Olympic year she'd been trying to help Lacey prepare for a new school and a new life without her father. She'd forgotten it was an Olympic year until Rory mentioned the opening ceremonies. "What about this past year? I haven't heard anything about Bryce trying to make the team again."

"He injured his shoulder in January trying to get another trial's cut," Vic said. "That was probably his last shot, and Joan told me privately that Bryce was relieved. He could finally see an end to his swimming career."

Nikki was trying to piece together the timeline in her head. "Trials are what, five or six weeks before the Olympics?"

Vic nodded. "In May, yeah."

"So early last year, Bryce hurt his shoulder and loses what's probably his last shot at making the team. Fall rolls around and school starts again. What was his mindset at the time?"

"Dave said Bryce was going to 'make it up to himself' and go on a rampage in the pool."

"You have any idea how Bryce felt about that?"

Vic shook his head. "He never showed his emotions, at least not to me."

Nikki would bet her salary that Bryce hated his father for the pressure he'd been under his entire life, and she wondered if his treatment of women somehow stemmed from the lack of control in his relationship with Dave. Regardless, even if he'd been out to prove something last year, he had to have been angry too. Kids had attacked their parents for less.

"Mr. Weber, did you try to prevent us from getting Bryce's phone records and searching his room because you wanted to protect his reputation, or is there something more to it?"

Vic locked his fingers together and rested his head on his hands. "Bryce and Dave have been fighting a lot lately. Bryce told my brother to his face that he hated him and wouldn't care if he was dead. At the time, I thought it was just anger, but now..." He shrugged, his words trailing off. "He wouldn't hurt his mother, though," Vic went on. "Never in a million years."

Nikki could hear the nugget of doubt in his voice. Vic knew his nephew well enough to be worried he'd had something to do with the attack on his parents. "Let's go back to the fight with your brother when you found out about the embezzling," Nikki said.

"I told Dave that I wasn't going to prison for something I

didn't do," Vic said. "He swore he would take all of the blame; he just wanted a little time to get things in order so that Joan was financially taken care of."

Nikki assumed that entailed moving money into offshore accounts, but she'd let the white-collar guys figure that out.

"I told him he had until the next week, or I was going to the authorities myself. If I'd known that he was going to take it out on his family, I wouldn't have given him the chance."

"Mr. Weber, we don't have evidence to support that right now," Nikki said, anxious to see his reaction. He'd found his brother's body, but shock had likely affected his memory of the event.

"God, I hope not," he said. "Joan was a good person. No matter what Dave or Bryce did, she deserved better."

Nikki knew that once the white-collar crime guys got hold of the case, a lot of records would be shut off from her, at least for the imminent future. "Mr. Weber, I appreciate your candor, and I know you're in a bad spot with your brother's financial misdeeds. I do think it's in your best interest to reach out to our white-collar guys and try to get ahead of things."

Out of the corner of her eye, Nikki saw Liam hide a smile. He knew what she was doing.

She wrote down a number on scratch paper she'd dug out of her bag. "Justin Nash is an old friend of mine, and he'll be fair. Give him a call and tell him that I sent you."

Vic nodded, pocketing the phone number. "Thanks for your help, Agent. Can you let me know about Ella and Gavin? When you find them, I mean?"

"Of course," Nikki said. "On the off chance you hear from Gavin, call us right away."

Vic stood to leave, running his hands through his thick, dark hair. "How do I get out of this place again?"

Liam stood. "I'll walk you to the front doors. This place is more of a maze than our offices in Minneapolis."

As soon as the doors closed, Nikki called Justin Nash. They'd worked together on Nikki's first case after Tyler's murder, and he'd recently moved back to work in the financial crimes division at the Minneapolis office.

"Nikki," he answered. "What can I do for my favorite dark and twisted agent?"

She rolled her eyes. "I just gave Vic Weber your number. He claims that his brother embezzled from their clients, and he's got the proof. He also says that he didn't know anything about it."

"Don't they all," Nash said. "Why'd you send him to me, though?"

"Because I need to be kept in the loop, and once the white-collar guys get his case, we'll be cut off. I know you wouldn't do that, right?"

"Of course not," Nash said. "You have his full financial records?"

"We're waiting on the warrant, but I think Weber's got influence with the judges. He seems cooperative, but he's also grandstanding."

Nash started laughing. "Nicole Hunt. You just want me to use my connections to speed up the information. Why didn't you just ask outright?"

"Because I'm making this up as I go along," she retorted. Both of Nash's parents were legends in the bureau and had a long reach with both the Department of Justice and the federal courts. "I don't think Vic Weber had anything to do with the murders I'm working, but he's hiding something, so I'm filing a warrant for his financial records. Can you rush that, too, along with his brother's?"

Nash laughed. "Text me the details. I'll do everything I can to have the warrant by the end of the day."

"Thanks," Nikki said. She hit "End" and started gathering up her things from the conference room table.

"Slick." Liam had returned, grinning.

"I thought so," she said. "Is Vic going to contact him?"

"He said he was, but who knows. Either way, we get the financials faster, and Nash will work with us a lot more than some of the other agents."

She closed her eyes, an unexpected wave of grief hitting her. Her ex-husband had worked financial crimes, and he used to be the one she called in situations like these. Nikki forced herself to stay in the present, grateful that Liam hadn't said anything about Tyler. "Let's head back out to the search site and see if they've turned anything up. Don't forget your notebook."

She pointed to the pocket-sized book he'd left lying on the table. She could see through the thin paper, and a heart with a note had been drawn on the other side. "What's that?"

Liam's face reddened. "Nothing."

"Can I see it?"

"It's not relevant to the investigation, Nicole."

She managed to keep a straight face despite the pink creeping up his neck. Liam's live-in girlfriend, Caitlin Newport, was known for leaving him "romantic" surprises in his work bag. She'd told Nikki that it really wasn't about the mushy-gushy—Caitlin just loved the idea of Liam getting all flustered over her at work.

"I hope it isn't, because the whole team would need a copy of it." She smiled sweetly, checking her phone to see if Brenner had texted anything about Jessica's cell-phone records.

"Miller just texted me." Adrenaline shot through her, her second wind suddenly blowing full blast. "They found Ella."

"Where?" Liam asked.

"Almost half a mile upriver. She's conscious but in shock and very cold. She left the tent in pajamas and a blanket, barefoot. Hasn't said what happened."

SIXTEEN

Nikki sent Liam back to the search area to assist Miller while she raced to the hospital. She showed her badge to the charge nurse at Lakeview Hospital's emergency room. "I need to speak with Ella Henderson."

The nurse glanced at her stack of charts. "They're transferring her upstairs. Her mother's with her. Let me see if I can find out which room."

"Excuse me, are you Agent Hunt?"

A young woman with dark hair and blue eyes approached, looking worried. Her black hair had been pulled into a messy bun, and she wore slipper booties that kids her age had deemed perfectly suitable to wear in the freezing cold and wet. Nikki's feet hurt every time she thought about how thin the booties had to be.

"Can I help you?"

"Oh, sorry," she said. "I'm Harper, a friend of Ella's. She called me from the hospital and said that you would be coming in to talk to her. Is she okay?"

"She was outside all night, disoriented," Nikki said. "I don't know much about her condition beyond that."

"What about Gavin? She said he was with her, and things got bad."

"Agent Hunt," the charge nurse said. "I can take you to Ella now."

"Thanks," Nikki said. "Harper, wait here. I'm sure Ella will want to talk to you when we've finished."

Nikki asked to speak to Ella privately, knowing she would say more if her mother wasn't around. No matter the situation, no kid wanted to hear their mother say I told you so. She could tell that Patty hated to let her daughter out of her sight.

"I'll be right outside, sweetheart." Patty smoothed Ella's hair off her pale face.

"Thanks, Mom," Ella said. "Could you see if Harper's here?"

"She is," Nikki said. "I just spoke to her."

Patty's eyes brightened. "I'll go find her."

"Your mother really likes taking care of you," Nikki said after Patty left the room.

"She worries about me all of the time." Ella's eyes filled with tears. "I feel so bad about what she's gone through the last year."

"What happened, Ella?"

She looked so small sitting in the hospital bed, her arms covered in scratches. The gash on her head had been cleaned and stitched but it had been open long enough that the wound still had a wild, angry look about it.

"Gavin wanted to go to the campsite by himself," Ella answered, her voice so quiet that Nikki pulled her chair closer to the hospital bed.

"But you were afraid for him to be alone," Nikki guessed. "Did he take that as an insult?"

"No," Ella said. "He understood that I just wanted to be there for support. He's going through so much right now. I promised him that I would stay out of his way. I'd got some work to catch up on anyway. I told him he could sit in silence all night and not even feel obligated to talk to me. I just wanted to be there if he needed me."

Because it was all about him, Nikki thought, barely managing to stop herself from saying the words out loud. "What happened when you got to the lake?"

"He was in a better mood. We watched the sun set and talked about stupid stuff. I got cold and went into the tent, but he stayed out to look at the stars. When he came in, I swear I could sense the change in him even though I was under the blankets. I asked him if he was okay, and he told me that he knew I'd been talking to you and that I should have checked with him before saying anything because you were on Jessica's side and didn't care about Bryce. I told him that wasn't true, you were doing your job." Ella closed her eyes. "That's when he punched me." She tugged at the neckline of her hospital gown, revealing a deep, purple bruise below her collarbone.

"That looks like it hurts," Nikki said.

Ella nodded. "It took the wind out of me. My chest felt like I'd been hit by a sledgehammer. I kept begging him to stop, but then he picked up the beer bottle and hit me with it." Ella buried her face in her hands. "I really thought he was going to kill me this time."

"How did you get out of the tent?" Nikki asked.

"I guess my fight or flight kicked in. My head was throbbing, and I felt like I was choking. I remember him standing there like a defensive lineman, just daring me to try to get by him."

Nikki was pretty certain that Gavin's wingspan was large enough to cover a lot of ground, and getting by him would have taken a feat of strength or sheer luck. "What did you do?"

"He came at me again, and I ducked. He twisted his leg or something. Went down somehow. And then I just ran. I kept running until my shins felt like they were going to explode. I got lightheaded, and that's all I really remember until I heard the searchers calling my name. Have you found Gavin?"

"We're still looking for him," Nikki said. "I know your mother lives across the river and it's a drive to school, but you can't go back to Gavin's apartment. We've got a unit keeping an eye on the place in case he comes home, but it's obviously not safe."

"I know it sounds awful, but I don't want to go home with her," Ella said. "She means well, but I'm already sick of hearing that she told me he was bad news from the beginning."

"What about Bryce?"

Ella worried her lower lip. "He's got anger issues too. Not like Gavin, but I've seen him be controlling on dates. He seems to think women are here to please him and that's it, you know?"

Nikki nodded. "You know about Jessica's accusation," she said gently. "Is it true?"

"I... I'm not sure," Ella said. "The last time I heard her name mentioned, it was more about Kai. Bryce was still steamed that Kai would challenge him, even though Jessica denied it. It didn't matter that it wasn't true and people believed him. He was more upset about the disrespect. He and Gavin talked about teaching Kai a lesson."

Nikki kept her expression neutral. "Did they?" she asked, already knowing the answer.

"I don't know, but I wouldn't be surprised if they did." She chewed on her broken fingernail. "Is Bryce going to make it? Gavin said he was going to die, and that's why he was so upset. He even said the stomach wound had gotten infected by the time Bryce was found and that it's probably in his bloodstream."

"I'm not sure," Nikki said. "He's in a medically induced coma for a few days at least. They'll probably reevaluate after that. What else did Gavin say about the attack?" Gavin had told them that he'd been Bryce's emergency contact, and Vic Weber had confirmed it. But Nikki knew that no one from her team or Miller's would have given any details to either one of them.

How could he know the wound had become infected by the time he was found?

"Something was spray painted on the walls," Ella said. "That's at least what Vic told him." She yawned and shivered, her eyes drooping.

"I'll leave you to rest in a second," Nikki said. "Do you have a safe place to go once you're released?"

"Harper said I could stay with her," Ella answered.

After she finished talking with Ella, Nikki checked in with the team.

"We're expanding the search area. Miller's contacted the media about Gavin, and he's got deputies from adjacent counties helping search. How's Ella?" Liam asked.

"She's keeping some stuff from us." Everything they'd learned in the last couple of days pointed to Gavin and Bryce somehow being involved in the murders, and Gavin's disappearing act initially supported that idea, especially when Nikki realized that someone had broken into the Webers' home and ransacked Bryce's room. Gavin could have been the one to plant the taser in Bryce's car and ran in a panic, but what had he been looking for this morning, assuming he'd been the intruder?

"I'm also not buying Gavin's trip to the campsite to clear his head," she told Liam. She also didn't believe he'd be foolish enough to go into the river, unless he felt like he'd been cornered with no way out. "We don't have enough evidence to make an arrest, so what could have spooked him enough to risk going to the crime scene and staging his disappearance?"

"Fingerprints, maybe?" Liam asked. "If Gavin left his prints at the scene, he would know that it was only a matter of time before we could prove he'd been in the Weber house yesterday morning."

Nikki agreed and sent a text to Courtney reminding her to compare the prints from the Weber home to the ones in the tent, paying special attention to Gavin's.

"Ella's memory's too good for what she's gone through." Nikki hated to doubt a victim, but Ella's story had way too many details. Nikki knew from experience that trauma memories were usually stunted and choppy, sometimes for a very long time. Either Ella wasn't telling the truth intentionally, or she was filling in the gaps in her memory with what sounded accurate. At least she was safe, but they needed to find Gavin before it was too late. He was now her lead suspect. Whatever crimes he'd committed with or without Bryce's help, Nikki was determined to make sure he was held accountable. "Ella's probably going to spend the night in the hospital, but I want to confirm that before I head back out to join the search."

The dreary day dragged into night, with no sign of Gavin. A fresh round of fall rain chilled them all to the bone. Between the wind and the shadows, the entire area had a creepy vibe. Nikki checked with the hospital and confirmed Ella had been admitted for the night and informed security to keep an eye out for Gavin.

Miller had set up a makeshift command center in one of the small park shelters close by and set up a gas space heater to help combat the wind rolling in from the river. He, Nikki and Liam huddled around it, planning their next move.

"We've searched the entire trail," Miller said. "Canvassed all of the houses in the area. No one has seen Gavin."

"What about his dad's house?" Nikki asked.

Miller shook his head, warming his hands over his steaming coffee cup. "He lives in Chisago County, north of here. They sent a unit over hours ago and said things were locked up tight. No sign of anyone. They've kept a unit on it just in case."

The MPD had also kept a car on the SAE house all day, but there hadn't been any sign of Gavin. Brenner had gone over to the fraternity house again this evening to make sure Gavin hadn't slipped in the back door.

"That's a dead end," Liam said.

"Agreed." Nikki wanted to throw her coffee cup. Her neck and shoulders ached, she missed her daughter, and she had lost track of how long it had been since she'd had a full night's sleep.

"Why don't you guys go get some rest?" Miller said. "We've exhausted the search area, but I'm going to leave a couple of guys out here. They won't be back on the water until daylight."

Nikki shivered. "I think Gavin's an abuser, but I still feel guilty not doing anything when he's missing."

"We've got bodies out searching," Miller reassured her.

"I'll stay a while longer," Liam said. "Seriously, go home and see Lacey. I'll call if anything comes up."

Nikki headed home on autopilot, trying to unpack everything they'd learned. Despite all the bits and pieces they'd uncovered, Nikki wasn't close to solving this case. She had a custody hearing on Monday, and it was starting to look like she'd have to reschedule. She couldn't lose half a day with Gavin MIA.

Would that cause her to lose Lacey?

A pit formed in her stomach at the thought. No matter how unlikely it was, Tyler's parents still had a chance at a custody arrangement. If they managed to get joint custody, Nikki knew they would start trying to find a way to finish what they'd started and take Lacey away from her as punishment for losing Tyler.

Nikki wasn't going to let that happen. She couldn't lose Lacey.

She parked in the garage stall Rory had cleaned out for her and made sure everything was locked before sneaking into the house. The television glowed from the living room, which meant Rory had probably fallen asleep watching the sports channel. She found him sprawled on the couch, snoring. But instead of football highlights, SpongeBob rattled on about the Krusty Krab, and Lacey was passed out in the recliner, the remote falling out of her small hand.

Nikki swallowed the lump in her throat. She knew the relationship between Rory and Lacey probably would have been different if they'd met after Tyler's murder, and there were times since she'd gone back to work that she'd been a little jealous of how close Rory and Lacey had become.

She realized how foolish that had been now. Nothing could change the bond between her and her daughter, and she was incredibly lucky that she'd found someone like Rory to help the two of them through losing Tyler.

Rory's king-sized bed was much more comfortable, but Nikki didn't care. She carefully slipped into the recliner without waking Lacey and snuggled against her little, warm body. Lacey shifted, sensing her mother, and buried her head in Nikki's neck. Nikki fell asleep quickly, content for the first time in days.

SEVENTEEN

The sun had barely cracked the sky when Nikki slipped out of the recliner. She showered and changed, leaving a note for Rory, who was still snoring on the couch. A few hours' sleep had done her some good, but she still felt sluggish. And hungry, she realized. Nikki wasn't sure when she'd last eaten, but her growling stomach demanded food.

She called Liam to let him know she'd be a few minutes later than she'd initially said.

"I was just about to call you," he said. "Nash came through with the warrant on Vic Weber's financial records," Liam said. "Jessica deposited a check for ten thousand dollars just days before she went missing. The account she used is at a different bank than her normal one. I'm assuming that's because her parents have access to her savings account, and she didn't want them to ask where she got the money. Anyway, and Dave Weber didn't write the check. His brother did."

"You're kidding," Nikki said.

"Nope. He's on the way in to talk with us now. I told him Miller would be here, and he wanted to bring him up to speed himself. He's back out at the search area, but I figured you'd want to come in and talk with Weber."

"I'm picking up food, but I'll be there in fifteen minutes."

She drove past the entrance for the sheriff's station and went to the Dunkin' Donuts around the corner. Carbs and sugar would backfire later, but right now, her sweet tooth held the power.

Somehow, she managed to bring the donuts, coffee and her heavy bag to the conference room at the sheriff's station, where Liam had set up temporary shop. Nikki dropped the box of donuts on the table and carefully set the cardboard container on the table without spilling much coffee.

"Jelly-filled chocolate long johns, just for you." She had no idea where Liam put it all, but he was a human vacuum, especially when they were on a big case. She waited for him to dive in, but he was staring at his laptop as though he hadn't heard her, his pale skin sickly.

"Liam, what's wrong?" she asked.

"I got into the external hard drive."

Nikki's stomach turned at the nerves in his voice. "And?"

"As best I can tell, Bryce and Gavin were into rape fantasy, real sick stuff. Some of it's homemade, starring Gavin and Bryce."

Nikki grimaced. She wasn't surprised, but verification of the men's depravity still made the donuts in her stomach churn. Had Bryce killed Jessica to keep her quiet? Had he tried to rape Jessica again at the house and it escalated and he'd killed her? Had he been that scared of it coming out that he'd killed his own parents too and faked his own attempted murder to cover it up? Nikki's head spun.

"Gavin and Bryce joke and laugh every time, but every girl I've seen so far is crying when it's over, and they don't seem like crocodile tears to me. The last one lay on the bed and sobbed until Gavin told her to get out of his apartment."

"His apartment?" Nikki asked. "How old are the videos?"

"According to the metadata, that one's the oldest. It's from last summer. And it's definitely the same bedroom we were in yesterday."

"Damn," Nikki said. "That's before Ella met him. But we still have grounds for a thorough search of his apartment."

"There are also some nude photos of girls on there, which seem to have been taken in the frat house. I want to stop by campus security when we're done at Gavin's apartment and see if anybody recognizes the girls' faces."

"Let me see what you've got."

He turned his laptop around, revealing screengrabs of a darker-skinned female, a redhead, and a petite blonde. Only one showed the girl looking directly at the camera, but Liam had done a good job in keeping the focus on their faces.

"Wish I could say that I recognized one of them," she said.

Liam glanced at his phone. "Vic Weber's here."

Vic Weber immediately looked frustrated as he walked into the room. "I thought I'd be talking to Miller today. Is he standing me up again?"

"He's tied up right now," Liam said airily. "Have a seat, Vic."

Vic glared at them, and Nikki had a feeling he knew why they'd called him in. It had only been a matter of time before the financial reports came back.

"Are there new developments in your investigation, Agent Hunt?"

"We need you to clarify some things for us."

"I'll do my best," he said warily.

"You told us that you'd never met Jessica Chandler," Nikki said. "Is that accurate?"

Vic nodded. "If you just brought me down here to ask questions I've already answered—"

"Why did you give Jessica Chandler a check for ten thousand dollars?" Nikki pulled out the photocopy of the canceled check she'd printed out before he arrived. Vic didn't say anything, so she carried on. "Because that's your signature. Jessica cashed it last week."

The color drained from his face. "I—that's—"

"No more lies," Nikki said. "This is a triple homicide, Mr. Weber. I shouldn't have to tell you that this puts you right back on the suspect list. So I suggest you tell us everything this time."

Vic slumped in his chair. "She called the office," he said. "She asked to speak with Mr. Weber, they sent her to me. I'm the senior partner. I think she assumed I was Bryce's father. I played along."

"Did she ask for the money, or did you offer?"

"I offered."

"Why?"

He stared up at the ceiling. "Bryce had been through enough. He hadn't fully recovered from his shoulder injury, and he was dealing with a lot."

"Dealing with something worse than being raped?" Nikki asked.

"Bryce told me it was a misunderstanding. They'd already had sex before. He didn't realize she wanted him to stop."

Lack of sleep had diminished Nikki's patience and her ability to put up with misogynistic BS. "You believed him?"

"He's my nephew."

"That means he's not capable of doing awful things?" Liam interjected.

"I was trying to protect them both," Vic insisted. "The truth was irrelevant at that point. If she went forward, Dave would have eviscerated her in the press long before the thing had a chance to go to trial. If she didn't and Bryce was being taken advantage of, Dave would have berated him for that. He said it was a misunderstanding," Vic echoed.

"You don't misunderstand rape, Mr. Weber." Liam leaned against the wall opposite her, effectively trapping Weber.

Vic shook his head. "He was going through a lot trying to rehab and deal with my brother's constant criticism. I just thought if he felt like he had someone in his corner, he might stay on the right path and get things turned around."

"Remind me"—Liam leaned forward—"when did you find out that your brother was embezzling from your clients?"

"Two weeks ago," Vic said.

"Here's the thing," Nikki said. "I want to believe you, but yesterday, you said your brother paid Jessica off, and you didn't know if Bryce had done anything to her or not. How do we know that you didn't do the same thing with the embezzlement money?"

"Are you serious?" Vic asked. "I'm cooperating on that. Once I found out what my brother was doing, I made sure to record our conversations. I'm not going down for what he did."

"Here's what I think happened, Vic," Nikki said, not bothering to hide her irritation. They were all too tired, and they still had a missing person to find. "For whatever reason, Jessica decided to cash the check after holding it for so long. You find out it's been cashed and say something to Bryce."

"Why would I do that?" he demanded.

"Human nature," Liam said. "Seeing the check cashed reminded you of everything, and you know he's got issues with his dad, so you probably asked how he was doing."

"You're wrong," Vic said. "I called him and left a message, but he never called me back. I never mentioned the check over the phone. That's the honest truth."

"I hope so," Nikki said. "You're only digging yourself deeper if you're still withholding information. Did Bryce ever say anything about Jessica threatening to come forward? Was he aware she'd had a rape kit done at the hospital?"

Vic's eyes widened. "I told you, we never discussed the accusation. The only reason I knew about it is because I took the call from Jessica instead of Dave when she contacted the office. I paid the girl and that was it. She told me that she'd had one done but after I offered money, agreed not to use it. I told her to use the money for counseling and school. I honestly didn't know whether she'd cashed it or not, because I didn't want to think about any of it after that."

Nikki sighed. She'd been on an adrenaline high going into the interview, and even though she knew she couldn't rule out the idea that Vic was the killer, her gut told her he wasn't involved beyond the check. He was certainly angry at his brother and didn't agree with the way Bryce had been raised—the pressure he was under—and he appeared to have some compassion for Jessica.

Courtney's number flashed on her phone. Nikki nodded to Liam and slipped out of the room.

"Hey, Court," she said, closing the door. "Do you have something?"

Courtney rattled off something, talking too fast and loudly for Nikki to understand. "Slow down," she said. "How many energy drinks have you had?"

"Tonight, or all day?"

"It's morning," Nikki said.

"Is it? I've been in the lab all night."

"Never mind. Just talk slower, please." Nikki turned the volume down a notch.

"Right, right," Courtney said. "Remember the blood I found on Ella's shoe yesterday?"

Nikki had almost forgotten about it. It seemed like days ago. "It was inside the shoe, right? On the side?"

"Yep," Courtney said. "I thought it was recently dried, but

I was wrong. Don't get used to me saying that, 'cause it doesn't happen very often. I ran the blood on the inside of Ella's tennis shoe to the rest of the blood in the tent, namely, the beer bottle, assuming that it would be a match, but it wasn't."

"She said he hit her with it," Nikki reminded her. "I saw the wound myself. She thought he was going to kill her that time. Even if she didn't get a concussion from it, she had to be dazed and disoriented. She just ran and finally collapsed."

"Can I finish?" Courtney asked testily. "The blood on the bottle was hers. The blood in the shoe wasn't. So that's when I went back to the shoe and realized that it was oddly clean. You'd expect it to have a fair amount of crud built up in the treads given how worn the shoes are, but it was just a thin layer of dirt. I kept going back to the blood on the insole, wondering if she'd had some kind of scratch and worn the shoes without socks—"

"It's Jessica's blood, right?" Nikki blurted, her heart pounding against her ribs. "Ella was at the scene, wasn't she?"

Courtney huffed. "Thank you so much for ruining my thunder. Yes, it's Jessica's blood. I triple checked the match, which is why it took so long. As for Ella being at the Weber house, I can't definitely say that she was actually there, just that a little bit of Jessica's blood was inside Ella's shoe."

The pieces of the story that had been whirling around her head like a tornado were suddenly landing in the appropriate spots. "What about her fingerprints? Do they match the unknown in the house? Or are those Gavin's?" she asked Courtney.

"The skate was wiped clean," Courtney said. "The print on the thermostat is a partial, and I'm not sure it's going to be good enough to hold up in court. Everything in Bryce's car had been wiped clean, too, including the taser. If Gavin touched anything else in the house, he cleaned it."

"We think someone stepped in Jessica's blood. Have you managed to figure out the shoe size?"

"There isn't enough of the tread marks to come up with a full shoe print, even with the Luminol," Courtney said. "I can tell you the person had wider feet, but that's it. Ella's shoes are a narrow fit, so no way it's hers."

"How did Jessica's blood get on her shoe, then?"

"Spatter, maybe," Courtney said. "Given its location, I don't think it would have transferred from Gavin's clothes to her shoe."

"Meaning Ella had to have been inside the house."

"Exactly."

EIGHTEEN

Ella remained in ICU for security reasons, and the new charge nurse wasn't very pleased about Nikki disturbing their morning routine. Nikki assured her that it was urgent she speak to Ella about a lead on her missing boyfriend, and the nurse finally granted her a few minutes.

Nikki was surprised to see that Patty hadn't camped out in the uncomfortable recliner sitting in the corner. Ella must have convinced her to stay at the hotel, which was less than five minutes from the hospital. She lay curled on her side, looking just as fragile.

"Is it that time already?" Ella asked sleepily. "I thought you were just in here taking vitals."

"It's Agent Hunt," Nikki said.

Ella opened her eyes and sat up, wincing. "Did you find him?"

"Not yet," Nikki said. "Ella, I need to ask you some more questions, and it's very important that you're honest with me."

Ella nodded. "What's going on?"

"I know you were at the Webers' during the time of the attack," Nikki said.

"What? I didn't know any of those people except for Bryce, and I wasn't hanging out with my boyfriend's best friend."

"We found Jessica's blood on one of your shoes left in the tent."

"That's impossible."

Nikki grabbed the stiff chair she'd sat in last night and pulled it to Ella's bedside. "You know it isn't. I need you to understand something. Right now, you're the only person we can prove was in the house. I'm sure I don't have to tell you that Bryce may or may not remember details if he wakes up, assuming that he even does. For your own sake, you really need to tell me the truth."

Ella's chin wobbled. "I couldn't stop him."

"Gavin?"

She nodded.

"Start from the beginning," Nikki said.

Ella sipped from her cup of water, her hands shaking. "Bryce called Gavin freaking out the weekend before everything happened. Jessica called and told him she was pressing charges, that her rape kit was still on file. Gavin told Bryce to come to the apartment. He told me to go for a walk when Bryce got there, so I did. By the time I got back, Bryce was gone, but I could tell something was up. Gavin was agitated and restless, like he always gets before something stressful goes down. I didn't ask what was going on because it was none of my business."

"This was before Jessica disappeared?" Nikki clarified. "She was killed this past Thursday. You just said that Bryce called Gavin the weekend before everything happened, so I thought you meant the conversation took place the weekend prior to her disappearance."

"Oh, sorry, everything's so jumbled in my head. It was the Saturday before the murders. Gavin was making fun of me for studying over the long weekend instead of blowing off school and having fun." Ella flushed and looked down at her hands. "He never stopped criticizing me."

Jessica had disappeared on that Saturday. "How did you end up at the Webers'?"

"Gavin told me that we had to go to Bryce's house to help him out with something," Ella said. "I really didn't want to go because I had a big test, but Gavin wouldn't take no for an answer. When we got there, he grabbed a duffle bag out of the back of his pickup truck. I didn't think much of it, but Gavin was so edgy and nervous."

"What time was this?" Nikki asked, thinking about the timeline the evidence and autopsies had established.

"Before dinner," she answered. "Bryce's mom answered the door and said that Bryce was upstairs, expecting us. Gavin told me to hang out with her because Bryce wanted to talk to him privately. So I went into the kitchen and made small talk with her."

"What did you talk about?" Nikki asked.

"School, I think. She asked me about classes. I mentioned getting ready to student teach. I don't remember specifics."

Nikki nodded. "How long were Bryce and Gavin alone?"

"Not all that long. Gavin texted me to come upstairs, so I did. They told me they needed to deal with Jessica's delusions before things got worse. Gavin said that no matter what I heard, unless he called my name, that I was to stay upstairs. They left me in Bryce's room."

"For how long?"

"I don't know, half an hour, maybe. It was dark, I know. At first, I didn't hear anything, but then I heard Joan shouting. And then she went quiet. Then out of nowhere I heard another female voice screaming and Bryce shouting." Ella put her face in her hands. "Someone was running upstairs—maybe more than one, it was so hard to tell—and then I heard Bryce call her a bitch. She screamed, and then there was this sickening thud. I'm pretty sure I heard that girl fall over the railing." Ella reached for the hospital tissues.

"Next thing I know, Gavin's back and says that we have to leave. He told me not to touch anything, and he had blood on his hands and shirt. He made me hold his hand and stay against the railing when we went downstairs. He covered my eyes and I wasn't supposed to look, but I did."

"What did you see?" Nikki asked.

Ella stared at her. "You know what I saw. Jessica lying in the foyer, all busted up. A man I assumed was Bryce's dad was by the door. I didn't see his mom."

"Do you know what happened to the stuff Gavin had in his duffle bag?"

Ella shook her head. "I never saw it again. I asked Gavin what happened and where Bryce was, but he told me to shut up. I didn't want him to hit me again."

Nikki couldn't imagine the fear Ella must have experienced. "Did you see Gavin with the taser?"

She shook her head. "No, but I know he owns one."

"Ella, when you were in Bryce's room and heard things happening, why didn't you call the police?"

"Because Gavin told me not to." Ella sobbed harder. "I know I sound like an idiot. I am. I'm weak and pathetic and—"

"You are not any of those things." Nikki grabbed the girl's thin hand. "Gavin spent a year mentally and physically abusing you. He traumatized you and, at the same time, isolated you from your mother and friends so that you didn't have anyone else to turn to. I'm sure the fear of what he would do to you was a lot more powerful than the fear of what he and Bryce might have been doing downstairs."

"That still doesn't mean I'm not a coward," Ella said. "I could have saved them, maybe. At least given them a fighting chance. But instead I just huddled in the corner and waited until it was over."

"I'm going to get you the names of some therapists," Nikki said. "They specialize in the sort of trauma you've gone through."

"What about Gavin?" she asked. "I know it's ridiculous, because he's not a good person. But I need to know that he's not going to come after me."

"We will find him," Nikki said. "I'll send a deputy here to take your official statement, and we'll make sure someone is posted outside the door until you leave. In the meantime, don't tell anyone beyond your mother where you're staying. He doesn't know where Harper lives, does he?"

Ella shook her head. "No, but we're actually going to stay at her parents' place in the country while they are away. There's no way he can find me there, but I can't hide forever."

Nikki wrote down the address Ella gave her for Harper's parents' place. "Did Gavin ever talk about what happened when you were upstairs?"

"He just said everything went to shit. He was so worried about Bryce not making it."

"Did he say how Bryce got hurt?"

"Fighting with Jessica is the only thing. He wouldn't tell me how she fell. He just said Bryce was bleeding and collapsed, unconscious. Gavin panicked and ran."

No wonder Gavin had been so uptight when Nikki spoke to him. He'd left his closest friend to die, and if Bryce woke up, he could blame everything on Gavin.

"What if he comes here?" Ella said. "I fought back and ran away from him. He's got to be plotting my murder now."

"I promise you, we won't let that happen," Nikki reassured her. "Someone will be outside the door, and if you decide that Harper's parents' place isn't safe, we'll send an officer there too. Did Gavin tell you why Bryce wanted his parents gone too?"

Ella shook her head. "I know he hated his dad, but I never heard him say anything bad about his mom."

Before she left the hospital, Nikki made sure a guard would remain outside the ICU until Ella was released later that morning.

NINETEEN

"I brought pizza," Nikki said, setting the box of steaming pepperoni and cheese on the conference table as she glanced at the smartboards. Liam had pinned aerial views of the property on the wall along with a rough layout of the crime scene so they could go through all of the possible scenarios. "Nothing new on Gavin?"

Miller shook his head. "Courtney's certain Ella was at the Webers' house?"

Nikki nodded. "Gavin's done quite a number on her." She went over everything Ella had told her at the hospital. "Like we thought, Bryce found out about Jessica going to the police and panicked. It sounds like he called Gavin for help, and the two of them plotted out this whole thing together. And poorly, considering how it played out. According to Ella, Gavin blamed himself about what went wrong at the house."

"But I thought you said Jessica cashed the check? Took the hush money?" Miller asked.

"Jessica cashed the check Vic Weber wrote her," Liam said. "But only recently. Perhaps Bryce didn't know."

"Why wait almost a year?" Miller asked.

"I don't know," Nikki said. She stretched and went to the smartboard. "We finally have Bryce's cell phone records, right?"

"Yeah, got everything late yesterday. I had the guys in the office go through it, and there's no sign of communication between him and Kai or Bryce and Jessica."

"What about the school email?" Nikki asked.

"Still waiting on that part. The judge isn't sure the university needs to be involved since the crime happened off campus." Liam rolled his eyes. "Ella tell you who spray-painted the message?"

Nikki shook her head. "He covered her eyes apparently."

"You don't sound convinced," Miller said, gulping his coffee.

Nikki shrugged. "I don't know. Gavin cleaned anything his fingerprints might have been on, so we can't directly tie him to the scene beyond Ella's testimony. I called Courtney and asked her to go through any other trace DNA she picked up from the tent and the Weber house, in addition to his fingerprints, hoping we might be able to forensically put him there. Without that, we're still looking at he said/she said." Nikki worried that if they couldn't find physical evidence putting Gavin at the scene soon, the media and the Weber family would target Ella because they needed someone to blame and hold accountable. Ella should have come clean immediately, but Nikki knew that a domestic violence victim's decision-making process wasn't like everyone else's. They thought in terms of survival, not right and wrong. Still, Nikki was certain they weren't getting the entire story from Ella.

Liam leaned back in his chair, staring at the whiteboard, chewing on his pen. "The spot was on the inside of the shoe, along the ankle. How do you get spatter if you aren't in the vicinity when the actual attack took place?"

"Gavin had blood on his hands and shirt," Nikki said. "It could have dripped off him, or he might have held something with blood on it while they were walking, and Ella just didn't see it. But that's been bothering me too. Her story almost seems too well put together, and I feel like we're trying to accommodate her version of events. She could have been forced by Gavin to do a lot more than she's telling us. It certainly wouldn't be the first time an abuse victim was coerced into crimes."

"I've been thinking about this all morning, and I have a different theory." Liam stood up and started to pace. "We have a swimmer who says she was assaulted, along with Jessica's rape kit at Mercy Hospital, if we ever get our hands on it. But he wore a condom, and scratches can be explained, so I'm not counting on that," Liam said. "We also have the student who reported seeing someone tall and athletic running from the girl who was attacked near the pool, and the spotlight was immediately on the team."

"Right." Nikki scrolled back through her notes, double-checking everything.

"Gavin was the resident RA," Liam continued. "Greg from the fraternity roomed with Bryce then, along with Kai. Greg specifically remembered seeing Bryce's reaction when he saw Samir after the assault was reported, and Samir appeared to notice too. He transferred out of the residence hall pretty quickly."

"What about the victim?" Miller asked.

"I've had Brenner trying to track her down. Since there is a police report, we didn't have to go through campus security and try to get warrants," Nikki said. "She moved overseas. That's all we know about her."

"So back to my theory," Liam said. "Between those rape accusations, which Ella's mother told her about, and the story about Jessica, Ella had to start wondering if her mother was right about Gavin, especially after the physical abuse started. Let's also assume, being Gavin's girlfriend who he effectively kept under his thumb, that she probably heard a lot of idle talk too. I'm sure Ella had at least an idea of what these two guys really thought about women."

"So?" Miller asked.

"So, what if she sought Jessica out? Or what if Jessica sought her out? They compare notes and eventually realize they're both a couple of louses. Maybe they even knew about the rape videos. Hell, Ella could be in some for all we know. I'm sure we haven't seen them all."

Something nagged at Nikki, a jagged piece that had been floating on the edge of her mind for the past few days. She kept thinking that she'd missed something extremely vital, but she couldn't put her finger on exactly what. "What exactly are you getting at, Liam?"

"Think about it," he said. "Why would Jessica cash the check now? Why didn't she just go to the police, especially since she knew her rape kit would still be accessible? That's the sort of thing that you do once you've decided to come forward, right?"

"Especially after likely agonizing over it for so long." Miller drummed his fingers on the table.

"Are you saying these two girls formed a revenge plan to kill Bryce?" Nikki asked.

Liam shrugged. "I think we have to consider it. After all, it's her word against Gavin's that he was even in that house. We've got his prints from the tent, and Courtney hasn't found a single match from the Webers' place."

Nikki hated to admit it, but Liam's theory made more sense than most of the ones they'd discussed. "But Bryce doesn't die, and Gavin's suspicious. He's gotten away with too much for too long not to be extremely perceptive," Nikki theorized. Someone had gone back to the Webers' house and ransacked Bryce's room, obviously searching for something. She'd initially assumed Gavin had done something to Ella and gone back to the house, but what if Nikki had judged too quickly? She flipped through her notes, trying to find any hint of what they were missing, a knot growing in the pit of her stomach, but nothing stood out. Jessica and Ella were both petite girls, and Nikki couldn't see them doing all of this alone. "Whoever fought with Dave Weber has to have some bruises. Neither girl really looked like they'd been in a fight. If Ella's involved, she had help." Nikki unlocked her phone and started going through the photos she'd taken that first day.

"Okay, but why take her camping intending to kill her?" Excitement swelled in Liam's voice. "Maybe he wanted to put the fear of God into her because he was afraid she'd talk to the police, and things got out of hand."

"But why would Ella help attack Bryce's family when Gavin's the one who's been abusing her?" Miller asked. "And why put herself in the position to be alone with the guy if he's so dangerous? Ella told Nikki that Gavin didn't want her to go, but she promised to be quiet, that she just wanted to be there if he needed her. I know domestic violence victims have a lot of trouble cutting ties, but that's because they're afraid of the consequences. Plus, Bryce's keys were at Gavin's apartment. Maybe Ella's story about going to the house with Gavin is true, but she just saw more than she's letting on."

"Ella could have easily planted the keys," Liam insisted. "But you're right, going out alone with Gavin doesn't make any sense, unless the intent is to frame him for the attack on Bryce and his family. But I don't think she would have had a chance against Gavin alone."

"She wasn't alone," Nikki said, feeling ready to throw up. She used her thumb and index finger to enlarge one of the pictures she'd taken of the many snapshots on the back of Bryce's closet door. Fortunately, she'd had the presence of mind to take a photo of each individual picture, so confirming her hunch wasn't difficult once things finally clicked together.

She shoved her phone toward Liam. "See the girl in the back row? With the dark hair and glasses?"

He nodded.

"It's Harper, Ella's friend."

Nikki was able to quickly find the same photo on Bryce's social media. Harper had been tagged, but the link wasn't active, meaning she and Bryce weren't friends on the app. But they'd both attended the university's swim banquet four years ago, when they were freshmen.

She clicked on Harper's profile information. "She graduated from Mankato State last year. And I can't find a single reference to swimming anywhere."

"Maybe she was his date," Miller said.

Nikki shook her head. "She's holding up a certificate in the picture, so I assume she had been recognized at the swim banquet. But this was clearly a university banquet, so the only way she'd receive an award is if she was part of the team. She must have transferred to Mankato State after her freshman year. But why would she stop swimming?"

"Injury," Miller said. "Career-ending is common in college. People's bodies are just pushed too far."

"You're sure?" Liam's voice carried from the hallway, where he'd gone to call the hospital. "Thanks."

The look on his face said more than enough. "Ella checked out this morning, before her mother even got there. A friend matching Harper's description picked her up." He tossed his phone on the table and kicked one of the chairs. "Damnit. Any clue where Harper might go?"

"Her parents' ranch south of Stillwater," Nikki said. "Ella told me they would be safe from Gavin out there."

Liam grabbed his coat. "Let's go."

TWENTY

"Miller's people are setting up check points on every road near Harper's parents'," Nikki said. "They aren't on any flight manifests, so if she and Ella are going to run, it'll probably be in a vehicle. Still, we've got agents at the airport, right?"

Liam nodded. "They have security at each terminal with copies of Harper's and Ella's driver's licenses, along with the BOLO."

"Good." The be-on-the-lookout order meant that every cop in the state would have the girls' pictures and information. "What about her parents? We're sure they're out of state?"

"Yep," Liam said. "Harper's mother updates her Facebook constantly. They're in North Carolina and don't plan on coming back for another five days."

Nikki still couldn't relax. They'd gone over every possible option Harper and Ella could take to flee the state, and all of their bases were covered. But she couldn't shake the feeling that they still weren't prepared enough. "You find the place on the map?" she asked, swerving to avoid a pothole. "I swear to God, these rural roads are hazards."

Liam had his tablet balanced on his lap. "According to

Google satellite, there's a ranch-style house, a decent-sized barn, and a fenced-in pasture."

"No other structures?" Nikki asked.

"Not in this picture, and according to the information..." Liam squinted at his screen. "This was taken last spring." His knees bounced against her glove compartment.

"I haven't seen you amped up like this over a case in a while," Nikki said.

"I'm just disgusted with the whole system," he said. "Bryce and Gavin are obvious abusers, but money and power protected them, including the school. Who knows how many others there are, and because they were too scared to come forward, Harper and the others took matters into their own hands. They'll do more time than Gavin or Bryce would have if they'd been arrested for rape."

"I know," Nikki said. "But this wasn't self-defense, at least not by Harper or Jessica. This was planned, and Ella's role was to frame Gavin, I guess."

"If that's the case, he's dead," Liam said. "That's the only shot they would have at pulling it off."

"I know." According to the GPS, the driveway was around the next turn. Nikki eased off the gas and pulled onto the gravel shoulder.

"Do you mind if I drop you off before we pull in? You can hopefully slip onto the property without them noticing. Search for Gavin in the barn along with the murder weapon and anything else they might have hidden. You should be able to cut across the pasture, hopefully unseen."

Liam nodded. "As long as it's just horses and not cows, that's fine. But if I see a bull, I'm not setting foot in the pasture."

Nikki smiled. "Fair enough." She dropped him off just out of sight of the driveway. It was a decent-sized ranch, probably built in the nineties when this part of town started expanding. A white fence surrounded a few acres of pasture, and a fat Paint

Horse rolled in the grass while another bay watched. She felt a twang of jealousy; she'd always wanted a horse, and the property seemed so quiet and peaceful.

After making sure that her gun was holstered beneath her coat, Nikki left the jeep unlocked in case Liam needed to get something and went to the door. Her heart seemed to pound against her chest, her legs twitching with adrenaline.

"Agent Hunt." Ella answered the door, looking much better than she had in the hospital. She had showered and changed, her hair was shiny clean, and her eyes seemed to have more spirit. They were also fearful. "What are you doing out here?"

Nikki smiled. "I wanted to check on you. The hospital said you checked out earlier than they advised."

"I didn't feel safe," Ella said. "The officer kept disappearing, and all I could think of was Gavin storming in and attacking me."

"Well, this is certainly private and very beautiful." Nikki pretended to admire the house, searching for any sign of cameras. "Don't Harper's parents have security cameras?" She feigned concern.

"Uh, I guess not. They've never had a problem out here." Ella twisted a lock of hair around her index finger. "Why?"

"I'm just used to everyone having a security camera nowadays." Nikki smiled. "Mind if I come in? I need to go over a few things with you."

"Okay," Ella said, glancing back into the house. "Harper's taking care of the horse stalls, but she should be back inside soon. I just made lunch if you're hungry."

"That's all right," Nikki said, debating texting Liam to tell him to watch out for Harper. She couldn't do it without Ella getting suspicious, and if Liam already had eyes on Harper, the sound of the text notification might give away his position. "I wanted to talk to you privately anyway."

Ella sat down on a barstool and picked at her sandwich. Her

foot bounced up and down, making the stool squeak. "Fire away."

Nikki noticed a large duffle bag near the entryway, along with a large suitcase and a tote bag filled to the top. "You guys planning a trip?"

"Why would you ask that?" Ella continued to twirl her hair, her eyes flashing between Nikki and the suitcase. "Oh, that. Harper went to Gavin's place and picked up a bunch of my stuff."

Nikki knew that was a lie because she'd asked Brenner to make sure an unmarked unit had eyes on Gavin's apartment on the off chance he came back. She decided not to press Ella for now. "When you and Gavin went to see Bryce the day of the murders, did Bryce say how he found out Jessica was going to go public with her accusations?" Nikki asked.

Ella thought about it for a minute. "No, I don't think so."

Nikki leaned against the counter, keeping the front door and kitchen sliding door in her sights. "There are just a few things that aren't adding up for me." Ella's fidgeting with her hair and constantly shifting her posture made it clear she was nervous. Since Ella had gone as far as to give Nikki this address, even when she and Harper must have already discussed their escape plan, Nikki had to believe some part of Ella wanted to tell the truth. If Nikki could push her enough while Ella was alone, she might be able to get her to come clean about everything. "What did Bryce have against his mother?"

"I don't know," Ella said. "Maybe he felt like he had no choice. After all, she never stood up to his dad about the swimming. Gavin told me that Bryce begged her to convince his father to let him stop swimming, but she didn't want to, because Bryce needed to finish what he started, whatever that means."

"Or maybe Gavin's the one who killed her," Nikki said.

"I hope not," Ella said. "I'll never forgive myself for not calling the police."

"When did you first meet Jessica?" Nikki asked, hoping to trip her up.

Ella looked at her in confusion. "I've never actually met her. I just know what Bryce and Gavin told me."

"That's right," Nikki said. "I should have checked my notes. It's hard to keep everyone's stories straight in my head sometimes. Given the way Gavin treated you and how close he was with Bryce, did you ever wonder if maybe the story about Jessica was true?"

Ella shrugged. "I told you that I did," she said. "But Gavin said it wasn't. I didn't want to think about it beyond that, and I sure wasn't going to pressure them about it. He didn't need a reason to hit me, so I didn't give him one."

Nikki retrieved the images from the videos taken off the flash drive found in Bryce's room at the frat house. She'd made sure to crop the images so only their faces were visible, but in at least two of them, Gavin's headboard was noticeable.

"Do you know any of these girls?" She turned her phone so that Ella could see the pictures as she scrolled through them.

Ella flushed. "Why?" Nikki saw her mouth twitch when she looked at the third photo, which had a clear shot of Gavin's headboard. "When was this?"

"Metadata shows it as last summer. That's before you met Gavin, right?"

Ella nodded. "Are there more?"

"Two, I think." Nikki gave her a few seconds to look at the next one before switching to the image of the picture on the back of Bryce's closet door, where Harper was clearly visible. She waited for Ella to acknowledge her friend in the photo.

"Agent, I'm not sure I can help you any more than I have," Ella said weakly.

Nikki increased the photo's size and zoomed in on Harper's face. "Can you help me now?"

"Oh, I didn't realize that was Harper." Ella forced a laugh, her face crimson. She was a terrible liar when the pressure was applied. "When was this?"

"Three years ago. Bryce and Harper were both freshman swimmers at the University of Minnesota. This was taken at a banquet. Did she ever mention that she'd swam her freshman year?"

"No, but—"

"Ella, I know the two of you are involved in the murders." Nikki gestured to the packed bags. "My guess is that Harper has convinced you the best thing to do is to run, but I promise you that isn't true. We have physical evidence tying you to the scene, and it's only a matter of time before we can tie Harper there too. If you want to have a chance at a lighter sentence, you need to work with me now. Tell me how this all started, for your own sake."

Ella's teeth dug into her lower lip. She wrapped her arms around her small frame. "I don't know what you're talking about, Agent Hunt."

Nikki leaned forward until she was fully in Ella's personal space, their knees touching. "Ella, I know Bryce and Gavin were bad guys. I want to help you, but you have to give me something."

Before Ella could answer, Nikki saw Harper striding across the back deck. She marched to the sliding glass doors and jerked them open. She brushed her black hair off her reddened face. "Agent Hunt. What a nice surprise."

Ella froze, looking at Harper with real fear in her eyes. Nikki wasn't surprised that she'd gone from being controlled by Gavin to under Harper's thumb.

Nikki shifted so that her feet were back on the ground. "Ella left the hospital early, so I wanted to make sure she was all right and that your parents' place is as secure as you thought."

Harper's gaze slid to Ella, her pleasant expression shifting to aggression. "You told her where we'd be?"

Ella stared at her friend. "Agent Hunt found a photo of you with Bryce and Gavin from your freshman year. You swam with them?" Her voice cracked.

Harper glared at her. "Save the wounded doe act for someone else. I know you're not trying to pin this all on me."

Nikki moved for her gun, but Harper was faster. She pulled a revolver out of her coat pocket. "Agent, take your gun out of the holster and remove the magazine, then slide that over to me."

"Harper, stop," Ella said.

Nikki kept her eyes locked on the older girl, her mind racing. She might be able to move fast enough to shoot Harper, but if she failed, Nikki and Ella would both die. Liam would eventually look for Nikki if she didn't return or check in. She did as Harper ordered, kicking the magazine across the floor.

"Put the gun on the counter so I can see it."

Nikki set the gun down, her mind racing. She had to keep Harper talking and hope Liam showed up soon.

"Harper, it's over," Ella tried again. "They've figured it out."

"Not if you shut the hell up," Harper shouted. "You and Jessica were never anything but dead weight. I should have taken care of you after Jessica."

Silence filled the room as the two girls stared at each other. Harper smiled smugly.

"You're the one who pushed her?" Ella shrilled. "You said Bryce did it. You said—"

"I know what I said. Just be quiet, okay? We can still get out of this if you let me handle it, El." Harper had lowered her voice, looking at Ella imploringly. "We're in this together, remember?"

Ella looked down, her hands trembling. Nikki seized her opportunity. "Ella, she's manipulating you. What she's doing is no different than what Gavin does, and she's using that to her advantage."

"That's not true," Harper yelled, stepping closer, the gun pointed directly at Nikki. "El, please. She's the psychologist, she's playing you. I thought we were done getting walked all over. You have to stand up for yourself for once in your life."

Ella's head shot up, anger brimming in her eyes. "Agent Hunt, Harper planned all of this. She convinced Jessica and me to go along with it. Both of us were too afraid of what she might do if we said no." Ella pointed a shaking hand at the other girl. "And we were right. You pushed Jessica. You killed her."

"You bitch." Harper raised the gun and pointed it at her friend, but Nikki stepped in front of her.

"Wait," Nikki said, sweat dampening the back of her neck. "Harper, listen. I know Bryce and Gavin forced you to do something you didn't want to do. I know what Bryce did to Jessica too. Right now, both of you can still be treated with compassion in court. But if you shoot me or anyone else, that all goes away."

"I don't care," Harper said. "I'm not going to jail for doing what needed to be done. And you know nothing."

"Then tell me." Nikki kept her gaze on Harper, but her fingers inched toward her cell phone lying on the counter. If she could distract her, she might be able to find a way to hit the emergency call without Harper seeing. "I want to understand. I want to help you."

Harper closed her eyes, her breathing quickening. She seemed to be willing herself to stay in control. Nikki started to go for the phone, but Harper's eyes flashed open. Nikki was taken aback at the rage shining in them. Her beautiful face turned dark with anger.

"They raped me during our conference awards banquet," Harper snapped, her entire body vibrating. "I'd already turned Bryce down twice, but I thought Gavin was different. I was wrong. Apparently getting drunk and making jokes about a threesome takes away your right to say no."

"It doesn't, I assure you. What they did was wrong." Nikki

understood the anger these girls felt—if they'd all suffered at Gavin and Bryce's hands. But how had this escalated? How had three innocent people died? "You have every right to feel betrayed and to want revenge. That's why one of you painted the Bible verse at the Webers', right?"

"It's the truth," Harper snapped. "I spent years swimming to earn my scholarship. They destroyed my life while they both go on like nothing happens. Bryce is hailed as some wunderkind because he swam at the trials against Phelps, and the school won't touch him. His father wouldn't allow him to be touched. By the way, where did you find that photo? It wasn't in Bryce's house. I didn't believe him when he said he had it, but I went back to make sure it wasn't there."

"His room at the frat house." Nikki had assumed Harper had been the one to come back to the Weber home and go through Bryce's room.

"Bryce convinced you that he was untouchable, but he isn't, I assure you. We've already built a case against him," Nikki said, trying to buy time until she could figure out how to get the upper hand or Liam showed up. She wasn't sure if Ella would fight with Harper or do the smart thing and try to extricate herself from the girl. As angry as Ella appeared to be, she was a follower. Nikki had to assume she was facing two against one.

"I was barely nineteen. I just wanted it all to go away."

"They drugged her, Agent Hunt," Ella said. "The date rape drug."

"That was only for the first rape," Harper snapped. "I was awake for the next two. I woke up tied to a hotel bed, tape over my mouth and bleeding from... they kept me there for more than fourteen hours. They said they recorded it and I had said yes. They showed me that clip. I knew I was drugged, but it wouldn't have mattered to a judge." Harper's eyes blazed with hate. "Bryce kept reminding me that the Stanford swimmer got a slap on the wrist, and that with my consenting on the video, I didn't have a chance at being taken seriously."

"I'm sorry," Nikki said softly. "It's not fair, and they should be held accountable. Everyone will know what they did."

"So what?" Harper snickered. "How does that help me? Besides, Bryce's dad would have protected him like always. Taking action was the only way to make sure they didn't hurt anyone else. It was Jessica's idea to fake her kidnapping by the way, not mine."

"How did she get into the house?" Nikki asked, trying to find some way to earn Harper's trust enough to either disarm her or talk her down. Ella's surprise about Jessica's death coming at the hands of Harper was genuine, and Nikki needed to find a way to use the girl's anger to their advantage.

"She convinced Mrs. Weber that someone was chasing her, and she needed help," Ella answered. "We were hiding, wearing dark clothes. Once the door opened, Harper used her gun to force her way in. She told Bryce's mom that we just wanted to talk to Bryce. I thought his mother was off limits, but Harper stabbed her before Jessica and me even realized what was happening." She glared at the other girl. "You promised us that Mrs. Weber would be safe."

"Shut up," Harper yelled. "It's not my fault you two were dumb enough to believe we wouldn't have to kill his mom when we realized she was home."

"You could have waited," Ella said. "We could have caught Bryce alone—"

"Jessica was supposed to be missing, remember that? We couldn't stop once things were in motion."

"Why was Joan off limits but not Bryce's father?" Nikki asked, watching the dynamic between the two women. Ella vibrated with fear, but she wasn't backing down, and Harper didn't seem to know how to handle it.

"He covered up for Bryce," Harper snapped. "And he enabled him."

"But Dave put up a fight," Nikki guessed. "He had defensive wounds."

"But I was ready for him," Harper said.

"Not ready enough," Ella snapped back. "Bryce heard the two of them fighting, so he came running downstairs. You should have just shot him and ran," Ella said. "Instead, you took him upstairs and tortured him for hours."

"Like he didn't deserve it," Harper said. "I finally had the power over him. He needed to know what it felt like to be a victim, and I wasn't about to give him any mercy. And bullets are traceable, stupid."

Ella gritted her teeth, her fists bunching up. "God, I hate you."

"I don't care," Harper said. "I knew the two of you didn't have the stomach for this. My mistake was thinking you were smarter than Jessica."

"Tell me what exactly happened between you two," Ella demanded. "I deserve to know."

"Isn't it obvious?" Harper asked. "She came upstairs and tried to take control, telling me to let Bryce off easy."

"That was after you tortured him for hours," Ella interrupted. "You were out of control and were going to get us caught. She went upstairs to talk some sense into you."

"There's no difference," Harper said.

"How did you torture Bryce?" Nikki cut in. "His injuries didn't reflect anything like that."

Harper smiled. "Mental torture is a lot more satisfying than physical. And I wanted him to have a taste of his own medicine."

"What do you mean?" Ella asked. "What did you do?"

"Whatever I wanted," Harper snapped. "Amazing he could

still get it up when he was so scared. Then again, he thought he could talk me out of it."

Nikki tried to hide her disgust. Harper had sexually assaulted Bryce, possibly more than once.

"Anyway, Jessica's pitching a fit when she sees he's naked. I told her to put on his sweatshirt so we could make it look like he'd been keeping her there."

"The plan was to make it look like a murder-suicide, with Jessica left to tell the tale?"

Ella nodded. "We were going to rough her up a little bit so it looked more genuine and leave her tied up in his room."

The cop in Nikki wanted to point out that leaving Jessica alive wouldn't have made sense in a murder-suicide, but it didn't matter. She just needed to keep the girls talking.

"I made him put his clothes on, and we went ahead and bound her hands. She was supposed to stay up there, but she freaked out about being left behind with a bunch of dead people. She was worried she wouldn't be found for days. Then I realized she hadn't put gloves on after we got inside like an idiot, and her prints would be on stuff."

"Because you didn't stick to the plan," Ella choked out. "Once we got into the house, it all happened so fast that Jessica and I could barely think straight."

Harper rolled her eyes. "She was more use to me dead at that point, so I told Bryce that if he shoved her over the bannister, I'd consider letting him live. He was so desperate not to die he didn't even hesitate, just barreled right at her. I'd hoped he would fall too, but he didn't. Instead, he ran to his parents' room, got the skate and ran downstairs."

"I don't think he realized there were three of us," Ella said, slumping against the counter. "He tripped and fell on top of the skate. I didn't know they were that sharp, but he started bleeding everywhere. He tried to crawl out of the foyer, but he collapsed. It was close to four a.m. by then."

"It was glorious," Harper said, her voice eerily steady. "He bled a lot, but I could tell it wasn't deep enough to kill him, so I cut him again." She scowled. "Then headlights came up the driveway."

"In the middle of the night?" Nikki asked.

"It was just after four a.m.," Ella said. "The newspaper was being delivered. Every light in the house was on, and we were afraid he would knock or call the police, so we ran."

Nikki realized they must have worn gloves and some sort of protective clothing, because there hadn't been a lot of trace evidence left behind.

"After he left, I went back in and wiped down the foyer where his dad and I fought," Harper said.

"Why did you tase Jessica after she was dead?"

Harper stared at her in surprise. "That was supposed to be how Bryce took her. I was trying to stick to our original plan. She hadn't been dead long, so I didn't think it would make a difference."

"Our medical examiner is good," Nikki said.

"You were trying to stick to the plan?" Ella echoed. "That's a load of crap. You were out of control."

"No, I took control," Harper spat. "After Bryce and Gavin ruined my life, I took control. You should be thanking me for helping you escape that abusive piece of shit, because you were never going to do it on your own."

Nikki could piece the rest of it together: they'd taken Bryce's keys, left the taser in his car, and then planted his keys at Gavin's. Jessica had probably taken Joan's wedding rings for the same reason. She glanced at her watch. Nearly ten minutes had gone by, and Liam still hadn't shown up. Was he waiting for backup?

"I understand how angry you must be," Nikki said. She saw Harper shake her head, unconvinced. "My high school boyfriend did something similar to me," she admitted, unable to control the sadness in her voice. "His actions set off a chain of events—"

"I don't care," Harper said. "Your story and mine aren't the same, we aren't going to bond over it, and you aren't going to talk me out of doing what I need to do."

"What you need to do is listen to me." Nikki kept her tone even and hoped Harper couldn't tell she was rattled. "How do you think things are going to play out after you murder an FBI agent?" She caught the flicker of nerves in Harper's eyes and doubled down. "And not just any agent, frankly. One that has a lot of name recognition, and that means as much to the Bureau as solving cases. They will hunt you down, Harper. My people know I'm here, and we knew there was a risk you'd try to run, so there are already check points set up. Your passport has been flagged, along with your driver's license. Every cop in the country will have that information by the time you get out of the area—if you can make it that far."

Harper's hand trembled, her bravado starting to fade. "You're lying."

"Am I?" Nikki asked. "Check my coat pocket. I've got a copy of the BOLO with your vehicle and license information on it. We also know your parents drive an Escalade, and they're in the Outer Banks right now, staying a couple of miles from Cape Hatteras. They weren't on any flight manifests, so I'm assuming they drove down there."

Harper paled. "How could you know all that?"

"This isn't exactly my first case," Nikki said, trying to walk the line between confidence and arrogance. "I came here prepared, and we live in a digital world. There's no place for you to hide."

"Listen to her," Ella pleaded.

"Shut up," Harper said. "Look in her pocket and see if she's telling the truth. And don't try anything stupid."

Shaking, Ella moved towards Nikki.

"Right pocket," Nikki said, her eyes on Harper. "Two papers folded together."

Ella took the papers out of Nikki's pocket, her face white. "There's one for each of us, Harper. You have to listen to her. We won't make it."

Harper shook her head. "I already killed an agent. What do I have to lose?"

Fear rocketed through Nikki. Liam wasn't coming, and he probably hadn't had the chance to call for backup. Bile started to rise in Nikki's throat. Had Harper really killed Liam, or was he out there alone, fighting for his life? "You lose any chance at seeing the outside world again," Nikki said. "I can help you in court, explain what you did from a psychological standpoint."

The doorbell rang, startling all three of them. Still keeping the gun trained on Nikki, Harper went to the window and peered out. "Shit, Ella, it's your mother. Get rid of her."

"How am I supposed to do that?" Ella asked. "You know how she is. If she takes one look at me, she'll know something is really wrong."

Nikki kept her eyes on Harper. "Other cops know we're here. It's over."

"I'll be the judge of that." Harper snatched Nikki's empty gun off the counter and picked up the magazine Nikki had slid over earlier, pocketing them both. "You two stay here, or Mom is going to get it."

The doorbell rang again, followed by Patty's loud knocking.

"Either one of you try anything, and I start shooting," Harper hissed. "This shit has gone so wrong I don't care what happens at this point."

She crossed the room, stowing the loaded gun back in her right coat pocket, and answered the door.

"Hi, Patty, how are you this morning?"

"Where's my daughter?" Patty's shrill voice echoed through the house. Nikki peered through the gap in the door. Patty wore a heavy, black parka that was too big for her and too warm for this weather, and yet it appeared to fit snugly. Had Nikki seen that parka before?

"She's taking a nap, but I can tell her you stopped by." Harper tried to close the door, but Patty blocked it with her foot.

"I went to the hospital, and she'd already checked out, without telling me."

Nikki edged toward the kitchen, searching for something to defend her and Ella against Harper. She motioned for Ella to do the same, but she shook her head.

"I can't let my mom get hurt," she hissed. "Harper will do it. She doesn't care."

Nikki wanted to tell her that Harper was going to kill them all anyway if they didn't do something, but Ella's mind was made up. Whatever bravado she had evaporated.

"I'm so sorry, Patty," Harper said. "I don't know why she didn't call you when she got here."

"Agent Hunt was going to stop by too," Patty said. "Isn't that her jeep out there?"

Both Nikki and Ella stilled, waiting for Harper's reaction.

"No, it's mine," Harper said evenly. "We must have the same one. Jeeps are awesome."

"I don't believe you," Patty shrilled. "If you don't let me in to see my daughter right now, I'll call the police."

Nikki saw Harper set her shoulders and knew the girl had made up her mind. Her heart pounded against her chest. How were they going to get out of this? She needed to get to Liam before it was too late—if it already wasn't.

"My goodness, relax." Harper opened the door wide enough for Patty to step inside, slipping her hand into her pocket. A muscle in her jaw twitched, her mouth pressed together in a tight line. Ella seemed frozen, unable to stand up to Harper even with her mother's life in the balance.

Nikki's hand closed around the handle of the heavy cast-iron skillet still sitting on the stove as Patty stepped through the door, sweating in the heavy Canada Goose jacket, and spotted Ella.

"Ella, are you okay?" Patty demanded.

Harper moved to shut the door, but it rebounded, slamming her in the face.

"Ella, get down," Patty screamed, hitting the floor.

Nikki grabbed the girl and yanked her down to the floor as SWAT rushed into the house. Harper managed to get the gun out of her coat pocket, but she was tackled before she could fire. She hit the floor face first, and the gun went sliding.

Nikki sprang into action and retrieved the gun while Patty rushed to her crying daughter.

She ran past the SWAT members pouring into the house. "Call an ambulance. We have an officer down outside." She nearly slammed into Miller. He grabbed her arms before she could topple off the steps.

"I don't know how you knew, but your timing is impeccable." She pulled up her contacts and called Liam, praying he would answer, but the phone went straight to voicemail. "Liam's out there—"

"He's the one who called me." Miller released her arms. "He said to secure the house, that he'd found something in the barn."

"She said she killed an FBI agent." Nikki sprinted down the steps, with Miller on her heels. She called Liam again, fear nearly choking her. How was she going to tell Caitlin?

Dirt swirled as she climbed over the fence and ran into the barn, her blood roaring in her ears. "Liam," she yelled. "You out here?"

She scanned the barn floor looking for any sign of blood but found none. All three horse stalls had been cleaned, and Nikki didn't see any sign of Liam. She scrubbed the tears out of her eyes, calling his name again, praying for the sound of his voice.

"Nicole, over here," Miller called.

Nikki whirled around and ran toward the back of the barn where hay had been stacked for the horses. Bits of blood stained a few stalks of hay, and she could see drag marks in the dirt.

Liam lay on his back, bleeding from his head, his face slack.

"Oh my God." Nikki dropped to her knees next to Miller. "Is he gone?"

Miller shook his head. "His pulse is weak, but it's there."

"Christ." Nikki knelt next to him, shrugging her sweater off. Blood dripped from the wound on the side of his head, and she could tell part of Liam's skull had been broken. She pressed her sweater against the wound. "Liam, can you hear me?"

Miller balanced his phone against his shoulder. "Officer down, repeat, officer down. We need medical asap."

Nikki stroked Liam's red hair, praying they'd found him in time. "Hang on," she whispered. "Help's coming."

TWENTY-ONE

Nikki sat alone in the ICU's waiting area, her head in her hands, the morning's events on repeat in her head. She shouldn't have sent Liam into the barn without backup or at least ensuring that both girls were inside the house. They'd known what Harper was capable of, but Nikki had overestimated her own ability to control the situation. She'd convinced herself that if she just found some common ground with Harper, they would be able to bring the girls in without incident.

Now Liam was in surgery, fighting for his life.

Miller had taken control of the scene at the ranch. She hadn't put it all together until right before SWAT burst in, but Miller had given Patty his coat to help hide the Kevlar they'd put on her. He also knew that Nikki would likely recognize it and know she had backup. Once Patty stepped inside and Nikki could see the Canada Goose brand logo, she'd realized it was Miller's. It had been a Christmas gift from his kids, and he rarely wore it because it was so expensive. Fortunately, he also kept it in his SUV in case he needed it.

"Nikki?"

Her head shot up at the sound of Caitlin's voice. Her former nemesis had become a friend, and Nikki knew how much she cared about Liam. "Is he going to be okay?"

Tears leaked out of Nikki's eyes. "He's in surgery. I'm so sorry."

Caitlin dropped into the seat next to her and put her hand on Nikki's shoulder. "I don't know what happened, but Liam trusted you. Whatever happened, it's not your fault."

Nikki wanted to argue with her, but this was no longer about her decisions. This was about Liam, and she needed to be there for Caitlin. Nikki took a deep breath and then patted her friend's knee. "A nurse came out about ten minutes ago and said surgery was taking a while, but he was stable."

"What happened?"

Nikki gave her the abbreviated version of events. "He must have called Miller before Harper attacked him from behind with the hammer." Miller had found the ball-peen hammer lying a foot away from Liam's body, the blunt end covered with blood. Harper had hit him at least twice and left him to bleed to death. "She had a gun," Nikki whispered. "Thank God she didn't use it."

Caitlin nodded, fighting to stay calm. Nikki knew they were both thinking the same thing: if Liam survived, what sort of damage had been done to his brain?

"By the way, what you found out about Tyler's dad, what you guys did for me—"

"You don't have to thank me," Caitlin said. "Lacey needs to be with you and Rory."

Courtney soon arrived with coffee and sweets. "I left my assistant in charge. I couldn't focus knowing the big lug was here." Her voice trembled. "He still owes me money from a bet on the Vikings missing the playoffs last winter."

Liam was a diehard Vikings fan, and while Courtney didn't care about football, she delighted in tormenting Liam.

"Twenty bucks, right?" Caitlin asked, wiping moisture off her cheeks.

"Yep. He's been paying me in installments," Courtney deadpanned. "I intend to collect, so he needs to pull through this."

"He will," Nikki said. "He has to."

The surgeon found them an hour later. Circles rimmed his eyes, and he looked dead on his feet. "Mr. Wilson's going to make it. His skull was broken in three places, and he had a subdural hematoma that started bleeding during surgery. We've got it under control, but it will be some time before he will be himself again. He'll likely need rehab for a few months."

"But he isn't brain damaged?" Caitlin asked.

"We don't know the extent until he comes around but given the size of the wound and the location, he's going to have some motor issues at least. Nothing that he can't recover from eventually."

"Can I see him?" Caitlin dabbed at her eyes with a tissue. "Even if he's not awake?"

The surgeon nodded. "I can take you to recovery, but it will probably be tomorrow before he's alert enough to talk."

Caitlin stood to follow him and then looked down at Nikki and Courtney. "I'll keep you both posted, but you should go home and rest. Especially you, Nikki. You look like hell." She winked before leaving with the doctor.

Courtney sank back into the leather chair and rubbed her stomach. "I need to eat some real food."

Two days later, Caitlin told Nikki that Liam was well enough for visitors.

"His head's too hard to be seriously injured." Caitlin kissed

Liam's forehead, the worry in her eyes betraying her light tone. Bandages covered his head, and bruises rimmed his bloodshot eyes.

Liam sipped on his water and rolled his eyes. "That hurt."

"How did she get the jump on you?" Caitlin asked.

"I sent him into trouble," Nikki said. "I knew they were dangerous, and I chose to underestimate them."

Liam grunted at her. "I can say no to you if I want to. I underestimated her too. Found Jessica's stuff and called Miller before Harper saw me."

Harper had buried Jessica's things beneath a mound of hay in one of the stalls, likely with the intent to burn or bury it later. She really believed they wouldn't get caught, even after the attack went so horribly wrong.

So far, she'd refused to talk, but Harper had likely caught sight of Liam and waited until she could sneak up on him with the only silent weapon she could find: the ball-peen hammer. Liam was lucky he wasn't in a coma like Bryce.

"Did you get any more out of Ella?" he asked.

"No, but her phone's been a wealth of information," Nikki said. "Ella and Harper met on an online chatroom for survivors. Eventually Harper figured out they were talking about one of the same people, so they got together. Once Ella told her the story about Jessica and Bryce, they sought her out and the plan was hatched."

Harper hadn't gone to the hospital after her rape, so it had truly been her word against Bryce and Gavin. The initial plan had involved Ella and Harper coming forward after Jessica's accusation went public, but Harper convinced the other two that the legal system would fail, and the only way to protect the same thing from happening to other girls was to take both men out.

"I still think they shot Gavin," Liam said. "I just hope his body is found so his dad can have some closure."

"Ella did admit that Jessica decided to deposit the check so that if something went wrong and she didn't make it, her story would still have a chance to be told. She also took Joan's wedding set to plant at Gavin's but never got the chance."

"I think we'll find out that Bryce surviving the accident changed their timeline," Nikki said. "They had to get rid of Gavin before he and Bryce connected and put two and two together."

"I wonder what the plan was if Bryce woke up from his coma," Caitlin said.

"I don't know," Nikki said. "But Gavin probably told them the head injury was so bad, they were banking on him not waking up or not remembering if he did. SWAT found Harper's car in the garage, loaded with both girls' things. My guess is we got there shortly before they planned to make a run for it. He's out of the coma but still pretty groggy. I'm going to try to talk to him later today or tomorrow."

Nikki checked her watch. "I need to head to the courthouse. I'm meeting with Tyler's parents, in the hopes we can hash things out instead of a custody hearing." After a long talk with Rory, Nikki reached out to Tyler's parents and asked if they were willing to work on things without going to court, reminding them that getting any sort of custody arrangement was going to be an uphill battle for them. "Lacey wants to be in your lives," Nikki had told them. "But sometimes it's hard for her to see you because you remind her of Tyler. We're working on that in therapy, and I'm willing to work out a schedule so that you can see her more, but she gets the final say. That's the deal."

After a lot of back and forth, Tyler's parents agreed to mediation. The spiteful part of Nikki wanted to bring Rory along so they could see that he was a permanent and important fixture in Lacey's life, but she knew that would only push them farther away. She patted Liam's hand. "Listen to the doctors and accept you will need rehab."

Liam scowled. "Guess I'm on official leave now. Tell Courtney not to be digging around my desk for candy, would you?"

Nikki laughed. "You know she's going to do it anyway."

Gavin's body was discovered tangled in debris ten miles downriver days later. Bryce admitted to the rapes and would stand trial when he was strong enough. Vic Weber was already building a defense centered around Gavin's influence. Ella pleaded guilty and agreed to testify against Harper for a lighter sentence.

Harper hadn't said a word since SWAT led her away in handcuffs.

A LETTER FROM STACY

I want to say a huge thank you for choosing to read *The Trapped Ones*. If you did enjoy it and want to keep up to date with all my latest releases, just sign up at the following link. Your email address will never be shared, and you can unsubscribe at any time.

www.bookouture.com/stacy-green

If you loved *The Trapped Ones*, I would be very grateful if you could write a review. I'd love to hear what you think, and it makes such a difference helping new readers to discover one of my books for the first time.

I love hearing from my readers—you can get in touch on Facebook or my website.

Thanks,

Stacy

facebook.com/StacyGreenAuthor
twitter.com/StacyGreen26
instagram.com/authorstacygreen

ACKNOWLEDGMENTS

This book has been a battle from start to finish, but I'm really happy with how it turned out. Thank you so much to my editor at Bookouture, Jennifer Hunt, for sticking with me through all of the ups and downs. And thank you to Laura Deacon and Kathryn Taussig for stepping in while Jennifer is on leave.

Thank you to John and Kristine Kelly for their help with all things Minnesota, and special thanks to Kristine for always making time for my books. Thanks to Jill Oliveria from the Minnesota Bureau of Criminal Apprehension for her assistance on warrants and other details on the state's legal system.

Special thank you to Jan Barton for being my second mom, and to my husband Rob and miracle baby Grace for supporting me even when I procrastinated and whined about how I couldn't stop procrastinating.

As always, thank you to my readers for their amazing support. The Nikki Hunt Series is continuing because of you, and I can't tell you how grateful I am for the chance to keep telling her story.

Printed in Great Britain
by Amazon